DEATH THE
PALE RIDER

DEATH THE PALE RIDER

VINCENT BANVILLE

POOLBEG

Published 1995 by
Poolbeg Press Ltd,
Knocksedan House,
123 Baldoyle Industrial Estate,
Dublin 13, Ireland

© Vincent Banville 1995

The moral right of the author has been asserted.

A catalogue record for this book is available from the British Library.

ISBN 1 85371 528 X

Cover photograph by Mike O'Toole
Cover design by Poolbeg Group Services Ltd
Set by Poolbeg Group Services Ltd in Joanna 10.5/12.5
Printed by The Guernsey Press Ltd,
Vale, Guernsey, Channel Islands.

A Note on the author

Vincent Banville was born in Wexford. A teacher in Dublin for many years, he is now a free-lance journalist and critic. He is the author of the popular *Hennessy* series for teenagers. His novel *An End to Flight* dealt with the Biafran war. His first John Blaine thriller was called *Death by Design*.

For Róisín
who makes it all worthwhile

And I looked, and behold a pale horse:
and his name that sat on him was Death.

Revelations 6:8.

One

It was the best part of ten years since I had last seen Max Morganthau, yet when he showed up in my office on that Monday morning he didn't appear to have changed in the slightest. He was still small, compact, muscular, his ash-blond hair in a razor cut that left most of his narrow skull bare, with only a rinse of it falling over his forehead. Under this fringe his eyes were the same deep blue, cobalt you might call it, his nose, broken, reset, but still slightly askew, his skin now and forever pocked by old acne scars, the insolent mocking smile a fixture that reached back into the past and nudged a small ache of nostalgia into my gut.

He stood in the doorway, framed in the vee of my size twelve sandals, where I had them propped up on the desk. One moment I was alone, sunk in bitter and hard to swallow thoughts, and the next there was the vision of Max, my old school pal – no, not the vision, but the real thing, grinning his grin, chewing gum and giving me that half rueful, half mocking look that conveyed the same message it always had, that he was sorry for something I didn't even know about as yet.

He was wearing a white tee shirt, and his faded blue jeans were tucked into brown, scuffed cowboy boots with high heels. He had always been conscious of his lack of height, going to great lengths to disguise it, so the heels didn't surprise me. He looked fit and well and in very good shape. Made me more than a little conscious of the thickening round my middle and my latest double chin – at thirty-three not a good omen for the future.

Now he winked at me and said, "Hey, Johnny boy, how's it going?"

I put back my head and glared down my nose at him. "It's going down the plug hole, if you really want to know," I told him sourly.

He tossed the fringe out of his eyes, folded his arms and leaned against the door frame. He was completely at ease, putting the onus on me to lay down the emotional field for our meeting. Should I be mad, glad or flippant, or should I get up and kick his arse through the window? I decided on a waiting game, so I indicated the visitor's chair. All in good time he would tell me what he wanted — and it was certain, knowing Max, that he wanted something.

"Take a pew," I invited him. "You're just in time to join me in a little TM. Good for the soul, not to mention the stress factor ..."

"I know," he said. "I read about it earlier on this morning. Old Wexford stripped naked and hung high on a cross. Different singers but the same old tune."

The Wexford hurling team had played Kilkenny in the Leinster Final the day before and had been thrashed. Because of it I had woken up this Monday morning with the taste of ashes in my mouth. Drowning a sorrow can be as emotionally draining as the sorrow itself.

I recrossed my feet on the desk top, then watched Max as he decided to take up my offer and sit down. He left the doorway and slid into the chair, his grace of movement as fluid as the passage of a globule of oil along a smooth surface. He had always possessed that same poetry in motion: on the hurling field when we were at school and later on during the couple of years he had spent at university before he took off to see the big wide world. During a game he would waltz around bigger opponents, avoiding their tackles with an insolent ease that was as infuriating as a spit in the eye. But he could be hard too when the occasion demanded. He was unscrupulous about getting his retaliation in first and was an expert at spotting the potential hard man and cutting him down to size, even before the initial eye-to-eye could be effected.

Now he worked his shoulders in the tee shirt, the corded muscles standing out under the flimsy material. It was obvious he pumped iron, for he had the physique of a body-builder: biceps, pectorals, the lot.

"Impressive," I said, enviously eying his frontage. "A pocket Charles Atlas ..."

"Hey," he interrupted me, "you're not with it. Atlas is out and Schwarzenegger is in. I burn rubber three times a day. You've got

2

to work hard to keep the tissue from slipping. We're not getting any younger, you know."

I made a face, thinking of man-mountain Harold, the gentle giant my ex-wife Annie was living with; he had his own gymnasium where he pressed weights that if I merely looked at would give me a hernia. Every night before I went to sleep I got down on my knees and prayed that he'd burst, the taut skin snapping and the insides shooting out like demented sausage meat.

Taking up the packet of Dunhills from the desk, I popped one out, put it in my mouth and lit it with my disposable Bic lighter. My doing so felt like a small act of rebellion against the fitness fanatics of this world.

"So," I said, "to what do I owe the pleasure of this call? If I remember rightly the last time I saw you it was on the occasion of your taking off with most of the contents of my house. I'm still in mourning for the inscribed piece of Waterford crystal, the bowl I won for ..."

"I know, I know. I always meant to reclaim that for you but I never could seem to get around to it. Same with the fifteen speed racing bicycle."

I winced, having forgotten the sleek machine in the purple and gold colours and with a saddle like a branding-iron that my mother had bought on the never-never. Max had ridden off into the sunset on it, my trusty steed that had only vibrated once or twice under my backside.

"Did you have to remind me of that?" I asked his far from contrite countenance. "You ... you bicycle thief."

He grinned, then leaned over and slapped the top of the desk. "Aren't you glad to see me, you old shit hawker?" he said. "Here we haven't seen one another for I don't know how many years ..."

"Try ten."

"... and you're as crusty as an old dog sitting on a tack." He paused, his lips moving as if he were counting, then he said, "Is it that long? How time flies. It takes a long time to see the world. But now I'm back ..."

"When?"

"When what?"

3

"When did you get back?"

Looking evasive, he said, "A while ago now."

I blew smoke at a stray beam of sunlight. "It's taken you long enough to look up an old friend. You haven't exactly come to see me fresh from the boat ..."

"You knew I was back?"

"I heard a whisper. Dublin's a small town when it comes to gossip and rumour."

"What'd you hear?"

"Just that you were around. Why?"

Again he looked slightly uneasy, shifting in the chair, looking sideways so that the morning light through the window bounced off his profile. I could almost see him hunting around for something to change the subject. Finally he said, "How's Annie? Still as gorgeous and sassy as ever?"

"I wouldn't know," I told him. "She left me last year. Packed up and went off in search of fresh woods and pastures new."

"You're joking," he said, his eyes disbelieving. "I always fancied you two were a permanent item. A bit rocky now and then" – he twisted his fist with a rolling motion – "but till death do you part. Definitely ..."

"I don't want to talk about it. It's like rubbing at an open wound."

"I know what you mean."

"You do, do you?"

"We all have our affairs of the heart. Comme ci, comme ça. A little of what you fancy does you good."

"Is that so?" I took my feet down and planted them squarely under me, ready to leap across the desk and throttle him. He had always been able to put me in a temper and then sit back and laugh at me while I fumed. This time, though, I decided that age had brought me wisdom, and instead I forced myself to grin at him. I took a deep drag on my cigarette and said in as honeyed a tone as I could muster, "Why don't you tell me the purpose of your visit? Not just to laze around and chat about old times, surely?"

"Well, that yes," he nodded, "and a little more besides. And stop calling me Shirley."

"Huh?"

"A joke, a joke. I thought you were into films. Haven't you seen 'The Naked Gun'?"

I pinched out the cigarette and dropped the stub into the cutglass ash-tray on the desk. "What d'you mean by 'a little more besides'?" I asked him. "If you're looking for a loan you can go whistle up your leg."

"The opposite, as a matter of fact," he said, appearing positively gleeful. "I've come like the good fairy to put some folding money your way. Maybe quite a lot. It depends on how you play it."

"Play what?"

"Well, not the big bass drum. And that's a fact." He gazed around my office: at the beige wallpaper, the roll-top mahogany desk in the corner, the more modern, glass panelled one behind which I was sitting, the Walter Osborne print on the wall, the undependable pull-down blind over the only window, the cabinet containing jars of mouldy false teeth, and none of it seemed to instil a start of aesthetic joy in his soul. "Looks to me as if this place could do with a bit of jollying up," he said. "A lick of paint, a strip of carpet, a sofa or two ..."

"I'll bet you know a good interior decorator?" I said maliciously.

"Could be," he replied airily, refusing to rise to the bait. "What's with the false teeth?"

"The place was rented by a dental mechanic before I took it over. I think he left them in lieu of his back payments. When the wind is right they start chattering away. Keeps me from feeling lonely. Satisfied?"

Again he put his own miraculously white teeth on view in a grin. Then he said, "Maybe we could find more salubrious quarters to do our talking in? A place of light and space, the quiet clink of bottles, the urgent glug-glug of amber liquid being poured, the lip-smacking satisfaction of imbibing it ..?"

"You're inviting me to go sit in a public hostelry with you at eleven o'clock in the morning? To take strong drink at such an early hour?"

"You've never done it before?"

I thought about his invitation, measuring out my length of

things to do. It was Monday morning, and the rest of the week stretched ahead of me as empty as a politician's promise. My telephone answering machine was full of wind whistling static, the post was composed of bills, bills and more bills, Batt, the one-armed eccentric who managed the video shop below my office and asked me questions about black-and-white films of the thirties and forties, was away on his holidays, and I had no work to engage my little grey cells or the sturdiness of my resolution. The odds seemed decidedly stacked in favour of the pub.

Hesitating no longer, I said, "You've convinced me with the force of your argument. And I also need a hair of the dog. Let's go ..."

Outside, the early July sun was high in the sky, with only a puff or two of cloud to keep it company. The video shop and my place of business above it are off the main thoroughfare, but the rumble of traffic from O'Connell Street could still be heard as a muted murmur. Parked on the pavement and painted in garish sunbursts of colour was a huge Kawasaki motor-bike. A couple of urchins were staring at it, their mouths open.

"This yours?" I asked Max, remembering his predilection for such machines. He had always had one when he was in funds and many was the time he scared the living daylights out of me, as, perched behind him, we thundered along unsuitable roads at a yammering rate of knots.

"Yep," he now said, caressing its shining flank like someone else might a woman's leg. "You like?"

"To admire, but not to ride. And you'd better bribe those street arabs with thirty pieces of silver or all you'll have left when you come back is its aroma."

"I've already done it. You're warding off invaders, aren't you boys?" he asked them, grinning in that way of his that immediately elicited a grin in return. Charm school hadn't been wasted on old Max.

We strolled through a number of interconnecting streets and ended up in Middle Abbey Street, in front of a pub called Destry's. It had a less than imposing facade, and the inside lived up to the promise of the outside by being even more downbeat.

It was a huge, barn-like building, with a long wooden counter running down one side, a number of sorry-looking chairs and cigarette-marked tables scattered about and, I kid you not, sawdust liberally coating the floor.

Cedric, the barman, presided over all this with an imperiousness that belied his surroundings, stumping along behind the bar on his wooden leg, insulting the customers, and frightening any non-regular who happened to stumble in. Up to recently he had kept a piranha in a glass tank and at set times of the day and night fed it a wriggling goldfish to devour, but to the chagrin of the more bloodthirsty of his *habitués* the animal rights people had kicked up such a stink that the toothy predator had to be put down. Now Cedric sulked and wrote letters to the papers in favour of hare coursing, fox hunting and otter baiting.

"You do a nice line in sleaze," Max remarked as we entered. "I can see why this place is a home from home from your office."

"Don't be like that," I told him. "My feelings are easily hurt these days. A dented sensibility. Comes from associating with low life like yourself.

He ignored the proffered insult and marched up to the bar. "What'll you have?" he asked me. "A Bushmills with a Guinness chaser? You see, I remembered ..."

I nodded, and stood beside him as he ordered. The whiskey and the stout were acceptable, but when he called for a vodka with grapefruit juice and water for himself Cedric summoned up his famous sneer. He did this by lifting his upper lip a fraction, letting it quiver for a few seconds, then putting it back where it belonged. This unwholesome exhibition was accompanied by a high pitched whinny like the sound of a jackass in heat.

In no way fazed, Max did a pectoral quiver, the front of his tee shirt undulating like the bishop's trousers when the comely young maiden did her rustle of satins at matins. Recognising a fellow showman, Cedric nodded happily and went off in search of the drinks.

Except for two pensioners staring into space and absent-mindedly sipping their pints, the place was empty, but Max still led me to a table far from the bar. He waited until Cedric had come and gone, paying for the drinks himself, much to my surprise, then he said,

"I was intrigued to hear you were in the private investigation business. Seems to me you had a secure job in insurance the last time I met you ...?"

"Yeah, promoted to claims analyst. But I was continually being pissed off by having my recommendations overruled. Seems it's easier to pay out and then raise the premiums. Less trouble, less paperwork, less fucking about in the courts. And then I had a boss who had a tasty little earner running scams with the more greedy of our customers. I sold him out and packed the job in. Now I'm on my uppers, but my virtue's intact."

"So it goes," Max said, shrugging. He sipped at his vodka and grapefruit juice, little finger extended, his nails nicely shaped and shining with some kind of transparent lacquer. The fact that he was gay, recalled as it was now, never failed to startle me. I've always equated that particular sexual orientation with the more feminine side of one's nature – Max was, and ever had been, as tough as an elephant's foreskin.

"Must be an interesting line of work," he now said. "Who do you model yourself on? Philip Marlowe? Mike Hammer? Spenser? Pretty glamorous.."

"Nothing glamorous about it," I demurred. "I'm either wearing out the seat of my trousers sitting down or shoe leather walking about. And doing surveillance is one of the most dog-weary pursuits known to man." Moodily I sucked in a little of the Bushmills, then threw it back and waited for it to hit. I was disappointed; the effect was as explosive as if I'd downed a glass of milk. Lately I'd been drinking too much, and the more one drank the less effect it had. Resignedly I took a draught of Guinness – at least it didn't taste like mother's milk.

I lit a cigarette and blew smoke into the dimness of the bar. "So," I said, "let's have it. Why've you suddenly appeared again in my life? And how did you know I was in the detective business?"

Max moved his glass about on the tabletop, forming wet rings. In anyone else it might appear as if he were looking for the best means of saying what he had to say, but from prior knowledge of his methods I knew he already had it cut and dried in his mind. He had always been one to check out a fence before he leaped it.

8

He started off mock-hesitantly: "Remember the Haly family? We used joke about them and call them the Holy Family. There was the old guy, Bart, and the two sons, Mossie and Alfie ..."

"I remember," I said, my glass halfway to my mouth as I stared at him over the rim. "What about them?"

"I work for them now. At least, I work for Mossie. Or Mr Maurice as he's now known. Old Bart died. They've branched out and the main office is now in Dublin."

"I know that. I haven't been asleep for the past ten years. But I can't believe you're working for those bloodsuckers, especially after the way they treated your father."

Max stared at me equably enough, but his hand around the glass was white-knuckled. He shrugged. "Bygones are bygones," he said. "Who was it said 'The past is a different country'? You move on. No point in dwelling on the bad times ..."

"In a pig's eye."

Again I regarded him over the rim of my glass, then took a long slug while I thought about a few things. The Haly family had been like feudal barons in the town where Max and I grew up. Protestant landowners originally, they had started up a steamship business, bringing in Polish coal, South American fruit and Ceylonese tea between the wars. The harbour had been a fine, deep-water port then; that was before it had silted up, the resulting sandbanks making it impossible for anything other than flat-bottomed boats to sail into the once busy quays. Most of the able-bodied men of the town had worked for the Halys at one time or another, forced into being a cap-doffing fraternity that set the old man and his two sons on pedestals from which they could piss down on all and sundry. During the good times, Max's father – from old Protestant stock like themselves – had been chief dogsbody of all their many businesses, but when the commercial side took a sudden tilt over into the red he had been apportioned most blame and had died a broken man. It didn't seem likely to me that Max, a ferocious holder of grievances to my certain knowledge, would now be trailing his coat on their side of the fence. But I held my tongue and instead asked him in what capacity he worked for Mossie, the smarter and more ruthless of the two sons.

"A little bit of this and a little bit of that," he said, his eyes once more on the glass as he rotated it between his fingers.

"What does that mean?"

He looked at me. "What's with the antagonism?" he asked, mildly enough. He put the glass down with a sharp click. "Here I am, your best and oldest friend, seeking to put a little business your way, and maybe to do a bit of reminiscing on the side, and all you do is growl at me. What's happened to you? We were pals, buddies, all for one and one for all. We stood back to back, repelling all foes ..."

"Cut the shit, Max. You're not going to put one over on me with that act. You want something from me, and it's not out of the goodness of your heart that you've chosen me. Let's be straight with one another about this ... That is, if you've ever been straight with anyone, including yourself, ever in your life."

I listened to myself saying the words, but inside I'd grown a tad mushy, remembering. It was true what he said: there had been a time when we were seldom out of one another's company. All through secondary school we had been inseparable, roaming the highways and byways of the town together, scouring the fields, rivers and low hills that surrounded it for fun, play and adventure. We had joined the local hurling team together and progressed through juvenile and minor ranks, winning everything available along the way. I was the more successful one, already six-two and built in proportion at the age of eighteen, but in a way it was he who had made my reputation. Known never to take prisoners, he had taken the brunt of the ferocious side of the game, leaving me to swan in and score goals and points, while he absorbed the punishment that I should have been shipping. Both of us had been selected for the county minor team and, when I was promoted that same year to the seniors, Max had been the first to congratulate me. He was also the one who stayed out long hours in all kinds of weather to help me improve my style, my overhead striking, my free taking.

I put down my empty glass and signalled to Cedric for refills. One of the pensioners had dozed off and his head suddenly slipped off his hand and hit the counter with a dull clunk. His companion, a little way down the bar, neighed an unsympathetic, high falsetto of a laugh.

"You see?" I said, indicating them. "No one has any feeling for anyone else anymore. You chose to disappear out of my life and I forgot you, and now you expect me to take you back in again. Like you said, what's past is past ..."

"No, you don't mean that." Max shook his head. "You were always the one with the soft centre. Remember when that biffo from Offaly was giving you a hard time? In the Leinster Minor Championship ... what year was it? ... no matter. He was tearing strips off you. And who was it who clocked him? Your's truly, that's who ..."

"All right, I'll grant you that one. And I owed you. But you settled that and many another account. You stole from me, left, right and up the middle. You took my affection as well as my worldly goods, and then you fucked off. Not a word from you over the years. And then I hear you're back, but you don't drop around to see me. Fuck that for a situation ..."

Max laughed, his eyes a darker blue in the dimness of the bar. "The point is, I'm here now, and I've got an assignment for you ..."

We waited while Cedric brought the fresh drinks, then I said, "An assignment? That sounds very grand. You mean you've got a job for me? Something dirty that'll suit my line of work?"

"If you want to put it like that."

"Oh, I do. Most certainly I do. Cards on the table and no room for regrets afterwards." I lit a fresh cigarette and this time blew the smoke in his direction. "Tell me about it."

"I want you to get something for me. A set of photographs and their negatives ..."

"That's it?"

"Yes."

"Why can't you get them yourself?"

He reached over and took one of my Dunhills, but instead of lighting it he twirled it about between his fingers. The white tube danced from knuckle to knuckle. I waited for it to disappear, but he continued to play with it as he said, "I need a third party. Someone to act on my behalf. You see, I'm fairly deeply involved myself."

"Obviously, if you're hiring me to procure them for you."

"I'm not."

"Not what?"

"I'm not hiring you. At least I'm not the one who'll be paying your wages."

"That's something on the credit side."

"I'm the middle man."

"Then it has to be Mossie Haly."

"There, I knew you were the right man for the job. You got it in one. Right on the button."

Max flipped the cigarette in the air and caught it in his mouth. He still didn't light it, though. Under the surface patina of easy matiness, I thought I caught a whiff of unease. But then, he had always been a consummate actor, and this subtle shading of disquiet might be his attempt at emotional blackmail. There had never been a time when he hadn't been able to work me like an expert fisherman his catch. I knew that, but the knowing didn't make me any less susceptible to his wiles.

"Let's have it," I said, giving in, but also intrigued in spite of my reservations. With Max around, life was liable to become interesting.

Grinning, he leaned across the table and said, "It's like this. Mossie is pretty big in the business community. A lot of it is outward show, but that's how it's done. You wash your dirty linen out of sight around the back. He also likes to be thought of as a bit of a philanthropist and he mixes with the social set quite a lot. His image is important to him. I think you know his wife, Louise, but he's also got a daughter, Mary, and a son, Archie. The daughter causes him no problems: she likes to spend money, but he's got plenty of that, and if she plays around some, she's discreet about it. Louise, as you might expect, is still the great lady ..."

"Then it has to be the son who's ruffling his feathers."

"There you go, getting ahead of me again." Max gazed at me mock-admiringly. He took the cigarette out of his mouth and laid it carefully on the flange of the cheap glass ash-tray. "Archie's a bit of a disaster," he went on. "He's only twenty-one but he's already been in trouble with the law a number of times. Fast driving, drunk and disorderly, drug-taking, that sort of thing. The usual rich young man's vices ..."

"We should all be so lucky."

"Yeah. But there's a further complication." Max stared at me under his eyebrows. "He also happens to be gay ..."

"Aha ..."

"Don't say 'aha' like that, as if it explained everything. Consenting adults can consent nowadays."

"So what's the problem?"

"Well, it appears that one technicoloured evening recently young Archie became a little high on something ... not an unusual occurrence. The upshot was that he allowed himself to be photographed in what is euphemistically termed a compromising position with another plonker named Richie Michaels. Now these same snaps have been offered to his Da for a cool quarter of a million, with the threat that if he doesn't pay up, they'll be flashed around in all the best circles. It's not something that Mossie would greatly desire, to have coloured two-by-fours of his beloved son with his crowbar up someone's blowhole tacked along his route as he whooped it up with the rich and famous."

"Nicely put, Max. Succinct and to the point, if I might pun a pun." I drank half of the second Bushmills, then damped it down with a libation of stout. "Let me guess what comes next," I continued. "Before he parts with his hard-earned cash, Mossie wants to try strongarming Michaels and getting the merchandise back that way. Am I right or am I right?"

"I wouldn't say you were wrong."

"If you're working for Mossie, why don't you do it? I would have thought you'd be a good man for a job like that."

"I'm too well known on that scene. They'd spot me coming a mile off ..."

"D'you mean that in the Freudian sense?"

He wet his finger and drew it along the edge of the table. "One up for you," he acknowledged. "What I mean is, this needs a straight up and down guy. Someone like you. You know, tread carefully, for you tread on my balls ..."

"I hope it won't come to that."

"I was speaking figuratively."

I eyed him. "I don't know, though," I said. "I've owed you a kick in the knackers for a long time ..."

"Maybe so. But could we get this bit of business out of the way first?"

I picked up the cigarette he'd been playing with and tried his trick of twirling it along the back of my knuckles. It fell on the floor. The lunch-time traffic was beginning to trundle in, clerks, secretaries, a number of die-hards who drank their collations instead of eating them. Max looked around at the assembling throng, getting restive. "So, what d'you say?" he asked me. "Are you in or out? You'll be well paid. Your usual rates plus a little extra to help smooth over the hassle I've caused you over the years."

"Mossie's footing the bill?"

"Of course. Haven't I told you that already?"

"He knows I'm coming in on it?"

"Definitely. I keep him informed of everything I do."

"That's a pork-pie for starters. You know, Max, you've told me so many untruths over the years that if they were laid back to back they'd reach all the way to purgatory and back ..."

"Purgatory is out. And Limbo. It's either heaven or hell nowadays. I remember all those missions and retreats you used go to when we were young. I'd wait outside for you in the churchyard."

"Yeah, you chased altar boys about for diversion. It's a wonder you weren't struck down by a bolt from above."

Max grinned delightedly, knowing he had sucked me in yet again into his sphere of influence. He said coaxingly, "Mossie remembers you well. He was a big follower of the county hurling team. Ploughed lots of readies into the training, getting facilities, providing steak dinners ..."

"Lot of good it did us, in the end of the day."

Moodily I drank off the remains of the whiskey. There was no doubt that I needed the work – well, the money actually. I'd been living on air and the smell of burning rubber for a while now, the skid marks plainly visible where my creditors had braked to a halt. But I was loth to get involved with Max or with his employer, Mossie Haly. They were too close to home, and you know what they say, never shit on your own doorstep. Max's reappearance in my life had awakened old hurts, old memories, the kind that one only took out for perusal on special occasions, like funerals, the death of love or starting up in the dog-hours of the night with no warm body beside you to help chase off the hawks of morning. Making a decision, though, was one half of a two-edged sword: if I refused to help Max I'd be left holding a burden of guilt, like Sisyphus his rock, while if I accepted the chore I'd probably be laying in enough trouble and strife to last me till I bought my next bed of nails. It was a nice little conundrum, with the only escape hatch a trapdoor poised to open under me. Being the reasonable man that I am – read, soft as a marshmallow dick – I tried to sidestep the problem.

"You know, Max," I said, "my instinct tells me to place my hand over my essentials and run like fuck. But unfortunately my sense of greed for Mossie Haly's money is also very powerful. I've a number of pressing debts, you see – they're pressing so hard I'm up to my neck in pitty-poo ..."

"Do I take it then you're about to give favourable consideration to my proposition?"

"It being?"

"That you go look up this Richie Michaels, of whose yawning orifices I have some knowledge, and that you'll twist his ear and get him to give me back what rightly belongs to me."

"To you or to Mossie?"

"To Mossie. I'll be handing the pictures over to him as soon as you place them in my hands."

"Oh, yeah?" I watched the expression on his face, which was neutral shading into oleaginous: if I were Mossie I wouldn't trust him as far as I could throw him. "I'm not going to get involved in rough stuff," I said. "I'll go and see this Michaels, talk to him, cajole him a little. Maybe he will listen to reason at that ..."

"Maybe he'll set fire to your foot and invite you to spit on it to put it out."

"It's like that, is it?"

Max shrugged and gave me another hit of that infuriating grin of his. "I'm only teasing," he said. "They're nice boys, really."

"Boys? There's more than one of them?"

15

"Michaels owns half of a public house over off Dame Street. His partner is a dipstick called Chinelio, Vincent Chinelio. He may be in on the scam. Someone had to operate the camera."

"That's pretty choice," I said, nodding my head. "It starts off with a couple of toerags bonking one another, moves on to include potential psychopaths like yourself and Mossie Haly ..."

"Hold on a minute," Max protested, interrupting me. "Don't include me in with the Mossie Halys of this world. I've still got some sense of honour."

"Have you?" I shifted in my chair, leaning forward to get a better bead on him. "Where've you been for the last few years, Max? I'm not like you, you see, when old friends disappear on me I do my best to keep track of them. The story goes that you've been doing hard time in a rat-house prison on the other side of the world. Would you like to tell me a little about that? Fill me in on your comings and goings, like?"

He blinked his eyes rapidly, then crunched down on his jaw muscles. Keeping in his anger had never been easy for him. After a time he said, mildly enough, "Who told you that?"

"That's not at issue. Let's just say I've got my sources. The business I'm in is grouted by favours. You do some, you earn some. The point is, is there any truth in it?"

"There could be."

"How much?"

"How much what?"

"For fuck's sake, Max." Angrily I drank off the last of the stout in my glass, then banged it down on the table. "You're playing games with me now. Why don't you be square with me for once?"

The interior of the pub had pretty well filled up by now and in the midst of all the chatter and noise Max suddenly looked somehow diminished, as if the crush of people was causing him to shrink. His natural bounce of cheerfulness and hail-fellow-well-met seemed to have deserted him and he looked cowed – like someone hunching his shoulders against an expected blow. I was dismayed by this change in him and instinctively reached out. I caught him by the arm, but it was as ropy and hard with muscle as a steel hawser. Was the seeming diminution in him merely a figment of my imagination, or had it been caused by the black shadow of some deeper possibility?

"I'm sorry," I said, without being exactly sure of what I was apologising for. "I didn't mean ..."

"It's okay," he said, squeezing my arm in return, but the realisation that he had turned the tables on me yet again changed my mood. Anger at his dexterity of intent again flooded my mind.

"It's called The Cock's Cuckoo", he said, causing me another mood swing: the nonplussed variety this time.

"What is?"

"The pub that Michaels and Chinelio own."

"You've got to be joking."

"Cross my heart and hope to die. At least it shows they've a sense of humour."

"I hope they see the humour in my coming over to ask them politely for something they're hoping will net them a cool quarter of a million smackers. I'm sure they'll hand over the photographs plus negatives, pat me on the head and send me on my way rejoicing."

"One can but try."

"And supposing I don't succeed?"

"The we'll just have to try something else, won't we?"

"And that something else might entail ... what?"

Max was back to his butter-wouldn't-melt-in-my-mouth expression, but it was overlaid by an element of slyness.

"Why don't we wait and see?" he said, spreading his hands, now plainly back in control of the situation. "You go on over there and talk to Richie and his friend Vincent, right? The sight of your imposing bulk and macho stance'll surely put the fear of God into them. You might even take out your denture and bare your gums at them. That could prove to be a banker in putting the wind up them."

"Very funny."

I thought about extracting said plate and stirring the remains of his vodka and grapefruit juice with it. Instead I held up my hand and rubbed my thumb along the tips of my fingers. He got the message.

"Too shy to ask, huh?" he said. He reached around to his back pocket and produced a roll of notes. It was impressively thick. He slicked off a number of twenties and passed them to me. Without bothering to count them I stuck them in the inside pocket of my light linen jacket. It was one that my aged father, who was beginning to shuck off his worldly possessions, had given to me. It was rather tight on me, so most of the time I merely carried it for effect.

"How will I get in touch with you? To let you know how things develop ..."

"Leave that to me. I'll ring you tonight."

"At home or in the office?"

"Aren't they both in the book? If I don't get you in one, I'll try the other."

"Home is where the heart is nowadays, Max. I've a mobile. I'll give you the number of that."

"Annie took the house?" he asked, as I wrote out the telephone number and passed it across to him.

"No, she just decamped. She's living with a body-builder called Harold. I sold the house. It was too big and draughty for me, and it held too many memories."

"Memories ..." he mused, fingering the skin of his face. For a moment I thought he was going to give me a blast of the big number from *Cats*, then he said, "They're as useless as a toothless comb. Looking forward is your only man."

"You think so?"

"I know so."

He seemed about to say more but then he abruptly stood up and leaned on the table. He really was in good shape, and yet he carried an aura of something, like a bright light tinged with a dark penumbra. Somehow I felt that if I scratched the surface I might well find an aging, scabrous substance beneath the cosmetic facade.

Maybe catching some hint of my insight he said hurriedly, "Take care those guys don't coax you into doing a photo spread of your own. They make look soft, but they can be tricky. And if you drop your hat on the floor ..."

"I know, kick it along the ground until I'm in the next street. I've heard that one before."

18

We had obviously come to the end of our conversation for the moment, and before an awkwardness could develop I said, "Go on, get outta here."

He made as though to depart, then he turned back and said, "When this is over we'll go out and tie on a session. There's much to catch up on. A lot of our water has gone under the bridge ..."

"Sure," I responded, putting my hands under the table and clasping them tightly. I was afraid I might make a show of myself by standing up and giving him a hug, so I said, "You'd better get going. I think I can hear your motor-bike calling ..."

He grinned one more time, then turned and strutted across the floor. It was only when he was gone that I realised how much I had missed him over the years.

Two

I stayed on in Destry's and had another pint of Guinness. It was part of the ennui of my mood that I found putting into motion the consequence of a decision so difficult. Sitting there I let the noise and the chat wash over me, not as an irritant but as a balm. As a matter of fact, it would have been nice to pass the length of the afternoon there, sipping stout, imbibing the odd whiskey, listening to the woodworm gnawing away at Cedric's artificial leg.

Then again I could ring Annie, my sometime wife. She was employed as a social worker with Dublin Corporation: a vivid, auburn-haired girl/woman whom I loved very much – and she loved me too, but preferably at a distance. Actually living with me annoyed the hell out of her. We had been married for ten, war-torn years; we met in university, found instant rapport, fought many the good fight, came together, drew apart, until finally she could stand the bitter sweetness of it no longer and took off, appropriately enough in the midst of a thunderstorm – or had I imagined that part of it? Whatever – when the noise and the smell of sulphur had dissipated I was left with a large rambling house on the Cabra Road, three suits, no job, an almighty thirst for strong liquor, and an emptiness inside me that I presumed was where my heart had been.

Setting myself up as a private investigator – trustworthy, reliable, and confidential – why do I always think the family dog would also suit that description? – had been a form of therapy, something to enable me to put some colour back in my life, to get me out and about to meet people, maybe solve a problem or two, stave off trouble in other lives that I couldn't prevent in my own. The concept was fine but the actuality turned out to be flawed: the more marital strife I encountered – and it formed the basis of most of what I was engaged to do – the more discontented and lost I became. For it was soon borne in on me that in personal relationships, and their breakdown, there were no ready solutions, no panaceas to bind, heal and caress. The opposite, as a matter of fact: family rows that started over trifles soon escalated into screaming knock-downs that pushed the interested parties further and further apart.

As to Annie and myself, we settled for a kind of quasi live-and-let-live arrangement; we met socially, went out to dinner, chatted, smiled, held hands, slept together occasionally, but then went our separate routes like old friends whose courses had diverged but who still waved to one another over neighbouring fences when the light was right.

The whiff of bar food had been impinging on my awareness for some little time, so I ordered a basket of scampi and French fries from Cedric's shuffling assistant, an antediluvian stick man whose simian aspect always kindled hope in my soul of funky gibbon antics — a hope, alas, so far unrealised. Cedric himself brought over the food, sniffing when I asked for a fourth pint of Guinness. He didn't like the regulars to let themselves down and he knew I sometimes became unpredictable with drink on me. Twice in the past month I'd torn the phone out of the wall with vexation when Annie pooh-poohed my suggestion that we should make yet another attempt to get back together. Life with Harold, it seemed, had put her sailing on a much more even keel.

It was after two and the pub had quietened by the time I finished the food. I swirled the remains of the stout about in the glass, then drank it down like medicine. I felt nicely light-headed and I probably staggered a little on my way to the gents.

In there I got rid of the liquid in my bladder, washed my hands, brushed my hair. I regarded myself in the speckled mirror over the washbasin, examined my bloodshot eyeballs, showed my teeth, growled at my reflection. A performance sure to scare small children, genteel old ladies, maybe a nun or two. A real hardcase would scoff, stick his finger in my eye, and give me a Three Stooges slap in the mush. So much for my tough guy routine. I got out of there before I started weeping into the urinal.

On my way towards the door I considered putting off Max's assignment and tying on a real bender, but the memory of the blackouts I'd been experiencing lately drove me on. I'd lost two whole days to the most recent one, two days from my life which

21

I could not account for; it was frightening even to speculate on what might have occurred during that dark and memory-locked absence.

The blast of sunshine when I tottered out into Abbey Street almost knocked me down. I reeled about and would have turned back into the cool dimness of the pub if the door hadn't slammed in my face. Probably Cedric, sussing my intent, was behind its abrupt closure. I shrugged, paused to light a cigarette, then strolled nonchalantly across the road. The car that I walked out in front of ground to a halt with an agonised screeching of brakes, but I pressed on regardless. Let he who had never taken a drink throw the first stone ...

The Liffey, when I came to it, stank, the low tidemark on its bricked sides an ugly green blazon of its polluted state. I crossed it, using the Halfpenny Bridge, then went through the arch into Temple Bar. People were sitting out in the sunshine under coloured umbrellas, instituting a facsimile version of Montmartre, or the French Quarter, or the Casco Viejo of any Spanish city. The Irish had finally caught up with Europe and the European mode of disporting themselves, even if still a little self-conscious with the brio and air of careless disdain to carry it off. I admired the naked female flesh on view, sneered at the youthful insouciance of the males, and wished fervently that I had Annie, in wide-brimmed straw hat and flowered summer dress, safely arm-in-arm and laughing adoringly up into my face.

Moodily I shuffled on. The sun was hot between the buildings, the light hard and brittle, and shadow, where it was present, was sharp and almost threatening in the overtness of its contrast. Traffic was slow and sullen, mirroring probably the ill-humour of its cooped-up drivers. There was an odour of petrol fumes and of hot tar, and any remnant of breeze that blew was limp and old and tired, shop-soiled by its journey through the sweating streets.

I crossed Dame Street and took the narrow entranceway that led into Mahony's Court. Clarence Mahony had been Lord Mayor of Dublin back in the twenties and thirties, a little bantam of a man in hard hat, morning coat, stiff shirt and high collar. Everyone loved his eccentric ways and he was elected for term after term. A true Dublin character, he had gone his slightly mad

22

way until he had been run over by a cart dragged by an out-of-control dray-horse. His funeral brought the city to a standstill and my father, who was working in Dublin at the time, told me afterwards that the whole place was awash in drink and sentiment for a week.

There was a lifelike bronze statue of him, hand doffing his hat, at the bottle-neck entrance to the little square that had been named after him. It was the custom for people to touch the base of it for luck, the consequence being that most of his thrust-forward foot was worn away by supplicating hands over the years. I gave it a rub as I went past – better to be in the swim of things than drowning.

Once one was in behind the high, red-bricked buildings, the court offered a little oasis, a tucked-away pool of quiet in the midst of so much activity and traffic noise. There were a number of shops with olde-worlde frontages, and the ground underfoot was paved with cobblestones. The sudden contrast between modern and quaint kindled in the beholder the suspicion that what one was seeing was merely the facade of some film set or other.

It was not difficult to find the Cock's Cuckoo. One of those old English inn type signs creaked over its front door, featuring the multi-hued figure of a crowing cock, and people sat outside at white painted, metal tables with dainty frilled parasols keeping the slanting rays of the sun out of their eyes. However, the inside, when I entered, was cool and shadowed, the furnishings this time wooden and polished to a shining brown benignity by usage. Every available surface was covered in graffiti, peoples' names, dates, little messages and drawings, most of them obscene. There were also old yellowing pin-ups, mostly of young men in various stages of undress. A Robert Mapplethorp study of a fist where it had no business being dominated the back wall, in behind the horseshoe-shaped bar.

A fat character with five o'clock shadow and little black button eyes was polishing glasses at one end of the counter. He had on a butcher's striped apron and was whistling tunelessly as he worked. When I came in he looked up and stared at me, then he grinned. The grin did nothing for me except to let me know that he was missing a few teeth, both top and bottom.

23

"Ooh, you are big," he said by way of greeting, glass in one hand, dish-rag in the other.

I remembered Bogie as Philip Marlowe in "The Big Sleep" replying to a similar remark by Carmen Sternwood, and I said, "I try not to be."

"I've no argument with big," the bartender assured me. "Especially if you're big all over."

I eyed him, then I said, "Well, I don't mean to boast but I'm sure you've heard the expression 'a horn like a cucumber'?"

"A cucumber, eh? You must be looking for a big orifice if so ..."

I felt the stout move queasily in my stomach and I wondered if I regurgitated a pint or two would my new friend be very dismayed. I settled instead for belching. Once upon a time I had been a mannerly young man, but time, tide and the seasons had effected a sea change and now I was as uncouth as the next guy — and the one next to next.

"What can I do you for?" the fat man asked, his words coming out with a slight hiss because of the gaps in his teeth. He grinned again and ran a moist tongue over thick lips. His hair was black and shiny and combed straight back, and it stuck out in little spears on his roly-poly neck. He didn't look particularly Irish — maybe Italian, Greek ... certainly Mediterranean.

"My name is John Blaine," I said, "and I'm looking for Richie Michaels. I believe he owns this pub, or at least a part of it."

"That's right."

"Which?"

"He owns a half share. Are you from the Inland Revenue?"

"No, should I be?"

He stared at me, and I could almost hear the little cogs revolving in behind those button eyes. Finally he put down the glass and dish-cloth and wiped his hands on his apron. He stuck one out and said, "I'm Vincent Chinelio. I'm the other half of the partnership."

I took the hand and shook it. He hadn't done much physical work in his life, but the grip was reasonable and he didn't try to tickle my palm. I let go, then sat up on one of the bar stools. The seat was contoured to fit and it clasped my backside lovingly. I wondered if I would have a struggle getting free of it.

"The reason I'm looking for Richie," I said, "is because a mutual friend asked me to look him up."

"Which friend?"

I thought about that one, then decided it would not do any harm to mention Max's name.

"A guy called Max Morganthau," I said, and watched a frown slide down Chinelio's fat face.

"Morganthau? I know a Maxie Morgan. Small and muscular and hung ..."

"That's him. He must have dropped the 'thau'."

"That's not the only thing he's in the habit of dropping." Chinelio leered but when he saw I wasn't going to join him he went on, "Why send you? He was in here himself the other night."

"Well, I'm in insurance and I guess he thought Richie could do with some."

"He must know something I don't. Is it personal insurance you're talking about?"

"That's it."

Chinelio went all thoughtful, gnawing at his lip with the couple of teeth he had left in his upper jaw. He looked as if he could do with a good insurance policy himself for his mouth.

Eventually he said, "Richie's not around at the moment. He could be anywhere, but he's most likely at home having a siesta. Although I don't think he'd like to be disturbed."

"Why not?"

"Why d'you think?"

"He's reading Nietzsche and thinking about wearing his underpants over his tights?"

"Huh?"

"Is it a bird? Is it a plane? No, it's Superman ..."

To stop the fat man's mouth from dropping any further open, I ordered a Bushmills. I was beginning to feel a bit hung over, headachy and a little parched. Another hair of the dog was on the cards – at least so I told myself.

He poured and I drank, then I lit a cigarette and blew a thin stream of smoke towards the ceiling. I noticed that it too had graffiti on it and wondered at the Michaelangelo who had taken

25

the trouble to so decorate it. Seemed a lot of trouble to go to just to carve one's name with pride.

"Where does Richie live?" I asked in a conversational tone, but my companion was not to be deceived.

"Why d'you want to know?"

"I thought I might amble out there and have a chat with him about cucumbers," I said. "Maybe he's got an allotment that we could cultivate together."

Chinelio looked me up and down, standing on tiptoe to do so. "Seems a pity to go all the way over there when you could do your sowing and reaping here," he said.

"I like to travel. See new places. Where's over there?"

"His address is in the phone book."

"But you could take the labour out of it by giving me it."

"Why would I want to do that?"

"Because you're an obliging git who enjoys helping out his fellow man?"

He didn't like that one but he forced the smile to stay on his gap-toothed face. I had the distinct impression he might be shrewder than he looked. There was something about the shiny button eyes, an opaque blandness as if the real he were in hiding and only peering out covertly when I wasn't looking. Then again it could be my over active imagination at work, sending out signals to confuse rather than enlighten me. I decided another Bushmills might help and, when Chinelio brought it, I downed it with an alacrity that surprised both of us.

"Richie lives out in Ballsbridge," my fat friend volunteered, possibly as a reward for the amount of whiskey I was buying. "He's got a flat in the Apollo apartment building. Filbert Road, opposite the RDS. You can't miss it."

I turned the shotglass around in my hand, thinking how small it looked in my large paw. I was approaching that stage of drunkenness where irresponsibility overlaps decorum; if I tossed back one or two more I would become either mischievously playful or meanly belligerent. Neither mood would suit the time, the place, the moment, so, regretfully, I made up my mind to leave my convivial companion and his nice dim and dark, cool place of business. Taking a lungful of the alcohol-tainted air, I said, "Well, I've got to be on my way. Duty calls. If I do manage to see Richie, shall I give him your best regards?"

Someone came in behind me and Chinelio's gaze shifted over my left shoulder, but it was only some guy on his way to the toilet. A stray beam of sunlight had winkled its way in from outside and was glinting off the bottles stacked behind the bar. I felt such a wave of feeling for that place, and a deep sadness because I had to leave it. But then, bars invariably have that effect on me.

"Don't tell him I gave you his address," Chinelio said, the grin still fixed to his face as if stuck on. I would have liked to have asked him about his teeth, or lack of them, but felt I should wait for a more opportune time. Instead I said, "What have Budweiser beer and making love in a canoe got in common?"

He thought about it, wrinkling his brow. "I give up," he said. "What have they in common?"

"They're both fucking close to water."

For a few seconds he didn't get it, then he began to giggle. I climbed down from the stool, my backside coming off the seat with an audible pop. Best to leave them laughing, I thought, so, giving him a parting salute, I made for the particulate suspension of dust motes in sunlight that marked the open door.

My car, a 1986 Renault 9, was sick again and in the garage, so I had to catch a number 8 bus out to Ballsbridge. The sun shining through the window made me drowsy, and I leaned against the warm glass and snoozed. Max Morganthau invaded my dreams, riding his giant Kawasaki backwards and forwards over my protesting head, shouting "Hup, ye boy ye," each time the wheels left tyre marks across my face.

I woke up, shuddering, as the bus was crossing Mount Street Bridge, causing the old lady who had sat down next to me hurriedly to change seats. My mouth felt as if someone had emptied a used ashtray into it, and my headache was high on the Richter scale and climbing.

I gazed out at the fine old redbrick residences we were passing. Lawns tended towards the scorched and flowers drooped their technicoloured heads. The weather had been fine now for a week, oppressively so; the sun shone from a clear blue sky, tarmacadam bubbled, people discarded more and more clothes, and the city seethed like a cauldron about to blow its lid. My friend Superintendent George Quinlan of the Special Branch was always uneasy in this kind of weather, believing that it further inflamed the minds of the criminally insane. He could quote facts and figures to substantiate his belief that more murders occurred in hot sultry conditions than at any other time. "Mark my words," he had counselled me at the weekend, "but this is surely killing weather." At the time he had been furiously blowing bottles off a rocky escarpment in the quarry behind his suburban home with a pump-action target gun, so the probability of his being correct about mass slaughter in the city was not lost on me.

I got off the bus opposite the buildings of the Royal Dublin Society. Towards the south a knot of deep purple cloudbank was beginning to shoulder itself into the sky and the clammy foretaste of an approaching thunderstorm was bleeding its way over rooftops and through gaps in the buildings.

Filbert Road was easy enough to find and I walked down it, traversing a level-crossing with its red-and-white striped barrier raised high and trembling as though readying itself to descend on my anxious head. I made a sign of friendship at the face in the station house window and got through without being clobbered.

The road curved, bending its way down towards Sandymount and the environs of Dublin Bay. I thought of Joyce's 'snotgreen sea' and 'scrotumtightening sea' and my own nether parts took a turn for the worse. What I would have given for Chinelio's bum-clasping stool, a place at his horseshoe-shaped bar and a warming bumper of fiery amber Bushmills. Instead, here I was standing outside the awful shiny newness of Apollo House, its balconied tiers of flats like teeth waiting to tear strips off my wholesome.

Shivering away the image, I went up the five shallow steps to the heavy, glassed front door and pushed at it hopefully. It was as firm and steadfast as a Reverend Mother's underwear. I shaded my eyes and peered inside. The vestibule was small, pinched and impersonal, and it boasted no doorman nor guardian angel to protect the inhabitants from casual rape, robbery or ransacking. Instead there was an intercom beside the door and, I presumed, a switch in each individual apartment to work the lock.

I gazed up at the face of the building and at the milky aspect of sky above it. Suction pads on my hands and knees would be the way to climb it, but I had no head for heights, not to mention the Spiderman accoutrement, so I gave up on that idea right away. Casting around for other options, I stared at the list of names set in metal brackets on the wall to my right. Richie Michaels had flat number 7, so I pressed his bell and awaited developments.

Time went by. The breeze had freshened and was blowing its hot breath in my face. Thunderheads were barrelling their way further and further up into the sky and there was a scent of incoming rain. There was a hush and to complement it I instinctively held my breath.

When it was eventually borne in on me that Richie was not going to respond to my summons I checked the list of names again. Selecting two, a Pat Howard and a Stephen Magnier, I squinted my eyes and thought about them for a while. Pat could be either male or female, so I pushed his or her bell. The voice that answered was depersonalised by the intercom system and I was no wiser as to gender. Quickly I said, "Sorry about this. Stephen Magnier here. I've mislaid my keys. Could you buzz me in?"

There was a pause, then a metallic whirr sounded and the door clicked and moved a fraction. Hurriedly I caught hold of it, pushed it further open and stepped inside. It settled back into place behind me with a polite sigh.

There was a lift facing me but I decided to use the stairs instead. Confined spaces are inclined to make me hyperventilate. My footfalls echoed on the cement steps but, confident in my assumed identity, I motored on.

At the first landing I opened the metal fire door and peered around it. Four varnished wood portals faced me, two to my right, two to my left. In the middle a red fire extinguisher in a glass-fronted case was fixed to the wall. The legend 'Break in an emergency' tempted me, but I steeled my resolution to act in a temperate and ruly fashion.

The door with the number 7 on it was to my right. I stood regarding it, then I unfolded my linen jacket and struggled into it. Squaring my shoulders and hoping the seams would not explode, I reached out and knocked softly on the wooden panel.

More time went by. I stared at the door, the door stared back at me. I wondered which of our stares was the more blank. I tried again, with the same result. Nothing. Either Richie was elsewhere or he was not in the mood, as his partner had prophesied, for receiving visitors.

I thought about knocking on doors 5, 6 and 8, in the hope that he had the habit of leaving a spare key with one of his neighbours and that I could convince whoever it was that I was his long-lost son, father, brother – knock off the one not applicable – but soon consigned that idea also to the rubbish heap. I probably didn't look in the least like old Richie, and from what I knew from Max of his base propensities I sincerely hoped not.

Furtively I gazed about, but the landing was bare of humanity except for myself. From behind one of the doors I could hear the faint sound of classical music, and there was an odour of food being fried. Near the ceiling a nervous-looking spider was doing a bungee jump on a string of his web, but I reckoned he was too busy to pay me any regard.

I took out my wallet and extracted my Access card. My fingers fumbled with it but I knew that if it fell on the floor it would bounce straight back up – my cheques did, so why not it? With great care I slid it into the crack in the door where I could discern the glint of the lock. I had been assured many times by those in the know that you cannot open a Yale lock with a credit card but had always wanted to try for myself. Like Doubting Thomas, I too would have needed to stick my fingers in the wounds.

I sawed the card backwards and forwards, sweat dripping into my eyes and causing me to blink. About to give up, I felt a resistance, pushed harder and heard the almost orgasmic sound of the bolt sliding back. If there was no mortice lock I was in.

There wasn't and I was. Quickly I slipped inside and closed the door behind me. I rested for a moment, my shoulders against the panel. There was a faint, high-pitched whining noise seemingly coming from inside the apartment, but otherwise no outraged challenge greeted my sudden and unlawful entry.

I was standing in a small hallway with further doors facing me, all closed. I tried the one immediately within reach and found myself looking into a minuscule kitchen, and an untidy one at that. There was an unpleasant odour such as one gets a few days after neglecting to mop up spilled milk. I shut that door and opened another.

This time I received a vista of carpeted living-room and an increase in the volume of the whine. I could also see the top of a person's head just visible above the top of what looked like a recliner. Shifting my feet, I coughed apologetically, but it brought no reaction: no one peered around the blue tufted cushion, the head didn't move, the sound of the whining didn't decrease in volume.

I got a sinking feeling in my stomach that had nothing to do with the amount of drink I'd consumed. On leaden feet I moved around until I could obtain a better view of the person occupying the lilo, then wished I hadn't. He was a medium-sized, blond guy wearing a silk dressing-gown, grey with just a suggestion of red fleck in the weave. His slippers were leather slip-ons, highly polished, his socks navy blue with pink dancing cupids, and the couple of inches of bare leg between them and his pyjamas were nicely tanned.

All this I registered before I reluctantly raised my gaze above his waist, past the vermilion cravat to the tip of the telephone receiver protruding from his gaping mouth. Someone had obviously made sure he got the message, for the cream laminated instrument had been rammed down his throat with such force that only the cord set into the base was visible.

His face was a bruised, purplish colour, his eyes bulging out further than eyes should ever bulge. Twin rivulets of blood ran from the corners of his ripped mouth and spread in blotched stains where they met the cushion under his head. His outflung arms ended in clenched fists, the awfulness of his death imparting a coiled spring attitude to his body as if he were about to leap up as soon as the obstruction in his throat were removed. The whining noise was coming from the telephone console, familiar to me now that I could see its place of origin.

I stood and looked at him, wondering if he were Richie

31

Michaels. The probability was that it was indeed he. I was beginning to feel slightly fragile, the drink I had consumed sloshing around in my stomach and endeavouring to find a way out. I returned to the small hallway, gagging as I went. I tried another door, found myself in a bedroom, walked through it to the en suite bathroom, got sick in the toilet, flushed it, drank a glass of water and tried to stop shaking. Even in the soft-focus mirror above the washbasin I was pale, haggard and furtive, like someone who had had an unfortunate encounter with the ghost of Hamlet's father.

I stood for a while until my stomach settled down, then I wiped my mouth with the back of my hand. A thought struck me and I picked up a pink fluffy towel and cleaned the outside of the glass I had drunk from and the gold-plated tap I had twisted.

Still holding the towel I went back into the bedroom. There was an oriental rug on the floor – a caliph with pointed slippers and a string moustache leering at a dancing girl in diaphanous veils was the motif. The bed was a brass four-poster with a canopy over it whose trailing drapes could be lowered to screen the occupants from prying eyes. The covers were rumpled as though recently slept in, cream silk sheets thrown back, the pillows in matching material indented. I sniffed and the unmistakable odour of marijuana fingered its way up my nose, promising naughtiness on a minor scale.

I wondered what my course of action should be. Getting out of there as fast as my legs could carry me seemed the obvious move, but I was tempted to have a quick search through the apartment in case the photographs Max had sent me to get might still be around. It was possible of course that Michaels – if it were he – had been killed because of those same pictures and that I had been sent along as the patsy. Then again maybe the naughty photos had nothing to do with it and it was the telephone repair man, grown weary of Richie gazing over his shoulder and proffering advice, who had done him in.

I was still trying to make up my mind as to what to do when a new sound was borne in on my consciousness, This was a low whimpering such as a puppy-dog might make when his bladder was full to bursting and he was too shy to lift his leg. I froze, an

32

icy finger tiptoeing up my spine. Was Richie an animal lover and would I have to slaughter the family pet to prevent him sniffing me out at a line-up sometime in the future? Was it a friendly little tyke that would gaze soulfully into my eyes and then do the dirty on me as soon as it got the chance? It was my heightened frame of reference that instigated such fantasising, the stuttering squall of fright that rooted me to the floor and set me to believing if I did regain my motive powers it would simply be to jump into the bed and pull those silk covers over my head.

Ah, to heck with it, I thought, am I a man or a mouse? Tentatively I approached the large, built-in wardrobe from which the sound was coming. I put my ear to its mirrored surface and tried to still my breathing so that I could listen. Yes, there it was, the painful mewling of a highly unhappy animal, inside the press, only inches from my ear.

I started back, my hand instinctively rising to shield my face. If I opened the door, whatever was inside would surely set about me with the ferocity of cornered desperation, a swirl of flashing teeth and salivating jaws. Then again, it might merely trot out, lift its leg and piss on my shoe.

I eyed the wardrobe; as ever where action was called for, caught in a dilemma. Go on, I told myself, take a chance. Only half convinced, I got a pillow from the bed, came back and, holding the soft satiny bulwark in front of me, slid the door of the wardrobe open. At first all I could see was a racked array of suits and sports jackets, more than I had ever owned in my life. Then my eyes were drawn to the pair of feet and bare legs that protruded from beneath them. Ordinary in every way, they had, no distinguishing features, no webbed toes nor fallen arches, no corns, bunions nor chilblains.

Working on the assumption that they were attached to a body, I reached in and parted the row of clothes. A slight young man, completely naked, was hunched into a corner of the alcove, one hand in front of his face, the other positioned in the air as though ready to claw and rend. A sad brown eye gazed out reprovingly, possibly blaming me for uncovering his nudity before he had the chance to robe himself.

It is very difficult to come up with the proper greeting on an

33

occasion like that, so I contented myself with a nod and a backing away to indicate my good intentions. I even reached into my pocket, took out my cigarettes and lit one. Nothing like the familiar for putting naked youths hiding in wardrobes at their ease.

As the suits had fallen back into place I could no longer see him, and he made no effort to emerge. Suddenly angry, I approached once more, bent down, caught him by the foot and yanked him unceremoniously into view. He came with a squeal like a stuck pig, then abruptly shut it off and lay on the floor looking at me, his hands cupping his genitals, his eyes wild and unfocussed.

I let him stew and went and sat on the bed and puffed at my cigarette, The room had grown dark and through the window I could see the heavy roll of cloudmass that now obscured the sky. It would not be long before the rain came. I imagined it pounding down and the vision had a pleasing effect on my mood. It would not wash away what was in the other room, but it would surely carry with it the illusion of a cleansing of sorts.

Young Lochinvar had sat up and was inching his way along the floor, not in the direction of the door but towards the dressing-table. There were clothes draped over the back of a chair and I guessed he wished to garb himself before engaging in pre-cocktail chat.

How wrong I was. With his right hand he suddenly took hold of the bedside lamp, hefted it and then threw it in my direction. Unfortunately for him, it was still plugged in, and it held, snapped back and hit him in his surprised mug. An unsettling clatter ensued as both he and the lamp fell on the floor.

Something boiled up in me and I got the urge to stub out my cigarette in his navel. I resisted, topped the burning end into the rug and rubbed it under my shoe. Then I got off the bed and met him as he once more struggled upwards. I caught him by the cock and pulled, hard but not hard enough to tear it off. He put both his hands around my wrist and tried to dislodge my grip, but he had no strength to speak of.

Face to face, we gazed long and deep into one another's eyes. His were wide and startled, but suddenly they went all soulful

34

and he leaned forward and kissed me full on the lips. I recoiled, stumbling back but retaining my hold on his willie. He groaned pleasurably and lurched along after me.

This time I let go and pushed him backwards. I noticed that the pupils of his eyes were enlarged, the whites splintered with tiny veins – a warning to me that he was on something a little stronger than fine water. I looked down at the hand that had held his ding-a-ling and I went once more into the bathroom and gave the offending paw a good scrubbing.

When I came back he was sitting on the bed, still naked. It seemed to be a state that came naturally to him. He was engaged in snuffling up lines of white powder from the surface of a pocket mirror, a finger damping down one nostril while he sucked with the other. He was totally absorbed in what he was doing, so I left him and began a desultory search of the apartment.

I really did not have my heart in it, and the presence of the body in the living-room did nothing to stir enthusiasm into my task. I plumped cushions, opened drawers, looked under the carpet. There was an open fireplace and I poked around in the chimney with an ornate brass poker. Soot cascaded down and did little swirls and arabesques against the red tiles.

I opened the one remaining door and peered into the spare bedroom. It was stacked with cardboard boxes and wooden crates containing empty beer bottles and had the dusty smell and feel of a place not too often frequented. I shifted a few things, but the feeling was becoming more and more insistent in my mind that it was time I got out of there. At any moment someone might unlock the door and push his or her way in: Chinelio, the partner, for instance, might be anxious about his colleague's health, or lack of it; or the killer might return to see if Richie had coughed up any messages.

I trudged once more into the bedroom and gazed at the boy stripper, where he continued to recline on the bed. The coke had taken the jelly out of his backbone and he gave me a look that was derisory in the extreme. He had a smooth, hairless body and looked younger than his twenty-one years.

"Come on, Archie," I said, my educated guess at who he was

occasioning a start of surprise. "Get some clothes on and we'll fly the coop. It wouldn't do for either of us to be here when the law arrives."

He scowled, an expression that slipped easily on to his boyish features; petulance, I imagined, would be his natural caprice.

"How'd you know my name?" he asked, his voice snooty and redolent of the confidence money and influence bring. Instinctively I knew he was a right little prat and deserved everything that life hopefully had in store for him. For the moment, though, I was being paid to look out for his welfare, the correctness of my identification of him as Mossie Haly's son indemnifying the fact.

"You've got it tattooed on your left buttock," I said. "Arse for Archie, or vice versa as the case may be. Throw some duds on and we'll make tracks, singing as we go."

He got up, all wobbles and shakes like Marcel Marceau doing a mime of a blancmange – either he was doing it to annoy me or the drugs had given him the jitters. Everything about him was on the miniature scale, including his private parts. He was so thin that if he turned sideways he would merely be a straight line. He had tight gingery hair cut plateau fashion, shaved on the sides and the back, wiry ringlets on top. His skin was bone white, his eyes, nose and mouth small, and he could have done with a sliver more of chin to lend definition to his face. As he gazed about him he reminded me of a ferret looking out of a hole to see if the coast was clear.

He began clothing himself: high-buttoned, red flannel vest with elbow-length sleeves, cowboy waistcoat, baggy cotton trousers held up by purple braces and a leather belt with a large ornate S buckle, and high backed red-and-white striped Michael Jordan air runners. The outfit imparted a cool and sassy appearance: Michael J Fox maybe, just as he was about to throw yet another beer can out the window of his stretch limousine. I felt a glitch of nausea rattle in one of my yards of gut and an accompanying poof of wind under my breastbone.

To prevent myself from bopping him one, I said, "Who killed your pal in the other room? And why'd he leave you around to tell the tale?"

Archie paused and I guessed maybe he had heard the mermaids singing, but then he produced a comb out of a back pocket and began settling his hair. He exhibited no particular unease, whistling between his teeth as he worked, using his left hand with open palm to pat this and that stray curl into place. He was as unconcerned about the pickle he was in as a gherkin in a jar.

"Listen," I said, "I've been hired by a friend of your father's to retrieve some compromising photographs that you were stupid enough to allow to be taken. Going on the supposition that my duties also extend to protecting your butt, I'm about to get both of us out of here in double-quick time. But first maybe you'd give me an inkling of what happened. Are you listening to me?"

The rain which had been threatening suddenly shook itself loose and gave a rat-a-tat-tat on the window, causing both of us to jump. There was a quick flicker of lightning, then a heave of thunder rolled overhead. It had also grown decidedly dark in the room, and cold, cold as the grave. I shivered, thinking of what was in the other room.

Not so young Archie however. Dredging up a supercilious scowl he said, "Ring for a taxi and get me home, if you're my minder."

I looked at him, then I said, "How the fuck can I ring for a taxi when the phone is wedged down your pal Richie's throat? Should I climb up his rear end and get at it that way?"

Archie thought about that one, then in the same superior tone he said, "Yes, I can see that might cause a problem. Maybe you could knock up one of the other tenants and use theirs ...?"

I blinked, screwed up my eyes, thought about extracting the phone from Richie's gullet and ramming it down his, but then relented, not on his behalf but on my own. I had deliberately gone into this on the back of Max's expectations of me and my capabilities. Was I now going to let a little prick like Archie chase me out of it? No fear. I was a fifteen-stone, ex-hurling star with balls; I could handle anything that came along, and that included a dead body, a vandalised telephone, missing photographs and a cocaine-sniffing rich kid with deviant sexual impulses.

"You know," I said, "in America the phrase 'to knock someone up' means to impregnate. If you said over there what

37

you just said to me, they'd think you wanted me to poke one of the other tenants ..."

He gazed at me with incomprehension starting out of his eyeballs. I passed a hand over my own eyes and said, "I know, I don't understand what I'm talking about either. It must be delayed shock. We can pick up a taxi outside. The rain'll provide cover. Keep people with inquiring minds indoors ..."

He shrugged and put the finishing touches to his coiffure. Then he replaced the comb in his back pocket. He wet an index finger and ran it over each of his eyebrows in turn. He was for the moment quite a composed young man. Behind him the rain poured down the window, creating wavery outlines. In the fading light the cream silk sheets on the rumpled bed were but a pale gleam.

In a coaxing tone I said, "What happened here? It'd be in your best interests to tell me. I'm John Blaine and I'm a private investigator. Max Morganthau, at your father's behest, paid me good money to do a search and retrieve mission on the glossies of yourself and Richie cavorting ..."

"Cavorting?"

"Whatever you were at. Forming a daisy-chain? Playing hidey-hole? Before Richie got the phone stuck down the wrong orifice."

That got to him. "I didn't have anything to do with that," he said sulkily. "We were in here having a good time when there was a ring at the door. Richie went out and opened it and I could hear him talking to someone. Then he came back in and told me to stay in bed and keep my head down. I must've fallen asleep and when I woke up ... well ..." He shrugged again and made a pouting expression with his lips.

"You didn't get up at any stage to have a look? Maybe put your eye to the crack in the door just to see what was going on?"

"No. To tell you the truth, I wasn't feeling too hot."

"Something you ate?"

"Possibly," he said, missing the sarcasm. "Anyway, when I finally went out I found him ... well, like he is."

With thumb and index finger I massaged my forehead, but my headache had been reactivated and was sending out exploratory shoots of pain. As though to exacerbate it, thunder again rumbled overhead. Archie's story had as many holes in it as a sieve, but now was not the time to begin quizzing him on its inconsistencies.

I looked about me, wondering what the best course of action might be. It would be difficult to disguise the fact of Archie's occupancy. There were too many of his fingerprints in the apartment, maybe more of his clothes and other belongings. And Chinelio, Richie's partner, he would know about him. However, the fact that he often visited, probably staying the odd night, would explain the signs of his being there. And he would most likely not have been the only young man to have been entertained there. If and when he was questioned, he could always say he had left Richie in the best of form – he might even have the audacity to remark that Richie was chatting away on the phone when he left. Providing he refrained from kissing the interrogating policeman on the lips as he had bussed me, he might not even be detained.. He didn't even look strong enough to have done the deed. Richie was no giant from what I had seen of him, but it would demand a fair amount of fire-power to subdue a man in such extremes of terror.

"What're we waiting for?" Archie suddenly asked me. "I thought we were about to split."

I went and got the fuzzy towel again and wiped down everything I remembered touching. I knew I should search the body, but I couldn't bring myself to do it. I did consider asking Archie if he would oblige, but he was sidling about the sitting-room like a dog seeking somewhere to lift its leg and I decided it was not worth the effort.

I opened the door of the apartment and peered cautiously about. The landing was still bare of humanity. Even the jumpy spider had given up and gone off in search of his mid-afternoon repast. Archie was standing uncomfortably close to me, so much so that I could feel his breath on the back of my neck.

"Doesn't it bother you that your ... ah ... friend is lying back there as cold as yesterday's mutton?" I asked him. "Aren't you scared you'll be implicated in his death? Maybe accused and convicted and put into jail forever and a day?"

He merely stared at me, his doe-like eyes only a couple of

inches from mine. I knew a girl with eyes like that once, demure, innocent, as clear as a spring well. One night she had set fire to the family home and danced around it while her aged mother and father fried and sizzled inside. One can't go by appearances where good and evil are concerned. Again the thought came into my mind that Archie might after all have killed Richie – where there's a will there is always a way, and someone like him, wilful, perverse, used to getting his own way, might do something like that and not think too much about it afterwards. Like a child tearing the wings off a fly ...

I pushed him away from me, wiped knobs and handles and threw the towel back into the sitting-room before I closed the door. We went down the backstairs like comic villains, on the soles of our feet, hands extended. Anyone coming up would have taken a decidedly rum view of our progress, but we were lucky and met no one, not even Richie's ghost.

Three

It wasn't just raining outside, it was whacking down with a ferocity that plainly bespoke the fact that it had it in for us humans. Dublin Corporation and contingency plans not being on speaking terms, the water was already beginning to flow and gurgle out of the gutters. Filbert Road, near the bay and low lying, was rapidly taking on the appearance of a minor lake and it would not be too long before anyone venturing out would be in dire need of crotch-length rubber boots.

We stood in the overhang of the entrance to Apollo House and gazed out at the downpour. The banked and landscaped beds of flowering shrubs were being denuded of covering clay, and the hard heavy rain drummed against the broad leaves of the trees that such a short time before had shaded walkers from the hot July sun.

"You haven't got a car?" forgetful young Archie asked me in a chiding tone.

"No, I came here by thought transference," I told him. "I'm really only a holograph."

The chance of hailing an idling taxi in that quiet secluded road was as likely as finding a little green man on Mars, but I was loth to wander off and leave Junior on his own. It was important to me that I get him home safely, a sense of duty to my calling as a fully paid-up member of the ancient guild of private detectives. The client always came first, and nothing must be allowed get in the way of what his paltry stipend buys. In this case, if it meant me getting wet to my drawers, then so be it. But if I were about to get pissed on, Archie wasn't going to remain in shelter and watch it happen.

I shoved him along in front of me, protesting loudly; down the five steps and along the path under the trees. Before we had gone a matter of metres we were drenched to the skin, but the sudden and total immersion brought with it an accompanying carelessness of outlook. How wet can you get, other than wet wet?

We splashed along, the urge nibbling at me to do a Gene Kelly and swing out of a lamppost while warbling a verse of "Singing in the Rain". I resisted it and we soon arrived at the top of the road and the more open and busy spaces of Ballsbridge – or "The Testicular Viaduct", as some wag once christened it.

It took a while to flag down a taxi and when we did the driver grumbled about the mess we were making of his upholstery. He was obviously car-proud, for the interior was spick and span and there was a smell of polish that would poison a duck.

I looked to Archie for guidance as to our destination and, when he provided an address in Rathfarnham, I passed it on to surly puss behind the wheel.

We sat in the clean-smelling interior of the cab and gave ourselves over to our thoughts. I can't vouch for Archie's or the driver's, but mine were as low as a corgi's belly-button. Max Morganthau – or Morgan as it seemed I was now bound to view him – was only a matter of hours back in my life and already I was in shite up to my eyelashes. Investigating insurance frauds, getting the dirt on errant husbands and wives, doing a little debt collecting, those were the staples of my livelihood. Not endeavours guaranteed to elevate one into the higher echelons of the social register, granted, but honest toil for an honest penny just the same. But now, for the second time in the space of a year, I was involved in murder and mayhem. Discovering dead bodies was becoming a usual occurrence for me. Richie, back on the recliner, might have been a life-size doll for all the effect he had had on me. Or on boy Archie beside me, either.

I looked at him out of the corner of my eye. He was as composed as a choirboy who had safely delivered a high C, his face in profile calm and unruffled. That's what drugs do for you, I told myself.

The rain had calmed now and was no more than a half-hearted flurry. As we journeyed through a built-up area of shops and pubs I spotted a telephone kiosk that looked unvandalised. "Hey," I told our driver, "stop over there. I want to make a call."

He pulled in and braked to a halt. When I opened the door I found myself regarding a sheet of what looked like ankle-deep water. "Could you move a little?" I asked him. "If I jump out here I'll drown."

He threw a glance at me over his shoulder and I was reminded of a bulldog licking piss off a nettle. But he did condescend to manoeuvre the cab further on a few feet so that I could get out without causing a splash. I went into the telephone box, dialled 999 and told the voice that answered that something awful had taken place in Flat 7, Apollo House, Filbert Road, Ballsbridge. The guy, cursed by curiosity, was inclined to linger, but I hung up and got out of there. Telephones, as far as I was concerned, were not exactly user-friendly.

We continued on our way and soon the rain ceased altogether and the sun came back out again to play. We were in suburbia now, the houses better spaced, green areas more prevalent. The clouds had pulled back to let the high blue sky shine out, and the light was being showy, sliding off wet glistening surfaces, etching pointillistic patterns through tree foliage, playfully dappling this and that obstruction in variegated lines, stripes and hot broad strokes. God, it seemed, was back in his heaven and summer was serene once more to put people's minds at rest. At least those who didn't have dead bodies and wayward, sulky rich kids to worry about.

When we came to the address that Archie had given – The Beeches, Old Pond Road – we were already into the early reaches of the Dublin Mountains, a fetching panorama of fields, thickets of pine, and the odd craggy outcrop of rock. The estate was guarded by a new stone wall that the builders had tried to disguise as an old stone wall, but the cement interstices gave it away. Two matching pillars with capped tops supported a heavy, ornamental gate. It was open and Archie imperiously signalled to the taxi man to motor on in.

We followed the curve of a winding, gravel drive, through smooth as butter, green lawns, trees, banks of flowers, odd bits of statuary, a tennis court the eyelets of whose net winked with the iridescence of the recent rain. The house itself was an impressive pile, all cut stone cornices, bay windows, climbing ivy and chimney pots with wire tops on them like soup strainers. I was impressed, and so was the taxi driver, his scowl replaced by an expression of incipient awe.

I paid him off and Archie and I climbed out and stood

watching as he turned and took off back down the driveway, the gravel crunching under the wheels. The sun was warm on my back and I took off my sodden linen jacket and draped it over a bush. I could have removed the rest of my clothes as well and hung them out to dry for they were in as sorry a state as the coat.

Archie watched me making myself at home, the taxi man's expression of disdain having now come to roost on his puny features. Plainly he was not enamoured of my behaviour.

"I'll collect it on the way out," I told him, indicating the already steaming garment.

He stared at it, then at me. "You're already on your way out," he said, the scowl in his voice as well as on his boyish mug. "Nothing for you here, skipper. Contact your friend if you need more money." He gave his shoulders a little hike, à la James Cagney, and flicked at his nose with his thumb. "Now, hop it."

"Are you not even a teeny-weeny bit grateful to me for rescuing you?" I asked him. "For plucking you from the jaws of a fate worse than death? Not to mention an uncomfortable few hours, if not longer, in the company of the boys in blue ..."

He frowned, then poked at the gravel with the toe of his shoe. Had I finally got through to his better nature? Was I about to see the good side of him? Not likely ...

"You can fuck off about your business," he sneered. "Otherwise I'll sic the dog on you."

I held my temper and counted slowly to ten. I said, "I want to see your father."

"He's not in. He's gone to Bangkok."

"To become a monk, I presume?"

I took my cigarettes out of my trousers' pocket. I could have wrung water out of most of them, but a couple had escaped the worst of the deluge. I stuck one of them in my mouth and tried to light it with a wooden match, but the sulphur disintegrated with a pathetic little snivel. There, that gave me a further reason for going inside: I needed a dry match.

I took the cigarette out of my mouth and stuck it behind my ear. "Who is at home?" I asked the brat. "Surely there's someone into whose care I can deliver you?"

This time he didn't bother answering, he merely spat on the ground in front of my feet.

I sighed and did my counting routine again, then I said, "Let's go in and have a look, shall we? Someone might offer me a bowl of soup. Or maybe something stronger to warm the cockles of my heart. It's not a dry house, is it?"

"What're you going to tell them?" Archie asked, still inclined to dawdle.

"Who?"

"My mother. My sister."

"Now we're getting somewhere. I'll reel off my name, rank and serial number. Then I'll get down on the ground, turn over on my back and wave my paws in the air."

"No, I mean about ... well, you know ..."

I gazed at him sternly, and it wasn't just the sun that was making me hot under the collar.

"Listen, you little shit," I told him, "you've got me involved in a situation that's not of my own making, and if the law catch on to the fact that I removed you and myself from the scene of a crime, a very very serious crime, a crime of which there is none more serious, then I'll be in danger of losing my licence, my freedom and possibly my balls. I want to talk to your father, your mother, or to anyone who's got control over you. I want to work out a strategy with them wherein you'll be hogtied somewhere safe while I go off and try to get both of us off the hook, either by approaching the minions of the law on my knees and pleading mitigating circumstances, softening of the brain cells, incipient madness, galloping amnesia ..."

"Or?"

"Or by finding the real killer." I stared at him keenly. "There is a real killer, isn't there? It won't be a question of me huffing and puffing around the city while the object of my quest is right in front of me all the time, will it?"

At least he looked me in the eye when he said, "What d'you mean?"

"Never mind."

"You think I knocked Richie off, don't you?"

"Don't get excited about it."

"I like tough guys," Archie breathed, a wistful note in his voice. "You could knock me about a bit, if you liked. Maybe tie me up ..."

"I could give you a good hard kick in the arse," I muttered, then regretted it as soon as I'd said it: a kick in the arse was obviously what he was angling for, he being into the sado-masochistic syndrome. "What is it with you?" I asked him. "Are you really gay or is it the fashionable thing to be this month? Are you getting your kicks from the shadow or the substance? Or are you using it as a means to annoy old Mossie? Getting up his nose, putting a kink in his comfort zone ...?"

"You know him, do you?"

"Oh, yes. Once upon a time I was one of his golden boys."

"He liked boys?"

"A figure of speech. He was by way of being a patron of this, that and the other. I happened to be involved in the other."

"Which was?"

"Sport. I was a massive sporting figure in my time, a colossus, a mighty man ..."

"Seems to me I might have heard of you."

"Flattery will get you everywhere." I stretched, enjoying the warmth of the sun on my face. "Enough of this chitchat. Let's go inside and find the ladies. I'm fed up with all this man talk. Jolly jocks are grand in the locker room, but when the air is balmy, the soft music is wafting clear and free, and the blood is up, a woman is your only man ..."

I left him to chew on that load of old cobblers and went and rang the front doorbell. I was in need of some fresh company to rekindle my trust in the innate goodness of human nature.

The girl who opened the door and stood gazing enquiringly at me fitted the bill just about to perfection. She was wearing tennis whites: a short pleated skirt and a cotton shirt with a red collar. Her hair was dark, with a burnished gleam where it fitted closely the contours of her shapely skull. She had green eyes, a small neat nose and slightly pouting lips that looked eminently kissable. The rest of her equipment also matched up: full breasts, a slim waist and long, sun-browned legs without a scrape or a scar to take from

46

their smooth symmetry. I couldn't have wished her any better.

As my eyes came back up to hers, she said, "Satisfied with the inventory or would you like the back view as well?"

I flushed, something that doesn't happen to me often. To cover my confusion I said, "I'm sorry. I've been having a bad day and the sight of you brought a sudden tear to my eye. You'll have to give me a moment to recover my equilibrium."

"Take as long as you like. I see you've got my little brother with you. Are you one of his passing boyfriends?"

"Passing?"

"As in ships that pass in the night. They go and they come. Or should that be the other way round?"

"A jolly thought. Who knows where the answer lies? The fact is I only met him a little earlier this afternoon. Not really enough time to have our relationship develop ..."

"Or not develop, as the case may be?"

I raised my eyebrows, but made no reply.

"But so far? Come on, give me a qualified judgement."

"So far he's been a pain in the ... neck?"

She looked cool, amused, in control, a veritable paragon of the confident young thing of today's generation. Putting her head to one side and giving me a long studied stare, she said, "I know you, don't I? Seems to me ..."

"The name is Blaine, John Blaine. I'm a private investigator. Nothing too small for me to snoop into. I've been hired to expedite a highly confidential matter for your father ..."

"Now I remember," the girl said, paying no attention to the in-between information I had supplied. "You're that Wexford hurler. For how many years? ... the best part of ten? ... you were never out of the news. You were my pin-up. I daydreamed about you. I had one of your old jerseys that my father brought home and I wore it to all the matches. It smelled of your sweat, so I never washed it. I think I've still got it ..."

I preened myself, imagining the girl's nicely rounded upper structure being caressed by my sweaty old jersey. Brought her to a certain level of earthiness, a warm musky tumble maybe on crushed grass, the pristine tennis gear becoming as crumpled as the sports shirt.

Brother Archie, looking bored out of his top, brought me back to earth and dispelled my wild surmise by saying, "Are we going to stand here on the doorstep for ever? Step aside and let me in. I've things to do ..."

"Such as?" his sister challenged.

"I need a shower. And then I've letters to write, photographs to develop, phone calls to make" – he said this last bit without so much as the flicker of an eye.

"Hah!"

"What d'you mean 'hah'?"

"You can't wait to get upstairs to give yourself a little pick-me-up."

This time he looked insulted, cocking his snoot in the air much in the manner of Margaret Dumont when Groucho came out with yet another outrageous remark.

"I'll have you know ..." he started to say, but his sister cut him off with, "Mother wants to see you. She's in the drawing-room, the spider to your fly."

Instinctively Archie placed a hand on the threatened area as he saw it of his anatomy, accompanying the gesture with a step backwards. "What's she after?" he asked suspiciously.

Amused, his sister gazed down at where he had put his hand. "Probably your balls. But for the moment I believe it's a matter of some bills. Like a small mountain of them."

Young Archie had more changes of expression than a Victorian music hall villain. This time he dredged up his relieved look. "Oh, that," he shrugged, moving into the hall past the two of us. Pausing, he gazed back at me over his shoulder. "About that other business," he said, letting the remark hang in the air.

I made no attempt to parry it, putting on my own give-nothing-away mien. He waited expectantly, his mouth slightly open; then, when he realised I wasn't going to reassure him, he flushed and began searching for his angry and injured expression.

It was the girl who broke the deadlock by putting out her hand. "I'm Mary Haly," she said. "I don't expect you remember me. The last time you saw me I had braces on my teeth and hair like a brush. I was at that silly age, no knickers and in a continual state of the vapours ..."

48

Once more gratified – it doesn't take much – I took her small but strong hand and gave it a gentle squeeze. Holding it for a little longer than necessary, I then gave it back to her regretfully. It was the mention of 'knickers' that got me – it always does.

We proceeded down a carpeted hallway that reeked of good taste and the no-expense-spared means of satisfying it. There was no opulence; rather was it the spartan discreetness of the furnishings that imparted an air of refinement. Underfoot the pile was rich but not clinging. The pictures on the walls just about hummed the fact that they were most decidedly not reproductions. A carved wood hallstand reposed in a pool of polished and expensive serenity. Even the air had a super-cool whiff about it, as though it were being hosed in fresh on the hour, every hour.

We came to a door which Archie proceeded to push open and go through. Before I could do likewise the girl touched me lightly on the arm and said, "I'd like to see you before you go. I'll be on the tennis court. Just follow the plink-plonk of the balls" – she said this last bit in a way that made it sound highly charged with promise, somewhat like the swish of a silk stocking sliding down a smoothly bare leg.

I stood and watched her walk away from me, gliding gracefully through the old gold radiance of the sunlit hallway, and I remembered Chandler's remark about a girl having legs that would cause a bishop to kick a hole in a stained glass window. Luckily the only window in range of my sandals had leaded panes that looked impregnable. I shrugged and went on my way.

The room I came into was decorated in the style of Olde English cottage, as defined by Hollywood in all those black-and-white films of the thirties and forties. The windows were mullioned, the armchairs and sofa softly sagging and covered in brocade, with lace antimacassars draped over their backs. The ceiling was all wooden beams, fire blackened and pitted, while the floor had been left rough, the knots in the pine rising up to tease the feet that trod on them. All that was missing was Nigel Bruce standing in front of the fireplace, holding a niblick and clearing his throat.

The woman who stood at one of the windows, looking out, was not of that period, though. She was much more modern, richly packaged, exquisitely made up, her hair a blond bouffant

49

swirl, her face youthful but tinged by a penumbra of aging, her stance stiff and regal, her expectation probably high but rocked by many a rebuff because of the man she had married and the son she gave birth to.

This was shown now as she turned to gaze at him, a look of disapproval momentarily cracking the paintwork. But it just as quickly disappeared when she beheld me standing behind him.

"You are?" she asked, clasping her hands in front of her as if to show that she would not give me one to hold until a satisfactory identification had been made.

I told her who I was and that I had been engaged to handle a certain matter for her husband.

"Concerning?"

I glanced at Archie, then at the floor, then at a stray beam of sunlight that was saucily fingering the furniture. It didn't take her long to get my drift.

"Can you leave us for a few minutes?" she said to her son, her voice as cold and chill as a defrosting fridge.

He shifted his feet, stuck out a hip, jiggled the change in his trousers pocket. "I'd rather stay," he finally said. "He's going to talk about me and I want to hear what he has to say."

"Archie!"

The single word was as effective as a wooden mallet: it deflated young Archie, took away all his braggadocio, left him bereft of cockiness. Turning, he slunk out the door, as crestfallen as any young pup with its tail between its legs.

"Do you mind if I smoke?" I asked Mrs Haly, resurrecting the bedraggled fag from behind my ear and putting it in my mouth.

She shook her head, then picked up a silver inlaid box from a coffee table, opened it and took out a gold-tipped cigarette of her own. She lit it and mine from a matching silver lighter.

I watched her, held by the grace of her movements. She pulled delicately on the tipped cigarette as if she were sipping tea, expelled a polite plume of smoke, waved it away. The dress she was wearing was a wool sheath, and it outlined a body that would stand comparison with that of her daughter. She had lovely, long hands, the nails carefully shaped, no brown age spots disfiguring them. Yet I knew she had to be in her late forties or early fifties, the former Louise James, much sought after in the Wexford of my youth and eventually settling for Mossie Haly, high class boor but rotten with his father's money. There was a story that he had once pulled her across the floor by her hair at a hunt ball – the cavemen of old had nothing on Mossie when he put his mind to it.

Hard to credit such a rumour now that I could see at close quarters the object of his attentions. I looked deep into her eyes and beheld a wintery landscape which made me doubt that even the bull-like Mossie had ever lit her fire. Best thing for me would be to tell my story, curtsy and wait either to be thrown out or offered a Bonio.

"This work you're doing for my husband, is it of a very private nature?" she asked me, the cigarette held between her thumb and index finger, her expression and her posture telling me she would brook no shilly-shallying, no beating around the bush.

I sighed, shifted my feet, then said, "I'd like very much to sit down."

She eyed my damp shirt and mud-streaked slacks, then gave the royal assent for me to rest my weary bones. I felt that if I sat into either the loosely-stuffed sofa or one of its offspring, the accompanying armchairs, I'd never be able to extricate myself, so instead I choose a wooden carver with a felt seat and sturdy-looking arms and legs and plonked myself into it. Mrs Haly remained standing, her feet together, her body tensed, only the smoke from her cigarette moving as it trailed in slow loops in the sunlit air.

"The answer to your question is yes, the matter is of a private nature," I told her. "I wasn't approached directly by your husband but by a man who works for him ..."

"What man?"

"Max Morganthau."

The look of pain that had flitted across her patrician features at the sight of her son now reasserted itself, but again as then quickly fled. She said evenly, "You mean Max Morgan, don't you?"

"When I knew him he was Morganthau. And you would have known him as that too."

"Obviously he found the name cumbersome."

51

"Obviously." I watched her, but it was plain she was determined to play her cards close to her chest. "He came to see me at my office and put me on a retainer to carry out a little chore for your husband ..."

"You've met him?"

"Your husband? No, not recently." I looked at her, attempting to gauge her reason for pretending not to recognise me. "Come on, Mrs Haly," I said. "You know who I am. You've seen me before, shook my hand, murmured polite considerations at me. You and your husband both."

She gazed at me placidly, not in the least put out; then she went to a small table, picked up her handbag and opened it, and took out a pair of shell-rimmed spectacles and put them on. Possibly it was pride in her appearance that had prevented her from acknowledging me, rather than any more circumspect motive.

"Blaine. Yes, I thought I knew the name. You've dropped out of the headlines in recent years. But you haven't changed much. You still look fit and slightly ferocious. It must be the scar over your eyebrow."

"Probably," I said, fingering it. The day I got it had been one of my finest hours, the newspaper picture of me the next day in bloody bandage and ravaged face having won the press photographer a prize. It didn't win me anything, though, except a sore head and a memento that I'd carry to my grave. We lost the match and the championship.

"Where is your husband?" I pursued, attempting to put a little authority in my voice to cover up my soiled appearance and crumpled manner. Where she was concerned I might as well have been trying to impress a debt collector with a roll of Monopoly money.

She sniffed, took another teeny drag on her cigarette and said, "He'll be away until tomorrow. On business. No forwarding address, no telephone number."

"Is there no way of getting in touch with him?"

"Why don't you ask Morgan? He's his latest confidant."

"I'm afraid he left no way of being contacted either."

She raised an ironic eyebrow.

"Then you're faced with a dilemma, aren't you?"

Suddenly stung, I decided a riposte was in order. I said, "Not half as much as your son."

"Archie? I thought as much. What's he done now?"

I found the second drooping cigarette and lit it with her silver lighter. It was shaped in the form of a miniature globe of the world, the countries standing out as ridged roughnesses. If she hadn't been watching me closely I might have put it in my pocket.

"Nothing or everything," I answered. Deciding to test the strength of her composure, I told her of finding her son in the dead Richie's flat, and of how we had skipped before ringing the police. Her face got a little more set during the telling, but otherwise she registered as much emotion as a dead fish on a slab. It was clear she was used to hearing the worst about her son.

When I finished she went and sat down, taking off the glasses, dropping them in her lap and then stubbing out the cigarette. Immediately she opened the inlaid box and took out a fresh one and lit it. We smoked for a time in silence, then the faint chiming of a clock somewhere in the house seemed to rouse her.

"He didn't kill that man, of course," she said, gazing earnestly if a little short-sightedly at me. "He's capable of a lot, but not that. You believe me, don't you?"

"If you say so. You're his mother, so I suppose you should know."

She nodded, accepting my agreement. It's amazing how the maternal instinct can dominate in even the most blasé of women.

"He and his father have never got on. A case of both of them being disappointed in the other. I suppose I spoiled Archie as a consequence. Gave in to him when I should not have, indulged him and his odd friends ..."

I shrugged, listening to her but not responding. I had no sympathy to waste on either her or her son. I was involved, I told myself, because I'd accepted her husband's money and the amount of my attention it bought. Otherwise I was as interested as a stone Buddha.

"That's all very well, Mrs Haly," I said, "but the time for recriminations is past. Our immediate task is to work up a good story for Archie to tell, because his relationship with Michaels will soon be known to the police. There's no point in his denying he was in the flat today. I've a feeling that Michaels' partner, a man named Vincent Chinelio, knew, and he'll hardly keep his mouth shut about it. Even if he does, the police're bound to find fingerprints, maybe even some of Archie's belongings."

"So what should he tell them?"

"That he was there in the early afternoon and that when he left Richie was still in good health. If he sticks to that story, he'll probably be okay. But you'll have to keep him off the crack until he's got it over him."

"The crack?"

"Or whatever. Don't be coy with me, Mrs Haly. You know full well what I'm talking about. Scrub Archie down, inside and out, and keep him on an even keel. In the meantime I'll poke around and try and unearth the real killer. As much for my own sake, as his, I have to admit. That is, if such exists."

"What d'you mean by that?"

I eyed her warily, not sure how deep her feelings for her son actually went.

"There is a chance that Archie did do Michaels in. Maybe in a fit of temper, or pique, or maybe as the result of a lovers' quarrel ..."

This time I did get a reaction, a quickly suppressed wince that flirted with her features and was as quickly banished. This woman had iron where others merely had resolve. She said, "That I won't accept. I know he's wilful and headstrong, but I also know he's not capable of violence. The opposite, as a matter of fact. The sulkiness and the arrogance are only for show. Behind that facade he's as timid as a mouse. Who should know that better than I?"

"Who indeed?" Again I watched her as she picked up her glasses from her lap and clicked them open and shut. The light in the room was mellow but it did not have the effect of softening her stern features. "Tell me, Mrs Haly," I said, "did you know Richie Michaels? Were you aware of his liaison with your son and the nature of it?"

Because of a sudden shaft of sunlight in my eyes I couldn't tell if she was looking at me or not. She said, "I'm aware of Archie's predilections, yes. They are a matter of some pain to me.

However I do not encourage him to bring his ... friends to my home. It would not be ..."

"PC?"

"I beg your pardon?"

"Politically correct."

"Exactly."

We mulled over that one for a time, then I said, "I find it extraordinary that your husband hasn't left an address or phone number at which he can be reached. Is he out of the country?"

She shook her head, her hair unmoving in its sculpted perfection. "My husband and I went our separate ways years ago," she said, her tone devoid of emotion. "Our marriage is merely outward show, a contrived arrangement to cover his philandering and my lack of interest. I host his dinner parties, am seen on his arm at social engagements, impart a certain air of respectability to soften the more vulgar excesses of his behaviour. In return, he indulges me with money and possessions. And he leaves our son alone and does not torment him as he used to."

"And your daughter?"

This time a look that I could not decipher passed fleetingly across her face – for a moment she appeared oddly vulnerable. But it quickly disappeared as she went on in answer to my question: "She does not need my protection. She is well able to look after herself."

"I see," I said, but really I did not see at all.

We sat and watched the light move in the room, the sun now lower in the sky, the rain-clouds all gone. It had the makings of a beautiful evening, and the landscaped view through the window of flowers, green lawns and quiet spaces was just about right. It was a pity that the lives of the inhabitants were not in harmony with this natural setting, which was steeped in tranquillity.

Reluctantly I got to my feet, feeling my shirt still clammy on my back, my trousers hanging in limp folds. It was borne in on me that I did not cut a dashing figure.

"I'll go back to my office and see if Morgan has left any messages for me," I told her. "It's important that we get hold of your husband and let him know what's happened."

"As you will," she said, giving an almost imperceptible shrug to show her lack of interest in that particular avenue of endeavour.

She got to her feet, her dress smooth on her hips, her hands once more clasped in front of her. "I'm grateful for what you've done for my son," she said. "You haven't told me why my husband involved you in the first place, but it's fortunate that he did. You've shown great tact in the face of a very difficult situation and I sincerely hope you do not get into trouble on our account. And I think I'd like to reward you in a more telling manner than merely by thanking you."

From the same table as before she took up her bag and extracted a wad of notes. Holding the money, she turned sideways so that I could admire her profile against the sunlight streaming in through the window. That would always be her panacea for present ills, I thought to myself: money and the power that it can encompass. In an attempt to disconcert her I said, "I'm afraid I'd compromise your husband's trust in me if I were to accept remuneration from you. He's the one who hired me and he's the one I have to report back to ..."

She looked at me. "You're mistaken if you take the honourable course where my husband is concerned," she said. "He is a devious man, who hides behind a cloak of bonhomie and joviality. This money is a reward for services rendered to me. A once-off payment for what you did for my son."

Regretfully I shook my head, wondering at the same time where all this nobility of intent had suddenly sprung from.

"Think of it as a favour," I said. "From one Wexford person to another."

Again she repeated, "As you will," and bowed her head to show that the audience was over.

Standing not upon the order of my going, I went at once. After all, did I not have an assignation with a beautiful damsel out on the tennis courts? So, it was with high thoughts of low business that I took my leave of Mrs Haly and made my way out into waning summer sun, the nudging scent of flowers, and the quiet fall of evening coming down.

Four

I retrieved my jacket from the bush where I had left it. It was still a little damp – the jacket, not the bush. I cut diagonally across through the flower garden towards the high net fence around the tennis court. A character in protective clothing and wearing a beekeeper's helmet passed by. We nodded at one another. I didn't ask him how the bees were doing and he didn't enquire from me what my business might be. The thought struck me that it could be a disguised Mossie keeping an eye on things. I turned and gazed after him, but he didn't pause nor look back.

Mary Haly was busy fending off tennis balls that a machine like an upturned hoover was spitting across the net at her. I stopped to admire her style as she dodged and struck, a forehand here, a backhand there, getting most of the balls back and in court.

Each time she batted one her skirt flew up, showing off her white pants. Her thighs were firmly muscled and there was no jiggle of fat. She was very fit, light on her feet, able to get around the wide spaces of the court with seemingly little effort.

She noticed me standing watching her, jumped the net and switched off the machine. She beckoned for me to come in through the latticed gate. I did so, feeling the heat of the tarmacadam under my feet. The sun was behind the trees, its light speckling the court in dots and dashes. It was very quiet now that the pop-pop-popping of the balls had ceased, a quiet oasis wherein to meet. If only I were visiting under more pleasant circumstances.

"Would you like to try a few hits?" the girl asked me. "There's a second racket ..."

I shook my head. "Got to get back to my office. Affairs of state and all that."

She raised an eyebrow disbelievingly, then she came over to where I was standing. There were beads of perspiration along her upper lip but otherwise she showed little sign of her recent exertions. Her hair was still tight against her head, her face warm and composed, her stance easy and loose. I wouldn't have minded dallying a little with her under the spreading reach of the sycamores further down the garden.

Her mind was on other things, though. "What trouble is Archie in now?" she asked me. "I've a feeling it's more serious than usual."

"Why d'you think that?"

"Woman's intuition?" She grinned, then owned up: "Actually, I was eavesdropping. Was that very naughty of me?"

I shrugged, thinking of a number of naughtier things she could do that would also be okay with me. It was with an effort that I dragged my mind back to business.

"What kind of trouble is Archie usually in?" I asked her.

We had moved across to a wooden bench and she took up a pink towel and wiped her face with it. When she bent over I could see her white pants again, the cotton fabric stretched deliciously across her taut haunches. The thought of eating a peach, or maybe two, came to mind.

"Oh, you know," she said, answering my question. "Drugs, bad company, bouncing cheques. Nothing as serious as this, though."

She looked at me, her eyes bright, teeth gently snagging a corner of lip. The thought of her brother being found in the company of a dead body seemed to impart a certain amount of titillation.

"What does he do?" I asked her, idly picking up her racket and swinging it against my leg.

"How d'you mean?"

"What does he do for a living? How does he earn his daily bread?"

She laughed, showing small white teeth that might nibble an ear just as well as bite into a steak. "That's rather a quaint way of putting it. He dabbles a bit in photography. And then Mossie makes him a generous allowance. Too generous, if you ask me."

"You always refer to your father as Mossie?"

She looked at me as if seeking a hidden agenda. "Yes, always," she said. "Can you imagine him being addressed as Dad or Pop or Pater?"

58

I dredged up a vision of his bulldog face, thick body and abrupt manner and agreed mentally that it seemed an unlikely scenario.

"And what exactly does Mossie do to earn his living?" I asked. "I've kinda lost touch since the Wexford days."

"Well, the business was broken up between the two brothers when old Bart died. Mossie got the construction side."

"Doing well, is he?"

She waved an arm to encompass the house and surroundings. "Look around you and make up your own mind. Not the estate of someone who's short of a few quid, is it?"

"Do you work for him?"

She squinted her eyes at me, maybe tiring of all the questions, but she answered readily enough: "No, I'm a PE teacher. In a school. A rather exclusive one on Dublin's southside ..."

"You know what they say about southside girls and northside girls?"

"What do they say?"

"Southside girls have real diamonds and fake orgasms."

She laughed again. I liked to hear her laugh — it had the tinkle of bells built in and also a certain throaty cadence that hinted at wickedness. Then again she could manage it and still look good. An amount of attractive women ruin things when they guffaw.

She watched me place the racket beside her towel, then she said, "Is there anything else you'd like to know? Maybe my vital statistics? My telephone number? Whether I wear a garter belt or a girdle on state occasions ...?"

I ducked my head in contrition. "I'm sorry. The questions go with the job. It's how I put in my time."

"It must be interesting being a detective."

"A lot of people think that, but don't be fooled. The best part of my day is spent walking, looking, sitting down, getting up again, talking to people who don't particularly want to talk to me ..."

"You must unearth a lot of grubby little secrets."

"Yes, that's what most of them are, grubby. Mean and nasty and furtive. It's a bit like turning over stones to see what's underneath."

"Has everyone got a secret?"

"I don't know. Have you?"

She looked at me as though she thought I was some kind of imbecile, then she said, "Of course. Are you going to try and prise it out of me?"

I shook my head and held the gate for her as she moved ahead of me. Her backside and her walk were works of art. We strolled by the serried ranks of flowers. The beds were beautifully ordered, a mathematical precision dictating which blooms should be where. There was not a weed in sight. The heavy scent from the massed formations was like an invisible mist that permeated the air and vampishly titillated one's sense of smell. I experienced a desire to put my arm around the girl's waist and have her lean her head into the hollow of my shoulder.

To keep from making a fool of myself, I asked her if she ever had the feeling that someone might be attempting to blackmail Mossie. That stopped her in her tracks and put a questioning glint in her eye.

"Is that why you're working for him? And is that why Morgan's been so much in evidence lately?"

"You think he might be blackmailing him?"

"I've never thought about it at all. But now that you mention it, he could be."

"Why d'you say that?"

"I don't think he likes my father much."

"How d'you know?"

"It's not a question of knowing. It's just a feeling I have. A lot of people have it in for Mossie ..."

"You watch his back for him?"

"What do you think?"

"What d'you think I think?"

The girl grinned wryly, her lips even without lipstick red and moist. She said, "Why is it that we Irish invariably answer a question with another question?"

"It's a trait we have, like never speaking well of one another until we're dead. How long has Max Morganthau ... ah, Morgan ... been working for your father?"

She shrugged. "For years, I believe. But he's only really been in evidence over the last six months. People like him come and go."

"People like him?"

She stopped, outlined against the vivid backdrop of a bank of snapdragons. Idly she swung her racket in its cloth cover. From somewhere a bird came out with a throaty warble. Evening light from the dying sun was pinkish, a soft even shade.

The girl said, "He's part of the Wexford mafia. There seems to be a good supply of them. You're one, too."

"News to me. But they say you can always depend on your own. Maybe that's why Mossie has them around."

"I wonder. It might be true if they were bound by ties of loyalty and affection. But when it's mainly money ..."

"Don't underestimate the power of money. It can grapple your friends to you with hoops of steel."

"That's old Polonius from Hamlet, isn't it? Look what happened to him. He was stabbed in the arse."

"Max is okay," I said, lying in my teeth – he had let me down many a time and probably would do so again. There was no reason to assume that he would treat Mossie Haly any differently.

"Maybe. But you still haven't told me why you think my father's being blackmailed. I bet it's got something to do with that shit of a brother of mine. It has, hasn't it?"

"In a way," I hedged. "But it needn't concern you."

I was becoming impatient with myself, the conversation and the trend it had taken. It would have suited me much better to walk in that beautifully tended garden, under drooping branches of elderberry, with summer-seeking swifts flitting here and there, and talk of ships and sealing-wax, and of love lost and regained, and of happy-ever-afterings – Ah me ... Instead I said, "You don't by any chance know where your father is, do you? It's important that I see and talk to him."

She shook her head, the descending sun aureoling her hair in pale light. "He comes and he goes. I'm closer to him than most, but he doesn't always confide in me. It might be a business deal. Then again ..."

"It's okay," I assured her, "I've talked to your mother. She told me a little of their relationship ..."

"Did she now?" The girl peered at me, then she crossed her arms under her breasts, the tennis racket protruding like a signal to turn. Suddenly the evening had grown chill, the air thin and cool now that the sun was on its last legs. What could have been a bat did a quick dart through the dimness under the trees, its silent swerving serving to startle us. "For someone who's just appeared on the scene, you've managed to win a lot of confidences," the girl said. "You bring home my brother, insinuating that you've kept him out of a compromising situation. My mother confides in you. And I ..."

"Yes?"

"I start remembering all those gooey girlish dreams I once had about you. Those awful, prepubescent twitterings that made me by turns exhilarated and depressed. And you didn't even know I existed."

"I do now."

"Ah, but we're all grown up now, aren't we? We've put away the things of youth."

"Like my used hurling jersey?"

"Maybe."

"Does that mean I'm not a god to you anymore? That I've turned up with feet of clay?"

She stood close to me and I could feel the warmth of her body. She said, "I always did like older men." Reaching out, she touched my cheek, letting her fingers slide down my jawline. It was an intimate gesture, yet also distant, as someone might make at the finality of a parting. I caught her wrist and drew her to me and kissed her, quite gently, on the lips. Her breath was sweet but her eyes were deep and unfathomable.

"You'll look out for him, won't you?" she said, our faces close, the moment trepidant.

"Archie?"

"No, my father."

I drew back, both to recover my breath and to get a better look at her, but it seemed I'd been given my lot for that evening. She wheeled out of my arms and walked rapidly away, along by the side of the house until her wavery white shape was lost to my view. I was alone with the night-flying creatures and the heavy sweet smell of the flowers. And the feeling that Mossie meant more to his daughter than the rest of the family put together.

I found a phone box a little way down the road and rang for a taxi. I had no cigarettes, so I plucked a stem of grass and sucked on it. Stars were beginning to wink in the cobalt vault of the heavens and the thin wind caused me to struggle into my linen jacket. The drink I had consumed earlier in the day was grown stale in my stomach, and the hot prickle of heartburn was playing tippy-toes with my gullet. Just the way a second-hand private detective should feel at close of day, I thought. At least, I consoled myself, I didn't have a cluster of knots on my head from being whacked by the bad guys; but then again, the night was still young and any number of hard cases could be lying in wait around the next bend.

And just then, as though by wish fulfilment, a car I knew only too well came slowly down the road towards me. It was a steel-grey Nissan Bluebird, its licence plate as flinch-making to me as a thorn under the fingernail. And the two thick-necked blockheads in the front seats were equally familiar to me, while, if the character in the back was whom I imagined it was, the threesome was complete and I was up shit creek without a paddle if they recognised me.

Carefully I retreated around the side of the telephone box, leaving only an eye showing to monitor the progress of the car. It went past me, its parking lights on, travelling nice and slowly and obeying the speed limit. I stuck my head out a little further and watched, fascinated, as it halted in front of the gates to the Haly residence. Somehow I wasn't that surprised when it turned in and took itself out of my sight.

Chewing furiously on the stem of grass, I marched up and down, wishing the taxi would hurry up and take me out of there. The guys in the Bluebird had no reason to come shake me by the hand and wish me well. They worked for a gangster known as The Waster, a low-profile though highly dangerous criminal with whom I had had an encounter some months before. Possibly in part due to the trouble I'd created, The Waster was now in a private hospital, hooked up to a life-support machine and being fed through a rubber tube, a stroke having laid him low. The story was that he would not recover.

The guy in the back of the Bluebird was most probably his chief dogsbody, a grade-A sleazeball, one Wilson 'The Whacker' Whelan, who fancied himself as a cool dude but who in reality was just as stupid and oafish as his comatose boss. When I thought about him, my scalp tingled at the memory of the way he had used a knuckleduster to straighten the parting in my hair. In my heart I'd always known that he and I were due another round.

The taxi finally arrived and I scrambled in and instructed the overly talkative young driver to take me back into the city centre. Huddled in the back I switched off listening to his chatter and instead tried to make some sense of my predicament.

I knew it would be a diplomatic move on my part to visit a copshop, especially before they had the chance to stir themselves and come looking for me. As soon as they talked to Vincent Chinelio, Richie's partner, they'd know I'd been asking after, and hinting I would visit, the deceased. The probability was that they were already scouring the highways and the byways for me, as I was not exactly unknown to them. The sensible thing for me to do would be to hightail it in to see my friend – acquaintance, he would term it – George Quinlan, Superintendent George Quinlan, that is, of the Serious Crimes Squad of the Dublin Metropolitain Police. and throw myself on his mercy. Problem was, George didn't exactly believe in the concept of mercy: justice, yes, neat, clean and down the middle, but when mercy was mentioned in George's presence it was his custom to raise an eyebrow, twitch and then take on the persona of an iceman, inscrutable in a field of snow.

Thinking of friendship and all that goes with it caused that other low-life, Max Morgan, as he was now calling himself, to pop into my mind. While not entertaining any high hopes that he would be able to extricate me from the mess he had got me into, I at least hoped he would be capable of shedding some light on what was going on. The blackmail thing with the photographs had seemed pretty cut and dried, but now with Richie's violent murder and the entrance on the scene of Whelan and his two stooges matters were becoming more than a little peculiar.

The taxi deposited me in Parnell Square and I paid off the still talking driver and made off in the direction of my office. Down a narrow street, it reposes over a video store called 'The Roxy': two rooms divided by a hear-through if not see-through partition; a humble place but mine own. Well, to be precise, it belonged to an entrepreneur from the County Mayo, who had bought the building with the compensation money from a farm accident that had left him with only one eye. Arriving in the big city determined to make his fortune, he proceeded to lose his shirt by purchasing the tenement I was housed in along with its adjoining twin; both were in a state of repair approaching the derelict site syndrome: to say they were condemned would be to praise them. Insuring them heavily, he tried on a number of occasions to burn them down, but they proved to be heat-resistant and highly antagonistic to spontaneous combustion. He, on the other hand, suffered a variety of burns and carried around with him a perennial odour of smoke and carbonised B.O.

I went into Pat's Grocery Emporium, a little way down from the Roxy and across the street, and bought twenty Dunhills and a box of matches. Pat was long dead but his widow carried on, a mountainously fat woman whom I had never seen stir from her seat behind the cash register.

On my way out, and in the best private eye tradition, I turned up the collar of my jacket, paused, lit a cigarette and tried to hide behind the pall of smoke. Everything seemed clear and in order. No suspicious-looking cars were parked in the street, there was no furtive glow of light in my office window, and the only animate life that paid any attention to me was a brindled cat that wore a flea collar and stared at me with that supercilious look that felines always seem to adopt with strangers.

I shooed it away and crossed the road. A church bell sounded, its tone hollow and solemn as it tolled over the old part of the city. I stopped to listen, and did a count-down. Nine peals. The rain-clouds had hunched their way back into the sky, and it was quite dark for so early on a July night. All the better to hide me, I thought, as I unlocked the outside door and ascended the rubber tipped stairs that led to my anteroom.

The floor creaked when I stepped on it and I knew there was someone in the office even before I crept across and opened the

65

door. Cautiously I reached in and switched on the light, at the same time flattening myself sideways against the door jamb to afford as small a target as possible. I need not have bothered. The occupant of my office chair was Max Morgan, wearing a baseball cap with a popped-up peak and a stiff-looking leather jacket with epaulettes and zippers. He looked cool, calm and unsurprised.

I wish I could have said the same about myself. "Christ, you put the heart crossways in me," I told him.

He shrugged. "Come on in," he said. "Sorry about taking over your chair. I tried the visitor's but it gave me pins and needles in my left buttock. Not that this one is much better. You really do need to get some renovations done ..."

"I'll renovate your mush. What d'you mean breaking in here and then complaining about the furniture? And I see you've helped yourself to refreshments," I said, pointing at the office bottle of Bushmills and the half-full glass by his right hand.

"You wouldn't want me to die of thirst while waiting for you, would you?"

"I don't want you here at all. You're bad news ..."

I clicked off the light and let the neon sign from the pharmacy across the way provide illumination. However, when I moved towards the desk my shin met up with the hard edge of the visitor's chair. I cursed, hopping around on one leg.

"Ballocks, ballocks, ballocks ..."

The pain subsided and I sat down. Then I got up again, took off my constricting linen jacket and hung it over the back of my chair. "For freedom of movement," I pointed out to my unloved guest. "In case I need to vault the desk and throttle you."

My eyes had got used to the gloom and I watched him fill a second glass and push it towards me. The reddish glow from the neon sign gave the liquid a rich ruby sheen.

I picked the glass up, took a sip, and heard the whiskey go "Aghaaaaa" as it made its way from my large intestine into the little one. I sent another shot down to keep it company, set the tumbler carefully on the desk top and said, "Michaels is dead. I didn't find the photographs. I did stumble across the real live Archie. And I'd say I'm up to my armpits in doody ..."

"And all because my lady loves Milk Tray?"

"Huh?"

Max leaned forward and put his chin on his hands. He gazed at me long and hard. So long and hard that I finally said, "Will you cut the shit? What's with all this meaningful staring? I need some honest answers to some hard questions ..."

"I didn't mean for you to get in that deep," Max said, interrupting me. "It seemed like a good idea to make an effort to be reasonable with Richie. After all, he's had more than his share of Mossie's wealth by way of Archie's largess. I thought when you talked to him he'd see the evil of his ways and stop killing the goose that was laying the golden eggs."

"And instead it was the goose that got him." I knocked back the remainder of the whiskey, then I said, "Max, that's a crock of shit. You set me up, you fuckhead. You knew all along you were sending me into a very tricky situation, otherwise you'd've gone yourself. And why aren't you surprised at Richie's sudden demise? You didn't even blink when I told you about it. And another thing ..."

"Yeah?"

"Take off that stupid hat. It makes you look ridiculous."

He grinned and turned the baseball cap so that the peak was to the back. The red glow through the window gave him a suitably demonic look, confirming my long-held belief that he was in league with Old Nick.

"I wasn't surprised when you told me Richie was dead because it's been on the cards for a long time. You don't go around threatening people like Mossie Haly and hope to get away with it."

"You're saying Mossie had him done in?"

"It's a possibility."

"But not with Archie there surely?"

"He wouldn't have known he'd be there. And even if he did, it might be his way of teaching him a lesson."

I poured some more whiskey and drank a little of it, thinking that our conversation sounded highly artificial, as if we were discussing the plot of a book or a film. I said, "He was killed by having a telephone receiver rammed down his oesophagus. Not exactly the *modus operandi* of a professional hitman."

"Maybe he was taught to improvise."

"He?"

"He, she or it. You think maybe the Beast from Twenty Thousand Fathoms got him?"

I squinted at him through the muted glow of light in the room. "You don't seem too put out by Richie's death. Wasn't he a friend of yours?"

"I knew him."

"How well? In the biblical sense?"

Max sighed. He put his hands flat on the desk top and moved them about as if he were polishing it. They made a low rasping sound. He said, "Have you ever read about Peter Pan?"

"Peter Pan? What's he got to do with anything?"

"I sometimes see myself as one of the Lost Boys. Waiting for Peter Pan to come and rescue me."

"Oh yeah? The next thing you'll be telling me is that you're full of Happy Thoughts, when really you're full of horse shit ..."

"If you had a Happy Thought it enabled you to fly."

"So?"

"Remember old Evel Knievel, the motor-bike daredevil? All those stunts he performed? Sometimes when he jumped it seemed as if he'd never come down. I tried a few leaps like that ..."

"But you always came down?"

Looking wistful, he said, "There's always that one definitive one, though."

"Which one is that?"

"The one you're most afraid to make. The one you think about all the time and it sends shivers down your spine and sticks your underwear up the crack of your arse."

"I can go with that. That's exactly how I felt this afternoon when I found Richie Michaels gagging on the telephone. And you're responsible."

"How d'you figure that?"

"You sent me there, you toerag. You can't have forgotten so quickly."

"Did you call it in?"

"Yep."

"A pity, that."

"Why?

He didn't answer immediately, merely shifted in the chair — maybe he was easing that left buttock of his, the one with the pins and needles. In spite of the fact that he had got me involved in this mess, I still felt a warmth of affection for him. We had been pretty close once upon a time, and that type of bonding doesn't exactly get flushed down the toilet too easily. We had seen good and bad times together, had fought and laughed and got through many a hairy situation. The matter of his homosexuality hadn't been a factor then for he had kept it well hidden, even from me. He had always been good at dissimulation, old Max. In the end it was another acquaintance of ours who had blown the gaff, a guy known as the Fart MacCoille, a shifty go-by-the-wall who followed whatever parade happened to be popular at the time. He had enjoyed telling me, knowing by the look on my face that it was news to me, even if I had half-suspected something of the sort.

When I put it to Max, he had merely grinned, ducked his head and acknowledged the truth of it. He offered no explanations as to why he had hidden the fact from me, made no attempt to concoct excuses or tell me he had done it to protect my feelings. That was Max, you took him as he was or you didn't take him at all.

Now I asked him again why he considered it a bad move to have informed the law about Richie's sudden and sad demise.

"It could have been covered up," he said, spreading his hands. "Maybe made to look like an accident."

"You mean that he swallowed the phone by mistake? Maybe mistook it for a cheeseburger? You're operating in cloud-cuckoo-land."

"The body could've been removed. There are ways and means. Burning, burying, sending into orbit. No one would've raised a hue and cry if Richie had simply disappeared."

"What about his partner, Chinelio?"

"Money talks, but not him. He'd've kept quiet if leaned on."

I put my teeth together and stretched my jaws until I fancied I could hear them creak. Since I'd taken up my present line of work, looking into other people's business, I'd come across a kind of subterranean world where the usual workings of human commerce became null and void. It is simply amazing what you are told when you set yourself up as some kind of father confessor figure; and when you begin to dig, no matter how superficially, under the surface of seemingly normal existences you can turn up dark vistas of the soul incorporating need, betrayal and desperation. If Max had suggested what he was now hinting at a year ago, I would have laughed in his face, but my new-found experiences had changed my outlook. Now I knew for a fact that in the shadow land that existed just below the surface of accepted society anything was possible, and that even in the most honourable of human endeavours, corruption can lurk like the worm in the otherwise burnished and healthy-looking apple.

I shook my head. "I don't work like that," I told him. "I need to know who killed Michaels, not cover it up."

"Even if it compromises your client?"

"Even so."

Max shrugged and turned the peak of the baseball cap to the front again. He said, "Have you ever thought about all the crap that's crapped around the world in a single day? Not even in a day ... in an hour, say."

"An awful lot of crap," I agreed.

"If it weren't biologically reducible, it'd take over. A great tide of shit, gobbling up everything in its path. Houses, fields, rivers, mountains, people, all going under ..."

"If it ingested the people there'd be no more shit."

"Now you're talking. That's my very point. Get rid of the crap makers, ergo, no more crap."

"Ergo?"

He filled both our glasses, then upended the bottle to demonstrate that it was empty. He placed it carefully on the desk and pushed at it daintily with an index finger. The bottle teetered, but regained its position. He tried again and this time it fell over, rolled to the edge and would have fallen on the floor except that I reached out and caught it.

"Why don't we go and see this Chinelio?" Max said. "Maybe we could convince him to keep you and Archie out of it when he talks to the law. I know him. He's easily persuaded."

"Don't you think that course of action may have passed its sell-by date? He's probably sitting on a three-legged stool, flirting with a few hardnosed coppers at this very minute. He struck me as the type who likes to pass on a few secrets, especially if they tend to stick someone else's head in the oven."

"You never can tell." Max tossed off the whiskey, then sat revolving the glass between his fingers. "It pays to be an optimist. Although as I remember it, you liked to think the worst in the hope that when it fell on you, it'd never be heavy enough to squash you flat. Come to think of it, that's a kind of inverted optimism, isn't it?"

"Maybe."

I repeated the dose Max had given his glass, then set mine standing beside the empty bottle on the floor. The whiskey warmed my insides, but it did nothing for the coldness in my mind. I was tempted to do a Pontius Pilate and wash my hands of the whole affair. The only thing binding me to these people was the money Max had paid me, and I could give that back. But as soon as that thought came into my head, I threw it right back out again. It simply wasn't true. This was something that had surfaced out of my past, unfinished business that had been lying dormant, waiting to pounce. Seems to me that old Jimmy Joyce knew a thing or two when he proclaimed that all history is cyclical; events come around again and again, although not necessarily any better than when they were first experienced. You're given one little plot of ground to till and whatever variations you impose on it, there's still always a piss-arse familiarity about the results. You may not be able to go down to the same river twice, but when you do go to have a look the water always appears the same, and so does the vegetation surrounding it, and the storm clouds rolling in.

I shuddered, stood up and put on my silly linen jacket. It too had been recycled, but maybe it would prove to be a lucky talisman, carrying my father's good emanations through the humming distance between us. It certainly wasn't much good for anything else.

Five

Max's motor-bike was nowhere in sight, so we walked along O'Connell Street, crossed the bridge, made our way up Westmoreland Street and around by the Bank of Ireland. The clock over the entrance to Trinity College stood at ten of the hour.

It was a balmy night, the rain-clouds having again disappeared, the sky a deep and vivid blue. The pavements were overflowing with people, and voices gabbled in a variety of tongues and accents. In the portico of the bank a number of young people sat and talked or plaited one another's hair; they looked grungy and there was the odour of leather, clothes needing a wash, armpits a reliable deodorant, and socks a pounding in sudsy water. Also the whiff of pot permeated the night air, a straight middle finger to the older generation of parents, priests and the parsimonious.

As we dodged through the press of bodies Max asked me how I knew he had been in prison.

"An acquaintance of mine is a Superintendent in the Garda Siochana. It seems it's routine for police forces to pass information about, especially news of natives of various countries who happen to be thrown into the slammer. George received this info from the mysterious East, noticed your place of birth was given as Wexford and asked me if I knew you."

"And?"

"I pretended I didn't know you from Adam Katzenjammer."

"Who's Adam Katzenjammer?"

"I don't know him either."

"Very funny. How come you're so pally with him?"

"With Adam Katzenjammer?"

"No, the policeman."

I paused to admire a willowy blonde in pink hot pants, cut high enough to show off the rising globes of her bottom.

"That's a man," Max said, following my gaze.

"You should be so lucky."

We were in Dame Street now, and motoring. A car honked and Max waved, but it was obvious the occupants were signalling to someone else. Nearby a screech of laughter ended in a hiccup; then it began again, more stridently.

"George Quinlan is his name," I said. "The policeman. We're hunting buddies. In the same gun club. He's more fanatical about it than I am. The hunting, I mean. He'd like to shoot the criminals, so he takes it out on the game."

"Did he tell you what I was in for? And for how long?"

"No, he clammed up when I said I didn't know you. I tried pumping him, but I might as well have been trying to get information from a Swiss banker. George is as tight as a duck's arse below the waterline." I stepped back to let a fat young man eating a bun pass by. "Why were you in?" I asked Max, letting my curiosity show.

"The usual thing."

"Stealing money from babies? Eating humble pie? Bestiality?"

"Drugs."

"Taking or transporting?"

"A little of both."

"Tell me about it."

"There's nothing much to tell. I was caught, literally, with my pants down. The old rectum is not what it used to be for secreting things. They don't go in for niceties like trials over there. I was on permanent remand. But I was lucky. I had a rich friend. A couple of years and I was out. Some other poor shits were left to rot ..."

"So you wouldn't recommend an Asian prison as a place to take a holiday?"

"Only if you happen to be a masochist with a death wish. As it was I crawled miles up the fundament of wickedness in order to be shat out a new man."

"Christ!"

"You don't believe me?"

"The fundament of wickedness?"

"Figuratively and sometimes in the event. I even gloried in it, like a dog rolling in excrement. But now that I've been burned like old Lear upon a wheel of fire, I've become tempered and

73

invincible. No more via dolorosa for me. I've joined the hero breed."

"You're nuts. A candidate for the funny farm."

He stopped in the middle of the pavement, the crowds opening out around him. "You know, that's a distinct possibility," he said seriously. "But it matters not a whit. Mad, bad or simply naughty, I've come to a kind of sunset resolution with myself. It just remains for a few old scores to be settled and then I'm on my way. In the meantime, stick with me, Johnny boy, and we'll leave a trail for men to wonder at ..."

"People are staring at you."

"You see, it's starting already. I'm Attila the Hun, Genghis Khan, Mr Midnight ..." – He took off his baseball cap and did a wide, sweeping bow to a trio of giggling girls, who responded with a collective "Jaysus". I felt like planting a boot up his rear but refrained with the thought that it might get stuck up there. I remembered the fist in the Mapplethorp portrait I'd seen earlier in the Cock's Cuckoo.

"Where are we going?" I asked him, as we continued on our way. I couldn't help but notice that we had passed the entrance to O'Mahony Court and the intersection with George's Street. Not too far away the outline of Dublin Castle stood out vividly against the skyline.

"You won't find friend Chinelio at home on a Monday night," Max said. "We are tracking him to the New Catacombs, as depraved a den of iniquity as you are likely to come across in Hong Kong, Rangoon or Lisdoonvarna. Under the very street even as we walk upon it, Hades is alive and blooming and open to all above the age of consent. Merely pay the ferryman and we'll guided safely across the River Styx ..."

It was actually the River Liffey he brought me to, and a tall old house that leaned to one side and had a bricked-up front door and blind, shuttered windows. We went down the steps to the basement and Max gave a rat-a-tat-tat on what turned out to be a new and solid metal portal. We waited and, when nothing happened, he knocked again, then gave the surface a kick that resounded out across the Liffey like the sound of a mighty gong.

A shutter immediately snapped open and a pair of eyes stared out at us. Recognition flared in them – for Max, I presumed – and the metal door was hauled back, emitting a swathe of bright, strobic light. It also released a discharge of noise like a rapidly widening pattern of buckshot.

"Skittles," Max cried, embracing the apparition that had opened the door. It could have been man, woman, or fowl, but was definitely not of the common variety of humankind. Attired in feathers, sequins, black net stockings, and a Lone Ranger mask, he, she or it let out a squawk like a violated hen and did a shimmy up against Max's jeans and leather jacket.

"Permit me to introduce my friend," Max said, holding Skittles at bay. "This is John, sometimes known as Big and Bad. He chews nails and spits glass. But if you get him in the mood, he can be as tender as a popsicle."

"Oooh, aaah," Skittles crowed, the eyes behind the mask rotating like symbols in a slot machine. I guessed he was an old and decrepit man, but he could equally have been an old and decrepit woman. Any flesh that was on view was raddled and hanging loose like a chicken's craw, and the stance was that of a carrion bird about to pounce.

We sidled in past him, into a vault with a low, sweating ceiling, pillared alcoves, guttering oil lamps and a mass of technicoloured humanity that should only have been glimpsed in a drug-induced nightmare. All kinds of characters were cavorting about to the pounding beat of some really hard rock, the smell of cheap perfume, perspiration and tumescence a miasma that hovered about them like steam off a fresh turd. I fancied myself as being fairly impervious to shocks to the nervous system, but this display set my teeth on edge and gave me palpitations of the lumber region.

"What is this place?" I yelled at Max, feeling myself swaying in the waves of sound that thundered from hidden speakers.

He moved me along into an adjoining cavern, where a stone counter had been set up and drinks were being served. Muscling into the throng of bodies, he soon returned holding two glasses. Motioning for me to follow him, he pushed further on into the eye of the maelstrom, then sat us down on a couple of stone plinths worn smooth by a succession of backsides. The noise level had dropped a little but it was still only just short of excruciating.

Max handed me a glass, then toasted me and the surroundings with a "Bottoms up" – a most appropriate form of salutation in the circumstances. By now it had dawned on me that we were in the midst of some kind of gay extravaganza, a belowstairs celebration of the joys of backdoor boring on the grand scale.

"Welcome to the new Catacombs," Max said, grinning his grin. "It's named after a place that existed back in the fifties, where people like Brendan Behan, Paddy Kavanagh, and Gainor Crist, the original Ginger Man, used hang out. There's a whole warren of caves burrowed out under these quays – dates back to Penal times when the clergy used them as hidey-holes. Now the bonny bouncing boys are after other holes ... It's nightclub land for the movers and the shakers."

"Great," I said, with about as much enthusiasm as a hang-glider in a down-draught. I drank from the glass and found I was taking in straight gin. About the only thing straight around here, I thought, and had another go at it. Gin is not my tipple, but any port in a storm, as the drunk said when he fell over the pig in the gutter. "I presume the reason we're here is to search out and find Chinelio?" I asked. "That is, if we're able to recognise him among this collection of weirdos."

"Weirdos? You're talking about some of my best friends. And there's a fine selection down here. The professional classes, for example, are well represented. A judge or two, a few barristers, solicitors, doctors, teachers ... I could point out a politician, a well-known society journalist, a television personality. See that guy over there" – he indicated a portly number in bouffant wig, pearls and floor-length frock – "he's a captain of industry and a county councillor. Worth his weight in influence, that old hag ..."

We finished our drinks, then Max suggested we split up and begin looking for Chinelio. I wasn't too happy about being on my own, but Max suited action to words and disappeared into the shifting throng. I stood irresolutely, the enormity of the task of finding any one person borne in on me by the density of the motley crew swanning here, there and everywhere, the faces dripping with make-up, trinkets clanking, arms and hands gesturing extravagantly, and voices rising and falling in screeching laughter or pretended outrage.

I watched them with a jaundiced eye, but also with the realisation that they were among their own and could do as they pleased. The gay community was like any borderline grouping pushed to the fringe of society: forced into being continually on the defensive, when they got the chance to let down their hair, they took it in full cinemascope, technicolour and dolby sound. And who was I to say yea or nay? It might not be to my taste, but there were quite a few dicey projects in the so-called straight world that were as preposterous and as gut-wrenching – jolly jocks on the rampage could be as off-putting in their way as any convocation of cruising queens.

Sighing resignedly, I started moving about, fending off clutching hands and shouted invitations, and the further I ventured into the maze of corridors the sparser became the press of people. Now I was among cooing couples, pairs of imploring lovebirds who had been hived off from the whirling kaleidoscope to linger and mope in shadowed recesses and hollowed-out alcoves. I'd need a crowbar to prise them apart to see if one of them was Chinelio, and even then they'd be liable to snap back together like released hair springs when I let go.

For a time I'd been conscious of being watched, and now again I surprised the same two characters regarding me with twin suspicious gazes. They were dressed conservatively in tuxedoes and exhibited the self-important air usually effected by professional bouncers.

They ambled over to me, the bulkier of the two glowering, the taller smiling amiably enough. I recognised the technique; the police used it in their "bad cop, good cop" routine.

Goody-Two-Shoes nodded at me and said, "Have we seen you down here before, sir? You are a member, I presume?"

"Let's not go into that member number right now, boys," I said. "It's been done to death."

Bad Bill scowled and showed me a matching set of crooked teeth. He also had a nose that had been broken and badly reset, and a pair of beetling eyebrows that he probably swept the floor with when all the punters had gone home. I'd say he looked like Maxie Rosenbloom, except who remembers Maxie Rosenbloom any more?

"If you could just show us your membership card?" Old

Goodie coaxed, at the same time placing a hand solicitously under my elbow and giving me the tiniest of warning squeezes.

"You know, I quite forgot to bring it with me," I told him, resisting the caress, but only enough to show that I was being playful rather than aggressive. "I must have left it in my pink pocket-book, the one that goes so well with the pastel mini and the matching twinset."

A frown nudged the caring expression on his face, then as quickly disappeared. He was a good-looking bloke, with nice curling chestnut hair and regular features. A thin moustache strutted its stuff under his nose and was complemented by the string dickey bow under his chin. He was neat and clean and well-advised, everything about him indicating that it would take a minor storm to ruffle his calm exterior. The thought was beginning to form in my mind that I might try.

"You from the press?" his companion suddenly growled, and we both stared at him as if surprised he had the power of speech.

"I've been accused of worse, but no, I'm not," I told him. "I came in with Maxie Morgan, the sweetheart of the forces. He'll vouch for me. He knows I'm true blue, the full shilling, high as a flag on the fourth of July ..."

"If you could just walk this way, sir?" the good twin instructed me – the 'sir' now given an ironic twist. "We'll go back to the vestibule and sort things out. All nice and regular and no fuss."

"Yeah, no fuss," the plug-ugly said, looking a bit down in the mouth as he spoke. He clenched and unclenched his large fists and moved his shoulders about in the jacket of the tuxedo, obviously disappointed at the lack of action.

"Which way would you like me to walk?" I asked. "Military two-step or galloping peg-leg?"

This brought renewed hopes of a fracas to the pug's face and he moved in closer to me so that I could smell his sweat and feel the hardness of his muscles. There was also a distinct whiff of mothballs, as if he were protecting his suit from being held to ransom by rapacious, cloth-eating insects.

Now, the majority of the time I am a most peace-loving guy, a friend to my fellow man, civil to old people, women and babies;

but now and then some sour streak in me gets the upper hand and I tend to fly off the handle. This was one of those occasions. I didn't like being pushed around by these two shapers in their hired suits – as a matter of fact, I took a decided aversion to the sight, sound and smell of them, the look of them, the way they took it for granted I would meekly obey the dictates of their urgings. While one could argue that they were merely doing their job, I sensed that they enjoyed it most when they could find an excuse for beating the shit out of some punter who had only come along in the first place to get his brownie fondled. Probably latent queer-bashers, in this case they took the money but didn't cease to sneer.

Going into action, I slammed my leather sandal-shod foot down hard on the ugly one's instep, the quickest recipe for bringing tears to the hardest of hard case's eyes. At the same time I gave the other one the benefit of a horizontal elbow, right into his moustache. The effect in both instances was eminently satisfying – for me, if not for them. The stocky one went 'ouf' and bent over, while his partner went 'arf' and leaned away in the opposite direction. To get them back together again I grabbed hold of them around the base of the neck and brought their heads into contact with a resounding clunk. This time they chorused 'ugh' in diminuendo and sat down on the flagged floor to take time out.

I left them to it. Our little roundelay had taken only a matter of seconds, so it had gone unnoticed by even those in the immediate vicinity. For that matter and in those surroundings, it could have been viewed as some kind of bizarre love dance, a bit of sado-masochistic cha-cha-chaing to get the blood up and other parts rising.

I retraced my steps, making a desultory search for both Max and Chinelio as I went. There was no sign of either of them. Skittles was still guarding the door, enviously casting glances back at the ring-a-ring-a-rosying that was going on inside. He reminded me of a praying mantis, cavernous jaws champing, limbs stick-thin, shiny sequinned dress like the carapace of just such a crustacean. I felt like grinding him into the floor also, and it must have shown in my eyes, for he meekly opened the portal, stood aside and even gave a half-hearted salute as I stepped outside.

In the night air I experienced the desire to yodel a Tarzan yell and, if there had been a vine handy, I would surely have swung on it.

I went up the steps and stood leaning against an iron railing. I looked at my watch. It was eleven-thirty. People would be leaving the pubs about now, hurrying for last buses. The night had grown even chillier, a glitter of stars down the spine of the sky accentuating the rawness of the air. For once I was glad of my father's linen jacket and its tightness around my shoulders.

I crossed the road and paused at the river wall. The stink from the Liffey was awful, a foul stench that permeated one's skin and caused the stomach to lurch. The city was no place to be in warm weather, the heat distending its belly and causing it to cut wind in its inhabitants' faces. I could take my gun and my rods and head for the mountains, do a little target shooting, maybe some fishing. Collect my father and listen to his ramblings about old times, old places, old friends. Sit beside a campfire taking in the scent of pine and the mouthwatering odour of a fat mountain trout sizzling on a spit. With the night all about, as soft and pressing close as velvet, and the air carrying a keenness that spoke of open spaces and sliding river rapids and the hard fastnesses of ice-honed crevices.

Shaking my head, I peered across the river, at the lighted insides of double-decked buses as they rumbled along, and at the people inside, intent on their destinations. Last month I had sold my house and it had been like cutting yet another link in the chain that bound me to the past. And to my sometime wife, Annie. We had lived there for ten years, had shared good and bad times, until one rupture too many had spread and become a yawning chasm. Now our furniture was incarcerated in a warehouse in Sheriff Street, our love also in cold storage waiting for a thaw, with me lighting flares and Annie blowing them out.

I put my back against the stone of the river wall and lit a cigarette and smoked it in a cupped hand. I knew what I had to do and where I had to go, but the knowledge didn't exactly fill me with joy. Sometimes it happens like that, one gets an intimation of what course of action to pursue, a déjà vu fluttering as if it all had happened once before. And equally the necessity to interrupt a set pattern and cause a breach in the accepted flow has to be dealt with: I could walk away from this, I told myself, leave it behind, go down to the warehouse in Sheriff Street that was owned by Lester Sprigg and to which he had loaned me the key, sit in my favourite chair, put a TV dinner in the microwave and listen to the lonesome lyrics of Janis Ian. Maybe the Port Authority might even let off a few forlorn blasts on their foghorn to impart greater depth to my mood.

Fuck that, I thought. I finished the cigarette and flipped the butt out into the road. It winnowed a shower of sparks, then died. I walked out after it, across the road, through Merchant's Arch and into Temple Bar. In Crown Alley people were still sitting out, talking quietly, sipping drinks, most of them huddled into their clothes against the night chill. Under a cone of light a girl with bright red hair, rings through her nose and ears, all black tee shirt and leggings and shiny Doc Martens, sat reading a paperback book. It suddenly was important to me to find out what its title was, and I leaned down to see, but she gave me a look of such sheer malevolence that I quickly went on my way, bemoaning the ways of the world.

Halfway up Fownes Street a man stepped out of a darkened doorway and I flinched, but he merely went on by leaving me with a whiff of garlic-scented breath and the more cutting aroma of alcohol. I could have done with a drink myself and I thought fondly of my office bottle of Bushmills. But then I remembered that it was empty, Max and myself having finished it before heading off for Hades-under-the-Liffey.

I moved along by the bulk of the Central Bank building, its grey slate and concrete solidity somehow reassuring, crossed Dame Street and went into O'Mahony's Court. It was silent, Monday night obviously not its busiest time of the week.

The Cock's Cuckoo was dark and shuttered, yet when I tried the front door it opened easily to my touch. I stood and listened, but not a creak or a rattle rewarded my anxious ear. I closed the door behind me, then, carefully taking baby steps and sliding my feet, I made my way towards where I remembered the bar to be. A little light filtered in from outside, but there were still enough deep pockets of shadow to house pop-up villains or assassins with guns and clubs.

I hit against a chair, half-fell over a stool. I was making enough noise to bring in a squad of security men, but I ploughed on manfully. Finally I made it to the counter and leaned on it, taking in long nervous breaths. My eyes had become accustomed to the gloom and I went in behind the bar, took hold of the first bottle that came to hand, pulled the cork and tilted a little of its contents into my mouth. It was some kind of thick sweet cordial that just about poisoned me.

After I had ceased coughing, I hunted about afresh until I found a triangular bottle of Black Bush. This time the liquid hit straight and true, a fiery stream that coursed down my gullet and bid howdy-do to my stomach. I took a couple more deep breaths and repeated the dose. Going for the three in a row then seemed the obvious thing to do, so I did.

Clutching the bottle, I went in behind the bar. There was a curtain which I parted and, taking a chance, I switched on a light. The hanging bulb was pink and it gave a nicely exotic air to a room that was furnished in the style of the East, loads of gilt embroidered hangings, embossed tapestries, stuffed birds, an ornate sofa with a high wooden back, a bureau whose top held stacked rows of vari-coloured bottles, what looked like a hubble-bubble for smoking opium on a silver tray, and a number of incense sticks whose musky scent still lay heavy on the air.

"Chinelio?" I called, then more seductively, "Vincent ...?" There was no answer. I tried again with the same result. My legs had become strangely reluctant to obey the messages being sent by my brain, so I took another pull from the Bushmills and waited for it to go to work on my locomotive joints. It did the trick and I was able to get moving again.

I poked around, wrapping my hand in my handkerchief to do so. The only object of interest I found was an inlaid box that clicked open to reveal the machinery for injecting some high-powered juice into the system: a silver spoon with a curved handle, a complementary silver dish with a blackened inside, a heavy, old-fashioned syringe and a packet of needles, and a length of silk cord to make the veins stand out. Putting it back in its satin-lined drawer, I imbibed some more of my type of stimulant from the Bushmills bottle.

Chinelio – or maybe it was Michaels – had a taste for pornography: I came across loads of magazines and photographs showing everything from bestiality to kiddie sex, but nothing depicting Archie and Richie in *flagrante delicto*. The collection of dildoes and other such implements I unearthed would have stuffed more orifices than Polyfilla. I put them back where I found them, going "Tsk-tsk" and taking numerous nips from my friendly bottle.

The time had come to venture in further, so I opened a door in the far wall and found myself in a narrow, dimly-lit corridor. Facing me was another door, which was standing slightly ajar. The riff of cold air from it gave me the impression it led to the great outdoors, a fact that I marked with uncommon concern – I might need an escape hatch in the not-too-distant future.

Trying to stifle a sneeze, I suddenly giggled instead, a nervous reaction to my creeping about in a dark place in the dead of night. I shook the bottle and it gave a reassuring gurgle. Still some diesel left to prevent ossification of the motor nerves.

Placing my hand against the first door panel I came to, I pushed gently. It was a storeroom and was full of mops, brushes, a couple of buckets, and the throat-clutching smell of disinfectant. I moved on, staggering only a little. Next in line was another cupboard, this time containing crates of soft drinks, and then the ladies' and gents' toilets. I took a desultory glance into each and was moving on when I paused and stuck my head more fully into the male depository,

There were two urinals facing me, then an alcove to my right with a door that ended before it met either the ceiling or the ground. In the aperture between it and the red tiled floor a pair of feet in shiny Italian shoes was plainly visible.

Normally in a situation like that I would have muttered a quick apology and diplomatically withdrawn, but there was something not quite right about the legs of the trousers above these particular shoes. When a man is taking a dump it is the usual thing for him to lower his pants, and the consequence is that it should reside in folds about his ankles. These trouser legs, however, were plumb lined and creased razor-sharp and were hanging as the tailor intended them to, just a soupçon above the line of the shoe. They could have been outfitted with a trapdoor, of course, but the more likely explanation was that the person sitting on the toilet was doing something other than evacuating his bowels.

Curious, I shuffled on in. The door of the cubicle was closed but, when I leaned on it, it swung open to reveal Vincent Chinelio perched on the throne, with a pink flower growing out of his face. I did a double-take, then saw it was a small, scalloped-edged parasol, the metal point driven deep into his left eye. The other one was staring at me accusingly, as if blaming me for the despoliation of its twin which had been so bloodily ruptured. I didn't need to feel for a pulse to know that he had departed this vale of tears: his stillness, the waxy colour of his skin, the unnatural posture, all told me he was now at play with his partner, Richie Michaels, in the fields of the Lord.

I leaned against the wall of the cubicle and toasted him one last time. It seemed appropriate somehow that it should be with his own liquor I was doing it. The small-wattage bulb from the corridor threw a pale sheen of light on the scene and I felt a weight of sadness descend on me, not especially for Chinelio himself, whom after all I barely knew, but rather for the circumstances of his death and for the fact that I should be the one to find him. Two violent deaths in one day and me left holding the after-image in both cases. It wasn't something I had ever been prepared for, nor would I want to have been. In my list of hoped-for vocations when I was growing up, that of finder of dead bodies had never cropped up even once.

Whatever disturbance I had created by lifting the bottle to my lips seemed to awake a last response in my companion – maybe the fact that I was drinking his whiskey for free served still to annoy him. His head moved slowly sideways, met the wall of the stall and slid along the smooth surface, leaving a bloody trail. It finally came to rest when the bamboo handle of the parasol jammed itself against his knee.

For some reason the slick points of hair standing out over the collar of his jacket attracted my attention. I lowered the bottle and gazed blearily, then I reached out, took hold of a few strands and pulled. The wig, for that was indeed what it was, came away from the scalp with a soft, sucking noise, and I was left holding it and gazing in horror at Chinelio's shiny head of skin.

Fixed to the bald crown by strips of tape was a rectangular envelope, and I automatically let the wig hang by its forward fastenings and yanked the packet free. I placed the Bushmills carefully on the ground and held the envelope up against the grainy light from the hall. Through its translucency I could make out two laddered strips of film negative.

I was afraid to shout "Eureka", so I whispered it instead. Chinelio had most likely been done in on account of what I was holding, but the killer had been no way as resourceful as yours truly in finding it. What a detective I was, what a champ, what a man!

I was about to reward myself with another belt from the bottle when there was a commotion at the front of the pub and I heard the heavy tread of feet and the murmur of voices that sounded highly official.

Waiting to hear no more, I stuck the negatives in my pocket, pushed out of the toilet, half staggered, half-ran down the corridor, made it to the back door and hurriedly went through it. I was in a narrow, cobblestoned alley, which I followed to its mouth. It led me into George's Street and freedom.

I took off, still clutching my bottle, weaving a little, but quietly elated. Now I had something I could use as a lever to prise out some information, a hold on Max and, more importantly, on Mossie Haly, and a way of getting them to leave their foxholes and come out into the open. I might be a small cog, but I intended to be a well-oiled one ...

And I was nothing if not well-oiled. With that comforting thought in mind I upended my faithful bottle and drank it to the dregs. It was with a pang of sorrow that I then deposited it in a rubbish bin – it had stood by me in my need, giving me strength, warmth and a pleasing carefree attitude in the face of desperate eventualities. What more can a man ask? I thought, and I shed a silent tear or two for its demise, and for Chinelio's, as I hurried along.

Six

It took a while for me to flag down a taxi, and then my state of drunkenness and the destination I asked for caused the driver to argue the score with me. I eventually persuaded him to take me on, but he insisted on my paying him at the start of the journey rather than at the end.

I had to be quick on my feet in getting out when we reached Sheriff Street, for the cab barely paused before it was off again. Although it was a dry night the cobblestones were slick and greasy, and I slipped and slid as I made my way down by the postal sorting offices to the warehouse where my worldly goods were stored and that I now thought of as home.

I got there without falling down and stood leaning against the rough-timbered entrance. A smaller door was fitted into the bigger one, and it was this that I opened with Lester's key. It swung back with an echoing clatter, the sound making me cock my ear and wait for the noise of falling timber. It died away and silence returned, but it was the kind of silence that the insides of all large buildings seem to contain: it had at its heart a sort of thrumming sibilance like the aftermath of a disturbance.

I reached in, found the light switch and clicked it on. The fluorescent tube flickered into brilliance, but there was a fault in it and it continued to blink with irritating regularity. Lester, a fast-buck merchant whom I had helped when the protection for sale hard men were leaning on him, dealt in a variety of commodities, and the interior of the warehouse was stacked with all kinds of odds and ends. A maze of corridors ran through them, some just barely wide enough to allow passage to a midget. Whenever I traversed them, I was accompanied by the fear that they would shift, topple over and bury me.

I followed the trail of coloured ribbons I had tied to this and that projecting piece in order to get to my little corner of heaven down by the back wall. This was where my belongings were stacked, the only material possessions left to me from my life with Annie.

Using the space available I had arranged things in the form of a furnished room, with my bed along one side, my ancient oak table another dividing margin, and my three-piece suite in brown buttoned leather the centrepiece. For cooking purposes I had a microwave but, as there was no running water, I had to join the early shift of postal workers to use their facilities for showering, shaving and shitting.

The accumulated stresses and strains of the day, combined with the not inconsiderable amount of gargle I'd shifted over the course of it, caused me to adopt a rather winding path in getting to my place of rest, and it was as well that I did. I took a number of wrong turnings, had to retrace my steps, had to stand and stare owlishly at numbered boxes, cardboard crates, rolls of carpet – and it was while engaged in one of those reconnoitring pauses that I heard a noise that did not sit right with the time, the place or my present admittedly untrustworthy state of awareness.

Was it someone clearing his throat? Blowing his nose? Farting? Whatever it was, there was no disputing the fact that I was not alone in the building. I thought about it, leaning against the nearest surface and blowing a little. It could be Lester, doing an inventory of his stock. At this time of night? Or an explosive expert, hired by Lester to reduce the contents of the warehouse to a pile of junk – it was a pile of junk, so I amended that to a pile of ashy junk.

Maybe it was Annie, the love of my life, installed in our queen-sized bed and awaiting her hero's return? Or Madonna in suspenders and steel bra? One was as likely as the other, me not being Annie's particular cup of tea just now. Or possibly Madonna's either.

Stop messing about, I told myself, but a giggle wriggled free and scuttled away before I could grab hold of it. To demonstrate that I was not completely out of my tree, however, I took the cellophane envelope I'd sequestered from Chinelio's cranium out of my pocket and slipped it under a Blueflite container at head height beside me.

I resumed my shuffle, even overdoing the stagger to appear drunker than I actually was. And that took a bit of doing, let me tell you. Eventually I found the proper gap in the piled crates and popped out in a rush into the centre of my converted living-room.

As the song says, there's no place like home, but when your sofa has been taken over by a tough like The Whacker Whelan and he is flanked in the two matching chairs by Humphrey and Sid, the Tweedle twins, the sentiment becomes a bit hard to swallow.

"Evening, men," I greeted them with forced joviality, at the same time swaying like a reed in the wind and wondering how far over I could bend without breaking. And there was no doubt in my mind that I was probably going to have to do an amount of bending.

Whelan stuck his chin in the air and made a face, either to ease his neck in the collar of his shirt or to show me how difficult it was for him to swallow his irritation. Humphrey and Sid, as usual, stayed as animated as a pair of wooden indians.

"Don't start in on that crap, Blaine," Whelan said. "You're in the soup and you know it."

I gazed at him and he stared back at me. He was very flash, with a narrow bony skull and a shaggy mane of fashionably ruffled ash-blond curls. He was wrapped in an expensive, lightweight wool sports coat, a knife-bladed creased slacks and a pale silk shirt. Jewellery dripped from him, the flickering fluorescence catching the highlights of neck chain, identity bracelet, gold wristwatch, and rings enough to spike the noses of a herd of bulls. I felt positively bereft looking at him.

Humphrey and Sid, in comparison, were like chalk to his cheese, both of them being arrayed in rumpled and baggy blue mohair suits, no-colour polyester shirts and ties that, in Sid's case, reposed under his left ear. They obviously had not bothered to change before coming to visit me, the heat of the day that had gone bringing out their natural fragrances and spreading them about like pig slurry. If they needed to torture me, all they would have to do would be to expose their armpits.

"To what do I owe the pleasure?" I asked, seeking to maintain a tone of light banter. I felt constricted by the linen jacket, so I struggled out of it and let it fall to the floor.

"Getting ready for bed?" Whelan said. "Don't mind us. We'll just sit here and watch."

"Maybe if I had a few silk scarves?" I offered. "I could do the dance of the seven veils."

Whelan frowned, chewed his lip, then growled, "Never mind the smart remarks. Just get the duds off."

"Really? You want me to disrobe?"

"You're a big boy now. You know how to open a button, unzip a zip. If you've any problems, Sid'll give you a hand. You'd like to give him a hand, wouldn't you, Sid?"

"Whatever you say," Sid said. He looked at me and I winked back at him causing him to blink.

I stripped down to my Y-fronts, seeing any further argument as being of little consequence. As I took them off, I handed each garment to a not-overly impressed Humphrey. He searched thoroughly through them, throwing my few belongings — a handkerchief, my frayed wallet, a bunch of keys, some loose change, cigarettes and matches — on the floor. The contents of the wallet he handed to Whelan.

He in turn picked through what I had left of the money Max had given me, my credit cards, a photo of Annie and myself, both of us looking young and happy and very much in love, some Pass machine slips, various other odds and ends ... but nothing detained him for very long. He let everything dribble through his fingers, then sniffed a few times to show how disappointed he was.

"The sandels and socks," he said, indicating them.

Obediently I bent down, took them off and handed them over, making sure to keep my unprotected rear end pointing off into outer darkness.

"If I knew what you were looking for ...?" I ventured. I felt cold and goose-pimply, and also embarrassed and more than a little angry. But I had done a round or two with Humphrey and Sid and knew that even though they might look like drapery store dummies they were still capable of inflicting pain.

"Something small and easily hidden," Whelan said in answer to my question. He let the sandels and socks fall to the floor to add to the growing mess, then he said, "Lower the underpants." He glanced across at Humphrey, then at Sid. "Which of you two boys is going to look up his crack?" he asked, an oily grin on his cosmetically enhanced mug.

"I'll pass on that one," Humphrey said, the words pushed out without any apparent lip movement. I think I did, however, discern a slight tightening of the facial muscles – it was as if a block of cement had winced.

"Aw, boss," Sid protested, "I ain't gonna do nothing like that. It ain't ..."

"Manly?" I suggested, putting on a brave front, but around the back I could feel my sphincter muscle clenching.

"Why not turn him upside down and shake him a few times?" Humphrey said. "Maybe somethin' will fall out."

"I'm not taking the underpants off," I said. "If it's going to come off, someone else'll have to do it."

Whelan glanced up at the winking on-and-off light. He made a face. He was good at making faces. Then he stood up, carefully arranging the crease in his tan slacks. He worked his shoulders in the expensive jacket. Wondering what was coming, I placed my spread hands in front of my genitals like a soccer player awaiting a free kick. Nudity is one of the most humbling of states; it reduces one to a very basic condition of anxiety. I've had nightmares of being caught in public without my clothes on, hopping along buck-naked with a derisory crowd hooting and sniggering in my wake. It's a dream that keeps on repeating.

Trying to put off the awful moment, I backed away, then fright released my vocal chords and I started talking: "You know, I do believe I've got it. It's been gnawing away at the periphery of my mind for days, hovering on the tip of my tongue. I'm sure you know the kind of thing? It's there but you just can't quite get at it." I paused, saw him open his mouth to speak, and forestalled him with: "Has it ever happened to you? I'm sure it has ... Wilson ... I can call you Wilson, can't I? Not being too familiar? Not taking advantage of your innate good nature? Although you did drop in uninvited. Not that I'm not glad to see you. Aha, two negatives there. They accentuate the positive ..."

"What the fuck ...?" Whelan narrowed his eyes, clearly wondering if I were genuinely about to tell him something or simply stalling for time. Adopting a wait-and-see attitude, he said, "If you've got something to say, spit it out. Things'll go easier on you if you do."

"Well, it's Oreste Kirkup, you see," I told him, hugging myself

90

against the chilly interior of the warehouse. I had never noticed all those draughts before.

"Huh?"

He gazed at Humphrey and Sid, who had stood up when he did and were now looking slightly more animated, somewhat in the manner of captive apes when the bolt clicks at feeding time. He made a signal and they came and stood on either side of me. Their feral odour went before them, as palpable as a force field.

"Who's this ... ah, Kirkup then?" Whelan asked, watching me closely.

"Now, don't be impatient," I said, holding up a hand. "I'll give you the whole story and then you can judge for yourself if I'm coming clean with you or not, Can't say fairer than that, can I?" I paused to give him a chance to answer, but he merely glared at me. I shrugged and plunged ahead: "In the fifties when the singer Mario Lanza was eating himself into the elephant league, film bosses began looking around for someone to replace him. And one of the pretenders to the throne that they came up with was a little guy with a big voice, a moustache and a breezy manner. No, it wasn't Groucho Marx, it was Oreste Kirkup — although he only used the first part of his name in his one and only film, 'The Vagabond King' ..."

"I'm not surprised, with a handle like that," Whelan mused. He frowned, then asked, "What's all this got to do with our business? I don't see the connection."

"Well, that's the beauty of it, you see. There isn't any. I just wanted to share this information with you. That guy's name has been going round and round in my head and I couldn't fasten on it. And now suddenly it pops up. Just like that. And it's all because you came along here and frightened the shite out of me ..."

This time Whelan's eyes narrowed to slits and a dark flush suffused his well-shaven chops. "Hold him, boys," he suddenly ordered, and he stood back to watch the brief struggle as Sid and Humphrey each got a grip on my arms. To expedite things and make me more cooperative, Sid stamped on my bare foot, sending a shot of pain licking like flame up my leg.

In no hurry now, Whelan turned to my antique sideboard and picked something up from it. When he was facing me again I saw that he was holding the miniature Toledo sword Annie had once given me for use as a letter-opener. The thin, three-inch blade glinted out a Morse Code message for anyone who wished to decipher it, but I personally did not want to know.

"Let me tell you something," Whelan said, his eyes on the little sword. "I saw a film once too. It was all about this smart ass private dick who was acted by ... what's his name? Jack Nichols?"

"Nicholson," I said. "I think you're alluding to a movie called 'Chinatown'."

"Yeah, that's what I'm alluding to." Whelan's eyes had gone all dreamy and he seemed fascinated by the trails of light streaming from the tip of the tiny implement. He did a few passes in the air with it, waggling his wrist from side to side. "It was a load of rubbish, all about this old fart who screwed his own daughter and had a kid with her. But there was one bit in it I liked. I wonder can you remember it?"

I had a bad feeling about what was coming and started struggling in the grip of the two gorillas.

"In case you've forgotten, I'll remind you." He gazed almost lovingly into my eyes, the look of someone who got his rocks off by inflicting pain on others. The thin spike of the blade was now upright in front of my face. "It's the part where the bad guy sticks a knife up Nichols's nose and pulls ..."

I eyed him, dragging again vainly at the restraints being put on me by Sid and Humphrey.

"You wouldn't dare," I challenged him, at the same time trying to pinch my nostrils closed.

"Wouldn't I?"

With his left hand he caught me under the chin to steady my head, then with the other he inserted the blade into my right nostril. He paused, and relief flooded through me with the thought that he had been bluffing, but then he suddenly jerked his wrist and ripped outwards. Pain this time was like a red-hot skewer, but before it blinded me I at least had the satisfaction of seeing bright crimson blood fountain out and spatter the front of his expensive sports jacket.

A lot of things then happened all at once. As though the mutilation of my nose was a signal, the ailing fluorescent tube abruptly gave up the ghost and went out completely. Even my tears of anguish couldn't hide that fact from me. With this sudden onset of darkness Sid and Humphrey relaxed their grip for a split second and I managed to wrench myself free. I went down on all fours and scuttled away, and more by touch than sight found an opening into which I was able to manoeuvre myself.

"Get him," I heard Whelan call, then shouts and curses as bodies came into contact with shelves and crates. There were crashes and bangs, and under cover of the noise I ceased my precipitate progress, got painfully to my feet and went on more slowly, one hand extended in front of me, the other cupping my poor pulsing nose.

As quickly as I could I got myself lost in the maze of passages, then stood in the lee of an outsize crate and listened to the drip, drip, drip from my proboscis. It felt as if someone were gripping it with a pair of pliers and gleefully twisting. Even the remembered pain from my hurling days paled in comparison to this latest outrage on my person.

I stayed where I was, measuring time passing by nodding my head like the toy parrot when you put your money in the slot. I didn't allow myself to think about my situation for fear my brain would burst.

Silence reigned throughout the length and breadth of the building as my erstwhile companions took a leaf out of my book and stood still to see what they could hear. It was a stand-off, and quite laughable if one could enjoy the humour of it: they listening for me listening for them.

In the end, their patience broke before mine, and they began blundering about, looking, apparently, for a way out. It seemed like an eternity before they found it, and Whelan's parting shout to the effect that they would be back was more like a benefaction than a threat.

What had they been after? I wondered. Odds on that it was the strip of film. Something small and easily hidden, Whelan had said. But would Mossie Haly have hired them as well as me to retrieve it? It would be just like the conniving bastard to play us off one against the other. A pox on his house, I thought, and on his lacquered wife, his sultry daughter and his creep of a son as well.

My hand was filling up with blood from my nose, and I sensed that if I didn't do something about it my brain would become dehydrated. Cautiously, like one of the blind men of Hindustan who came in search of the elephant, I made my way up and down a few aisles, stubbing my toe here, knocking some skin off my bare shin there. The only thing that kept me from sitting down and wailing was the thought of getting back at Whelan for ruining my nose. Playing "He loves me, he loves me not" with his guts, I journeyed up corridors and down corridors until finally my feet found purchase on what I recognised as my genuine one hundred percent Indian wool rug. I was back in my makeshift sitting-room, all alone and palely loitering.

I knew there was the possibility they were still in the building, having slammed the door from the inside to give me the impression they had done it from the outside, but I decided to take a chance. I would bleed to death anyway if I didn't soon stuff something up my weeping conk.

I went to where I kept a torch, found it and switched it on. My handkerchief was where Humphrey had dumped it and I picked it up and corkscrewed it into my nostril, cursing heartily at the renewed pain. I then dressed myself, all the while flicking blood about like holy water. What I would have given for a snort of Bushmills. Idly I wondered if I supped up some of my own blood would it still have a high-enough alcohol content to give me a lift.

When I was decently clothed I hunted about until I found my mobile phone. I stuck my wrist in the beam of the torch and saw from my watch that it was a quarter past three. Not a companionable hour to be ringing anyone, but I needed help for my injured nose. The nearest and most close-mouthed medical man who could help me was Leo Quinn, still a student, who was making the pursuit of the Hippocratic oath his life's work. An aunt of his had stipulated in her will that he should receive an annual allowance for as long as he was a student and, funds appearing to be inexhaustible, Leo remained an acolyte rather than a master. He maintained the nucleus of a surgery in his basement flat in the North Strand — as I had cause to know, for he had patched me up on a number of occasions there in the past.

He wouldn't mind the lateness of the hour, but whether he was in a sober enough condition to do some stitching was another matter entirely.

I thought about walking over there. No good, I would lose too much blood. Then I considered ringing for a taxi. A stab of pain from my nose convinced me I was in need of a little tender loving care, immediately if not sooner, so I sat down in the chair so recently vacated by Sid – his scent still hovered, like a melody lingering on – and dialled a number that would either bring me succour or the mother of all rollickings.

It rang and rang as I sat listening, my head tilted to one side and a steady stream of blood flowing across my face and into my ear. Finally it was picked up at the other end and a sleepy voice said, "You better have a good reason for ringing me at this hour, otherwise you're dead."

"How'd you know it was me?"

There was what could only be called a pregnant pause, and I tensed myself for the sound of breaking glass, but then the voice spoke again: "Who else would get me out of a sound sleep at ... what time is it? Christ, is it really three-thirty? In the morning? You great, thundering ballocks ..."

"Hold on. Don't go off into a tantrum. You know I'd only ring you at this hour in the gravest emergency. I'm hurt. My nose has practically been yanked off my face ..."

"Oh yeah? Well, if I had another part of your anatomy in a firm grip it'd be yanked off as well."

"It pains me even to think of it."

"Good."

"Seriously, I do need your help. I've got to get over to Leo's to have a few stitches put in. And my car's in the garage. Any chance you'd come over and do the Good Samaritan?"

"At this hour?"

"It's not as if it's late. It's early in the morning ..."

"I suppose you could put it like that."

Sensing a weakening of her resolve, I pressed on: "You know where I'm dossing down. Just give the gate a kick and I'll open up for you. Wait, on second thoughts you'd better give it three quick staccato kicks ..."

"Staccato?"

"That'll be the signal. So I'll know it's you."

"Who the hell else would it be at this time of the morning? Mother Theresa on a mercy mission? Egon Ronay with your *cordon bleu* breakfast? Give us a break ..."

"A Kit-Kat?"

"Huh?"

"One of us is delirious. Is it me?"

"Not today nor yesterday, buster."

"Annie, my nose is on fire."

"I'll bring a fire extinguisher. In the meantime put an icepack on it."

"I've no ice. The fridge is broken."

"Then you'll just have to bear with it, won't you? Offer it up in expiation for your sins and for getting a good Catholic woman out of her bed before the cock crowed ..."

That brought back a memory of Chinelio sitting on the toilet seat with the spike of the parasol transfixing his eye, and I said, "The cock has already crowed. If only you knew ..."

But I was talking to a hung-up phone, Annie having slammed it down. That usually marked the cessation of our conversations in recent times: me making her mad, she cutting me off. Maybe one of these days she'd do a Richie Michaels on me. The thought set me to hyperventilating and made my nose whimper in agony.

Awaiting her arrival, I went back and retrieved the cellophane envelope from where I had hidden it. Most likely it had been the cause of my ruptured nose, and my having to strip down in front of three leering neanderthals. I vowed to make good use of it in exacting revenge.

While I had been crashing about the fluorescent tube had come back to life, steady as a rock this time and exhibiting no surreal stuttering. I went back to my little nook and hunted about until I found a brandy bottle that was still about one quarter full. I lit a cigarette, put on a CD of the young Irish soprano, Regina Nathan, sat in my therapeutic rocking-chair and let the pure liquid notes of the aria 'Ebben ne Andro' from Catalani's 'La Wally' caress my aching brain.

I was still rocking at my ease, brandy bottle in one hand, cigarette in the other, and the bloodied handkerchief poking out of my nose, when three loud knocks came a-knocking on my door. It took an almighty effort on my part to stagger the distance to the door and let Annie in.

She was dressed all in black: knitted teacosy hat, roll-neck sweater, a short woollen jacket with shiny insets at the shoulders, leg-hugging tights, Doc Martens − a little soot applied to the face and she could have been a member of the A-Team come to rescue me.

Taking off her cap and shaking out her short red hair she said, "Was that staccato enough for you?"

"The knocks?"

"No, the lovebites. What d'you think?"

"I think I'm glad to see you too."

Concern suddenly flooded her face as she got a good look at the extent of my injury.

"Who did that to you?" she asked. "You look as if you've been given a nose transplant. But instead of a replacement nose they gave you an overripe plum."

"That bad, eh?" I fingered it gingerly, patting around it and finding to my horror that it appeared to be spreading over my face. "It feels more like a vegetable marrow to me."

Examining it critically and frowning, she said, "I don't think Leo will be able to stitch it until the swelling goes down."

I thought about that, then I said, "Maybe we'd better sit for a minute and have a chat. No use going over to his place if the trip proves in vain."

"Pity you didn't think of that before you rang me."

Preceding me along the passageway, she moved in the direction of my abode. As we went I couldn't help admiring the play of her hips and backside in the figure-hugging tights, and I felt a lick of desire rise in competition with the nagging pain in my nose.

Regina was now giving her all to the heroine's 'Mi ciamano Mimi' from La Bohéme, the soaring Puccini aria redolent with incipient love and impending tragedy. We sat and listened to its dying fall, then, as the CD wound down, I switched it off. The sudden silence was almost shocking in its abruptness.

Annie broke it by saying, "I can't understand why you're living in a place like this. With the money you got from the sale of the house you should be able to afford better."

"I've put it in a trust fund."

"For whom?"

"Us. Our children. And their children's children."

"That's ridiculous. You'd be better off spending it."

She sighed and pulled at a curl of hair that had fallen loose over her forehead. Her face was pale, the skin untouched by the summer sun except for a light dusting of freckles across the bridge of her nose. She had the colouring of many red haired people, a bone-like luminosity that was impervious to interference from the elements. She was not beautiful, but the nearest thing to it. Maybe her eyes were too widely spaced, her nose too emphatic, her mouth too generous, but the whole effect left little to be desired — certainly where I was concerned. I loved her so much it hurt.

Now she wrinkled her own untouched nose and sniffed suspiciously at the air. "What's that stink in here?" she asked. "It's enough to bring a dead cat back to life. Have you been storing your unwashed socks again?"

That was my cue to tell her about Sid and Humphrey, and their sometime boss, the Whacker. How they had entered my home, violated it and me, and left me sniffing up my own blood.

"But why? D'you know what they were after?"

"Well, yes and no."

"What's that supposed to mean?"

"You remember Max Morganthau? The friend from my Wexford days?"

"Of course. He always reminded me of Shane ..."

"Shane?"

"He did a great Alan Ladd imitation."

"That was no imitation. He was really like that."

"The whole works? Hat, boots, spurs ..?"

"Come off it, he didn't wear spurs."

"Are you sure? It seemed as if he did. It must have been something else that made the noise. Jinglebollicks?"

I looked at her, but her face was as innocently serious as if she were discussing dogma. Only the glint of amusement in her grey-green eyes gave away the fact that she was joking. As I remembered it, she and Max had got along pretty well, neither intruding on the other's space, but sharing the same sense of humour and laughing a lot.

Now I proceeded to tell her about his visit to my office, how he had hired me to find the film negative, and the consequences of my taking on the assignment. By the time I came to the finding of the second body the expression of fun was long departed from her features.

"I can't understand why you didn't get out as soon as you found ... what's his name?... Michaels."

"Me neither," I said, sighing. I shook the brandy bottle, but it was as empty as Mother Hubbard's cupboard. So was the cigarette packet. I rocked in my chair, felt my violated nose, gave another sigh. All the while Annie watched me, a suspicious look in her eye.

"Is there something you're not telling me?" she asked. "I get the feeling ..."

I made a face and shook my head. Even that motion caused my nose to scream.

"So, what're you going to do? Seems to me you should get in touch with George Quinlan and open up your heart to him."

"Before or after he cuts it out?"

"He won't like it much, granted. Your running away from the scene of two murders, I mean. But he will listen ..."

Again I shook my head, then grimaced as a stab of pain fibrillated the membranes of my nose. Praying that it wouldn't bring on a sneeze — the possible consequences of which left me weak with wonder — I said, "It's not as simple as that." I made a pass in the air with my hand. "I feel I owe it to Max to be ... circumspect? He's been in trouble with the law before. Drugs. Not here. In one of those Asian countries. But his record has gone before him. And then there's also the Wexford connection ..."

"How d'you mean?"

"It's difficult to explain. It's as if some unfinished business from my past has resurfaced, something I didn't attended to at the time. A sin of omission."

99

"A sin? You're not going to go all religious on me, are you?"

"No." I tried a grin, an occurrence that for her as an onlooker must have been ghastly. "But I think I'll leave George to stew for the moment. Let him find me. In the morning I'll pay Leo a visit and get the nose seen to. And I'll have the film I found developed."

"Where? You can't just breeze into a chemist's shop and say, 'Rustle me up a half-dozen of these and keep your eyes closed while you're about it'. If the pictures are as kinky as you say you could be arrested under the porno laws."

I looked down my nose at her, or at least tried to: it was beginning to feel as if I had a potato strapped to my face.

"By happy chance, I have a friend who is deeply involved in the art of photography, and, by an even happier chance, he owes me a favour. He'll do the business for me and forever afterwards hold his tongue."

"That's all right then, isn't it? Forget about the dead bodies, forget about leaving the scene, forget about suppressing evidence ..."

I gave a theatrical groan and slumped in my chair. "Could we not leave all that for another day?" I asked. "In case you haven't noticed, my schnozzle is taking on the proportions of a dinosaur turd, I have lost at least a gallon of blood, and I'm out of cigs and strong drink. Could you not see your way to procuring some aspirin for me, holding my hand and administering a little comfort and cheer? I would be most grateful ..."

Compassion won out over exasperation and in no time at all we were reclining on the bed, with Annie cradling my wounded head and whispering sweet nothings into my unbloodied ear. And scarce another cock had crowed before we were under the sheets, playing my patient to her doctor, with another part of my anatomy rising to rival the swelling magnificence of my nose.

Seven

Some time during the night Annie cried out in her sleep, and I held her until she settled down again. In spite of the pain from my nose I felt good about having her there with me, her breath fluttering against my chest, the familiarity of her warmth. In our ten years together she had never tried to argue me out of anything. When I gave up my safe job in insurance, basically for a principle a lot of people could have lived with, she supported my decision, then went out herself and got a position as a social worker. She had been studying for a degree in Pure English, but she threw this over without so much as a murmur and fell headlong into her new endeavour.

She showed amazing grit in dealing with the reams of red tape that the social services always seem to trap themselves in. She fought for her old people, her drunks and her down-and-outs, the chaff of life, with a ferocity that belied the even temper of her usual disposition, insulting terrified submanagers, riding roughshod over decrees from their masters and, when all else failed, turning abruptly to charm and blandishment to get her way. In the space of a little less than two years she became known as the patron saint of lost causes, the female equivalent of St Jude, and a true heroine to her legion of needy cases.

I was still holding her when dawn light began smudging its way in through the frosted glass skylight above us. Soon the dinginess of the place was brought into focus, causing me to spend a few moments dwelling on my situation in life. I was thirty-three years old, six foot two in height, in reasonably good shape except possibly for my lungs and liver, had a potentially thriving private detective business, my own furniture and an accountability to no one except the Man above.

On the debit side on this particular morning, of course, I was probably in the bad books of the security forces for finding two murdered men and only telling them about one. I had also had my nose ripped asunder by a low life while on the trail of a strip

101

of film showing two consenting adults – if Archie could be termed an adult – engaged in homosexual grappling.

Not details your ordinary Joe Soap can boast about when he struggles out of sleep in the morning. Whatever else could be said about me, there was no way I was a victim to dull routine.

I gazed at Annie, then plumped a pillow and sat up against it. With the disconcerting habit she has of coming from sleep to full wakefulness in an instant, she opened her eyes, showed her teeth and grinned at me. Then the events of the night came flooding back and the grin froze as she realised she was in the wrong bed with the wrong man, after saying things she probably meant but would have wished to keep locked in the inmost recesses of her heart. At least that's what the expression on her face implied – another explanation could be that she had not yet become accustomed to the devastation wreaked on my nose.

"Let's take off and find a bee-loud glade," I said. "Somewhere in the heart of the heart of the country. We could plant nine bean-rows. And have a hive for the honey-bee ,..."

"How are you on rustic gates?" Annie responded. "I've always fancied a rustic gate. One that squeaked."

"I see it leading into a thatched cottage with clematis climbing up the walls."

"Ah me ..."

I gave her a kiss, then slid out of bed, stood and flexed my muscles. Except for the dull throb in my proboscis, I felt fine.

"How do I look?" I asked her.

"Hard to tell. Your nose is covering most of your face."

"Thanks a ton."

"Don't thank me, thank the Whacker Whelan who did it to you."

I opened my wardrobe, took out underwear and put it on: a red vest and matching boxer shorts. A shower would have been nice, but I wasn't in the mood for trading insults with the postal workers.

"Fetching," Annie said from the bed, indicating my scarlet unmentionables. "You never wore anything as daring as that when we were cohabiting."

"I bought them to cheer myself up. And the socks," I said,

holding them up for inspection. They were also red, with beige cherubs disporting themselves as cherubs are wont to do. "You like?"

"Dazzling."

She threw back the duvet, stretched without any trace of coquetry, then got out naked and gorgeous on the wool rug. "Where's the bidet?" she asked.

"Thrown out with the baby and the bathwater."

"A washbasin?"

"There's a mop and pail."

"You're joking. You mean there's no way I can perform my morning ablutions?"

"Not unless you're content with a dry run. A bit of shining and burnishing. I've got a tin of Mansion polish and a rag around somewhere."

"Very comical."

With a look of distaste she got into her clothes of the night before, *sans* knickers, which she couldn't find. She pulled at her hair with her fingers, gazing critically into the mirror that stood precariously on the chest of drawers. "What do I look like?" she asked her image.

"You look like a million," I said, coming up behind her. When I caught sight of my own face I nearly fell out of my standing. I had two definitive black eyes, somewhat in the manner of a silent film villain, and a nose like a hot cross bun. Not exactly the kind of visage to win friends and influence people. "Do I really look like that?" I asked her. "Or is it the mirror?"

"What do I say?" she replied, spreading her hands. "Do I spare your blushes and assure you the mirror lies, or do I give you the bare, unvarnished truth?"

"Knowing you, it'll be the pain that kills."

"Right then. You could be arrested for showing a face like that on the public thoroughfare. Think what it'll do to old ladies and small children. The return of the Elephant Man ..."

Sulking, I put on a pair of jeans, runners, a Notre Dame sweatshirt, and a rainbow-hued waistcoat. Maybe my gear might take away some of the attention from my Hallowe'en mask of a face.

"Where'd you park your car?" I asked Annie, watching her furiously scraping at her hair with one of my onyx-backed brushes. I felt so good about having her there that I contemplated doing what Terence Stamp did in the film 'The Collector' and imprisoning her down in the cellar. I didn't have a cellar, but she seemed to divine my thoughts just the same, for she put down the brush and sidled away.

"It's right outside the door," she said in answer to my question. "I was in such a hurry to get in and administer the kiss of life that I left it any old way. I think I even left the keys in the ignition."

"Probably the safest thing to do in this neighbourhood. If there's no challenge, they won't break in. Anyway, who'd touch that pile of junk you call a car ...?"

She made a face, then asked me what time it was.

"A little after eight. You'll breakfast with me?"

"What've you got?"

"Percolated Bewley's coffee, hot croissants, truffles, fine cut orange marmalade ..."

"Really?"

"Only in my dreams. I could offer you a cup of tea. Yesterday's teabag. No milk, no sugar."

"Another time? I need to go home and clean up."

"Home? I thought this was your home?"

"Don't confuse me. It's too early in the morning. D'you want a lift to Leo's or would you prefer to jog?"

"I'll walk," I said, standing on my dignity, but all that elicited was an I-don't-care shrug and an exaggerated waggle of her knickerless backside.

Outside, the morning sky was high and pale, giving promise of another sweltering day. Already the air had an incipient warmth and the smell of engine fumes and closed-in spaces imbued one with the wish to be away to the seaside, with bucket and spade, swimsuit, snorkel and flippers, and enough corned beef sandwiches to last the length of a long day. I mentioned as much to Annie, but she was too preoccupied in examining her battered Citroen to take heed. I couldn't make out what she was looking for: there were so many indentations and rusty bits that any extra vandalism would have been like garnishing the town dump with sprays of flowering weeds.

"Is Madam's car not in the shape to which she's accustomed?" I enquired.

Again she ignored me and struggled into the driver's seat. Sticking her head out the window, she said, "I suppose there's no use advising you to go to Quinlan with what you know and then take a holiday, is there?" She stared at me, then shook her head. "I thought not. Of all the bull-headed, stubborn ... All I can say to you is, if you can't be wise, be careful." With that she switched on the ignition, bringing the engine to life with a ferocious clatter.

I leaned down to her and she presented me with her lips, pursed. I kissed her, gently but with feeling. Her lips were cold. I said, "Your lips are cold," but the words were lost in the stuttering roar as she manoeuvred the squeaking little car away from the path and down the street. A receding, waving hand bade me farewell, leaving me alone and breathing the sun-warmed air in noisily through my mouth. My nose was about as useful as a blocked sewer.

Leo Quinn had a basement flat in the North Strand. The house itself was three-storied and leaned on its neighbours as though out on its feet from neglect and old age. Three cement steps led up to the front door and enough foliage grew out of the cracks to keep a goat chewing for a week. The windows were blind eyes, cataracts of ancient lace curtains draping them, plus a liberal coating of dust to shield the insides from the prying gaze of rent collectors, bill wavers and men from the corporation with thoughts of condemning the building on their minds.

Many of the rooms were occupied by ladies of the night, a passing trade that came and went, mainly the former. The girls were a good-natured lot and Leo helped them out in matters of hygiene and the like, giving them the odd shot when it was needed. In return they provided material comforts, cleaned his flat, cooked and played at being housewives to his indulgent husbanding. It was an arrangement that suited both parties, and more than once I felt the prickle of envy when I beheld Leo surrounded by his bevy of surrogate wives.

The sun was up and climbing when I opened the iron gate that gave entry to his little nest in the bowels of the earth. I went down and banged on his door. Above my head traffic noise hummed and buzzed, but down here I was immured in solitude. I crossed my ankles and leaned against the wall and waited for some sign of life to manifest itself. There was a small postage stamp of garden, overgrown but with one small cultivated area. Looked like a couple of marijuana plants to me, nestling there, but I could have been mistaken. Dock leaves have their uses too.

I put my face up to the emergent sun to see if it could do anything for the persistent throbbing in my snout. Outlined against its rays another face was staring down at me. Two eyes, an ordinary-shaped nose, a brightly lipsticked mouth, the whole lot cuddled in a mass of very black, ringletted hair. As I started, the mouth opened and a voice enquired, "'ere, wot yeh doin' down there? Them's private steps and private property."

"Since when?" I challenged, cupping my conk in my fingers in case she dropped something on me.

The face disappeared from my view, the gate opened, and a well-upholstered body in a tight sheath of some kind of shiny material hove into view. A hip-high slit in the dress allowed a sturdy, nylon-clad leg to strut its stuff, but its owner only came down a couple of steps and then stopped.

"How ya, Lil?" I greeted her. "What's the occasion? You're done up like a dog's dinner."

"I'm only after comin' from a high society do, amn't I?" she answered. She stared short-sightedly at me. "Do I know yeh, sport? I've got so many gentleman friends ..."

"I'm a pal of Leo's. The last time I saw you, you were cooking a leg of lamb with mint sauce. Wearing an apron and nothing else. You, not the lamb."

"Is that so? How'd it come out?"

"The lamb was very tasty, and so was everything else."

"Well, yeh know wot they say: 'A little of what yeh fancy does yeh good'." She advanced down another couple of steps and squinted her eyes. The waft of her perfume made me feel as if I'd been socked by a scented marshmallow. "What's up wit yer nose?

106

Looks as though someone used it as a mallet to drive in nails."

"It's a long story, Lil, and I haven't really the time to go into it. D'you happen to know if Leo's about?"

"Leo's always about. Specially in the mornings. He's prob'ly feelin' the worse for wear. Fragile, like ..."

She came down the rest of the way and stood beside me and examined my face. "Nasty," she said, "but I've seen worse. Let Leo at it and in no time at all it'll be as right as ... well, the nose on your face." She laughed, then turned to the door and gave it a kick. "He's a bit hard of hearin' sometimes," she explained. "Sleeps with cotton wool in his ears."

While I put my face back up to the sun she continued walloping the door. Eventually it was opened by a tousled and unhappy Leo, a sight not guaranteed to do much for my peace of mind or my throbbing nose. Leo is a stick-thin, L S Lowry man with a decided slant to his ambulatory gait: when sober he leans forward, when drunk in the opposite direction. This morning he was at an in-between state, sort of vertical but with a wobble. His scant hair was messed up, his eyes were of the fried egg variety, and his mouth kept opening and shutting like a goldfish's in a tank. As an example of the ravages drink can have on a man, he was a prime exhibit.

"Wakey, wakey, Leo," my female friend said. "Yeh've got a customer. And by the look of him, he's in need of instant stitching. Maybe even a bit of crocheting," she went on, with a belly laugh. "I hope yeh've got the hands for it."

She brushed past him, leaving a small tornado of scent in her wake. Leo looked at me, did not like what he saw, produced a coated tongue and proceeded to run it slowly over his upper lip. I could hear the rasp from a yard away.

"Aren't you going to ask me in?" I enquired. "It's nearly ten o'clock. Time for all good men to come to the aid of the party."

"What party?" he croaked, sticking his head out the door like a tortoise seeking to see if the coast was clear.

"Merely a figure of speech. What I mean is that you should be alert, on your toes and eager to sally forth to heal your fellow man. Aren't you by way of being some class of doctor?"

"Only when the sun is over the yard-arm," he said grumpily.

He gazed at me through eyes that were now half closed and meanly red. "And stop taking the piss."

"Leo, would I do that?" I spread my hands to show him I had nothing up my sleeve. "I caught my nose on a nail and I'm here to have it seen to. A nuisance, but there you are."

"How'd you catch your nose on a nail?"

"I was trying to pull it out of a wall."

"With your nose?"

"What else would I use?"

"How about a pair of pliers?"

"Aw, Leo, real men don't use pliers ..."

He sniffed, shook his head to show it was all beyond him, then beckoned for me to follow him down the hallway. He was wearing a red flannel shirt that was much patched and faded and a pair of trousers held up by blue braces. Lil could have got into the trousers with him – and for all I knew quite often did – and there would still have been enough room for me and a few more.

I followed him into his surgery and watched while he picked up a flask of what looked like rubbing alcohol and took a hefty swig from it. He blanched, belched, took a step backwards, then came to attention. Looking on with interest, I saw colour return to his sallow face, a glint kindle in his eye, and a smile slowly materialise, Cheshire Cat-like, on his raddled features.

"Must be good stuff," I said, indicating the flask. "The elixir of life ...?"

He put it down, then came and tilted my chin and gazed up my nose. His breath was like the blast when the furnace door is opened.

"Pretty swollen," he observed.

"You don't need a doctor's diploma to tell me that. Can you stitch it?"

"I suppose." He stood back and spread his hands, palms upward. There was a discernible tremor. He used one of them to take up the flask and he sank another snort, then he regarded them again. Satisfied, he busied himself with gathering together the necessary apparatus for sewing together the frayed edges of my injured olfactory organ.

"Aren't you going to give me a shot?"

"A shot of what?"

"An anaesthetic."

"Here," he said, offering me the flask of alcohol. "Get a few ounces of that into you and you'll soon be as numb as an eskimo with frostbite."

I did as he advised, gagging on the raw spirit, then sat reasonably still while he performed his duty by me. He was surprisingly deft, and his touch was as light as an angel's kiss. Just the same, I did a few exaggerated flinches and grimaces to keep him happy in the knowledge that he was getting his own back on me for rousing him so early in the morning.

With a final snip he finished, then stood back to admire his handiwork. He put his head on one side, pursed his lips and went, "Dum diddly um dum, dum dum."

"They should let you at the Shroud of Turin," I said, looking at my face in his mirror. "You'd have it invisibly mended in no time."

"I didn't know it was in need of repair."

Tentatively I felt around my bloated nose. More than ever it felt like a foreign object on the front of my face.

"Will it be as good as new?"

"It wasn't new to begin with."

"You know what I mean."

He was at the flask again, sipping contentedly. He said, "Not if you continue pulling nails out of walls with it. Otherwise, yes. It may not regain its true Roman contours, but it'll be recognisable for what it is."

"Well, that's something. How much do I owe you?"

"You'll have to see my secretary about that."

"Your secretary?"

His eyes veered away from mine and towards the aroma of fresh coffee that was stealing in from the kitchen.

"Lil? You've employed Lil as your secretary? How're you going to get her to keep her uniform on? She'll be straddling the customer while you're swabbing down your hands."

"It'll save on painkillers."

"Then why wasn't she in here when you were pushing red-hot needles up my snout?"

"She doesn't come on till eleven. Strict union hours."

I looked at him. "Please don't make me laugh, Leo," I said. "I'm afraid the stitches'd burst."

He shrugged, finished off the contents of the flask, smacked his lips. Then he ushered me towards the door. The last I saw of him, he was sashaying down the hall, his shirt tail sticking out, but with an urgency about him that betokened a possible training-in session with his new secretary.

Out in the sun again and my face felt as if it were being held together with safety pins. Two rude little girls who should have been in school stood and stared, then one of them asked me, "Hey mister, did youse run into a bus?"

To get away from them I hailed a taxi and told the driver to take me up to Phibsboro. I don't know if he was getting at me, but for the length of the journey he whistled the tune of 'The Music of the Night' from *The Phantom of the Opera*.

We went through busy, sunlit streets, with me admiring the shapely female limbs so readily on view and wishing I were chasing Annie up and down the sand dunes on some beach or other. Then I had a renegade thought about Mary Haly and how her short, pleated tennis skirt shifted up and down against her firmly-muscled thighs as she walked. Guilt made me tense my nose until the newly-inserted stitches creaked.

I told the taxi driver to stop at Byrne's Pork Butcher shop and I went in and passed the time of day with Michael and bought a pound of narrow pale back rashers, a string of sausages and some black and white pudding. We then proceeded up the North Circular Road, turned into Manor Street, off it into Phoenix Avenue and pulled up in front of number 13 in a row of neat artisan cottages. I paid the driver, then waited while he took himself and his vehicle away back down the quiet backwater. If anyone was following me, he or she had made contact with H G Wells and wormed the secret of invisibility out of him.

I rapped on the red panelled door, heard nothing in reply, thought for a minute and then stuck some fingers into the letterbox. The key was there was usual, hanging from a piece of frayed cord, and I pulled it out, put it in the lock, turned it and let myself in.

The hallway was packed with cardboard crates and rolls of developing paper, plastic trays and bottles of solution, and bundles of squeegees and negative wipers. A harsh, graphite-like smell permeated the air, with below it the more mundane bouquet of many and frequent fry-ups. A large black cat sat crouched on a bright yellow Kodak box, his ears in the air and his unblinking gaze fixed warily on me. When I made to move, he hissed, then sprang away out of sight.

"Yo, Charlie," I called. "It's me, Blaine. I come bearing gifts. Drop your cock and grab your sock, I'm on my way."

I pushed on through to the back of the house, having to pass the gauntlet of two more unfriendly cats on my journey. I went by way of a grease-impregnated kitchen into a perspex-roofed conservatory and there was Charles Fitz Moore Oppenheimer himself, sitting in his wheelchair and basking in the sun that bellowed down on him through the clear corrugations above him.

He was attired only in gaily striped Bermudas, the grossness of his immensely fat body in stark contrast to the patrician gauntness of his head and face. It was as if some mad scientist had sewn the physiognomy of a suffering Christ on to the body of Buddha; the effect was startling and when people first met Charlie they were inclined to stand back and wait for him to shrug off the rolls of fat and reveal himself for the thin man he really was.

When I knew him first he was as fine a specimen of athletic manhood as one would wish to encounter. That was at university where we had often worked out in the gym together. His interests lay in mountaineering and photography, and it was not unusual for him to go missing for as much as a month at a time, climbing in the Alps, the Andes, or up any man-sized mountain that happened to get in his way.

The irony of his fall, when it did come, was that it occurred on home territory, down in Wicklow where his family had a stately home. High on a mixture of pills, booze and the strung-out desperation of the confirmed manic depressive, he had decided to go hang-gliding from the battlements of the ancestral castle, while at the same time neglecting to equip himself with the necessary apparatus. The result was that he did a magnificent

111

swan dive into the moat, a circumstance that did him no good at all, as said moat was completely devoid of water.

Among other major injuries, he snapped his spine and, after months of hovering between life and death, he woke up one morning to find himself confined to a wheelchair for the remainder of his life. A minor miracle had occurred, however, in that he left his depression somewhere behind him in the black void he inhabited for so long, and he now emerged as a cheerful, fun-loving and quite stable human being.

One other quirk manifested itself: he had become addicted to food, especially the greasy spoon type of takeaways, Burdock's best fish and chips, and hamburgers by the score. This accounted for the meaty immensity of his body, but everything seemed to lodge below the neckline and his head and face stayed Gandhi-like and austere. He was quite a sight and, because of it, seldom went out. This little house in Phoenix Avenue was now his home, his hearth, and his place of business. It was from here he operated his photographic web, sending his scores of young trainee apprentices out to snap the images and developing them himself with much loving care and not a little tentative genius.

It was like a hothouse under the perspex and beads of perspiration popped out all over me as soon as I set foot inside. Charlie looked like a beached whale, the rubbery, overlapping folds of fat slick and glistening. He was wearing mirror shades and these now turned in my direction, their lenses showing twin reflections of my handsome mug.

"Not working?" I asked. I showed him the plastic carrier bag I was holding. "Sausages and rashers from Byrne's. A little gift."

"A bribe, you mean." Charlie's voice was blubbery, to match his body, and it was accompanied by a continual wheezing, like the wind in the rafters. "No pudding ...?"

"Yeah, I forgot, pudding too. Black and white. No discrimination here."

He put out an arm that dripped wattles of fat, took up a glass from a high bamboo stand near him and drank from it. It contained a thick oily liquid, purple in hue, and his tongue, when he opened his mouth, was stained the same colour.

"What're you drinking?" I asked him. "Hammerite paint?"

112

"It's blackcurrant cordial and vodka. An attempt to stimulate the taste buds. They're getting a little ... frayed at the edges? Like the rest of me."

"Feeling a little down, are we? What you need is the pick-me-up of a good fry. Get your stomach juices working. I'll throw on a panful. Maybe two. One and a half for you, and the rest for me. Aren't you feeling a mite peckish this fine morning?"

He grunted, placed the glass back on its moist ring on the stand, then turned the wheelchair to face me. He flexed his neck muscles by moving his head from side to side. Pools of sweat had gathered in the dimples at his collar bones and they flowed like minor rivers down his chest and into his lap.

"What happened to your nose?" he asked, now that he had a full frontal of my injured appendage.

"Cosmetic surgery. I wanted to be like my hero, Jake Gittes."

"Who?"

"A character played by Jack Nicholson in the film 'Chinatown'. Don't worry about it. I'm thinking of having a placard made that I can hang around my neck. It'll say, 'Don't ask about the nose. It's a sore point.'"

"I get the picture. But before we leave the subject forever, what did happen to it?"

"Over-eager picking? Leave it be, can't you ...?"

Charlie chuckled, his mountain of blubber quivering. He wheeled himself ahead of me into the kitchen and helped and hindered me as I cooked the food I had brought. He ate most of it, sopping up the grease with doorstops of fresh white bread. He was slightly younger than me, but both of our life expectancies were about the same, short to none at all; his from lack of exercise and over-eating, mine from sticking my nose in where it wasn't wanted and an inability to keep my mouth shut.

When we were finished and smoking, he a cheroot that smelled like dried and wrapped dogshit, me a Dunhill, I produced the strips of film I had found under Chinelio's head rug and asked him if he'd be kind enough to develop them for me.

"I knew I was being bribed," he said. He took the negatives and held them up to the light, lifting the dark glasses at one side to expose a sunken eye.

"I think the pictures are a bit rude," I said. "But you're a man of the world and you've seen it all before. It's to do with some business I'm working on, in case you think I've gone kinky. Or at least kinkier ..."

"It's no problem. I get my kicks in wondrous ways nowadays."

He wheeled himself out of the kitchen and down the hall, the electric wheelchair going like the clappers and me trying to keep up. His darkroom was to the right, guarded by a curtain, a door and two cats – or was it one cat with two heads? No matter. We shut ourselves in and Charlie switched on a Safelight and began.

I've got a dentist who insists on explaining every move he makes, in spite of the fact that I'm sitting there terrified and wishing he'd get on with it and spare me the gory details. Charlie reminded me of him now as he set about taking me through the process of negative and print development.

In his rather grand voice – he came of old stock and could trace his lineage back to the first of Cromwell's blow-ins – he droned: "We place the roll of film in the spiral, place the spiral in the tank, and pour in the developer liquid. Agitate," – he thumped the tank, then turned it upside down. "We do that every minute for maybe five minutes ... Pour out developer ... Rinse with water ... Pour in fixer ... Pour out fixer. Rinse again and place in hot press to dry ..." He packed the interstices between these more-emphasised remarks with enough technical jargon to fill a good-sized textbook, but I quit listening and went and sat in a corner to ruminate and gently caress my injured nose.

Charlie brought me out of my reverie by asking if I wanted a gloss or matt finish.

"They're ready?"

"Yes. But I'm afraid you're in for a disappointment. Nothing kinky about these, unless you're into men in raincoats giving parcels to one another."

"Let's have a look."

I took and studied the series of semi-dried prints he handed me. There were six of them in black-and-white. I laid them in order, as I saw it, along the counter top. They showed two cars drawn up beside one another and facing in opposite directions;

then a man getting out of one of them, being greeted by a character in a raincoat from the other one, what looked like a thick A4 envelope or Jiffy bag being passed from one to the other, a close-up of the two guys, and one final long shot of the two cars. The only thing that caught my interest was that the figure handing over the envelope was my old dancing partner, the Whacker Whelan.

"You know these people?" Charlie asked me. "I suppose the guy in the raincoat could be a flasher ...?"

I shook my head, puzzled. I didn't recognise the fellow with Whelan. He was a heavy-set individual, with black hair and a moustache. He appeared to be in his late forties or early fifties, settled-looking, a professional type, maybe. He was the sole occupant of one car, but there were two others in Whelan's Bluebird, one behind the wheel, and another in the back. It looked like Humphrey in the driver's seat, but I didn't think it was Sid in the back.

"Can you enlarge that one?" I asked Charlie. "I want to see if I can make out the guy in the back seat."

Charlie squinted at where I was pointing.

"Shouldn't be any trouble. But it'll take a little longer."

I gathered up the prints, shuffled them, them studied them again. The cars were drawn up in a field, a field that appeared to be in the process of development. Either that or someone had dropped a bomb in it. It might have been in the early stages of being prepared as a building site. There were trees in the background and a kind of sprawling lean-to or shed. I could also make out the spire of a church and through the trees what looked like a small village. There was something familiar about the scene, as though I had actually seen not the place itself but another photograph of it, and in the very recent past at that. Like Oreste Kirkup, it just wouldn't come to me.

"Does that look familiar to you?" I asked Charlie.

"Sure, I printed it out for you just a minute ago."

"No, I mean the background. That piece of countryside."

He looked askance at me — at least I presumed it was askance, he was still wearing the shades.

"How would I know it? I never go out. And especially not into the countryside. The only thing I like about cows, sheep and pigs is that they're edible."

"No, I mean in a photograph. I'm sure I've seen it recently, but I can't work out where."

"What about the kinky ones you promised me? Where are they, then?"

"I don't know." I scratched my head, pulled at my ear, shuffled the photographs again. "It's a mystery. I was led to believe that I was after prints of two boyos poking one another. This opens up a whole new can of worms ..."

Charlie dipped his fingers in the fixer tray and blessed himself with the solution as if it were holy water. "I think I hear the Angelus," he said. "Time for my noonday snooze. That will take exactly half an hour. I will then enlarge the print for you and fax it to your office."

"I haven't got a fax machine."

"Okay, I'll send it by courier. What time is it now?"

"Eleven-thirty."

"You'll have it by one. You'll be in situ?"

"In my office? Yes. I need to catch up on my correspondence, pay a few bills, write a further chapter or two of my memoirs."

"Do I feature?"

"Indubitably."

I took my leave, cradling my nose as I again ran the gauntlet of the hissing cats. I let myself out and stood for a moment in the blast of sunlight. A weird feeling gripped me as if someone had walked over my grave. Something had just turned the corner of the avenue and was out of my sight, but a ripple of the familiar still reverberated in the close confines of the street. A feeling, a scent, a sound?

I moved quickly to the corner and loped into Manor Street, but it was clogged by a snarl of traffic. I got up on my toes to sight over steaming car roofs, eager for something out of the ordinary, but no apocalyptic vision greeted my straining eyeballs. Yet intimations of something important that I'd missed continued to ruffle my awareness.

As I walked back up the pathway a wino with a scarred face and a wild look in his eye approached me with his hand out. I

116

brushed past him and as I did, he pirouetted and threw an empty VP wine bottle into the middle of the road. It exploded under the wheels of a passing car.

Envying him the definitiveness of his gesture, I continued on my way.

Eight

I walked into town in the summer sun, taking my time and getting a fiendish enjoyment from the startled looks people gave me when they came face to face with my battered nose. I cut off after what used to be the State Cinema but was now a skating rink and strolled along Royal Canal Bank Walk. Grass was mown, flowers bloomed, lunches were probably being prepared in adjoining houses but, try as I might, I could get not a whiff. If the king of B.O., Ethelred the Unwashed, had gone past me I would not have given him a second glance. For the moment at least, my sense of smell was as dormant as a hibernating skunk's.

A rectangle of artificial lake with some flowering shrubs bordering it connects the Walk with Blessington Street, and I went in there and sat down on a ribbed metal seat. A bewhiskered old guy in a plaid lumber jacket leaned on a stick and dozed at the other end of the bench, while a woman with a little boy in tow trailed a bamboo pole with a net at the end of it in the water. The boy whinged because he wasn't allowed to hold the pole and the woman kept shaking him as though he were wet and she was trying to dry him out. In the background the hum of city traffic was a low waspish burr.

I was still puzzled as to the significance of the photographs I had found. According to Max Morgan they should have been prints of young Archie Haly doing a nude fandango with the late and possibly lamented Richie Michaels. The fact that they were not would naturally lead me to believe I was in possession of the wrong ones. Then why should Chinelio go to such lengths to hide them? After all, you don't just stick any old film negative under your wig; they would have to have had some value to be afforded such a warm and snug, not to mention personal, place of concealment.

I took them out of the A4 envelope Charlie had given me and gazed at them again. The probability was that I was seeing a pay-off of some kind: drugs? arms? maybe protection money? The

118

character being handed the package did not look right for such a transaction; he was too respectable, too settled, too well-fed. People in the line of business I was supposing this guy to be involved in were usually lean and hungry, like yon Cassius.

And then, who was the person in the back of Whelan's car? I held the photograph up close to my eyes, then further away at arm's length. Maybe when Charlie's blown-up print arrived, I would be able to put a face and an identity to him. If it turned out to be Sid, photogenic and all as he undoubtedly was, I would be sorely disappointed.

I put them back in the envelope, lit a cigarette and smoked it contentedly in the hazy rinse of sunshine. The old guy at the end of the bench was leaning further and further over and looked as if he might at any moment topple into the lake. The little boy had a jamjar with a couple of anxious minnows swimming around in it and, as I watched, the woman raised the net from the water, droplets forming an iridescence of colour in the sparkle from the surface of the pond.

Through the dancing eyelets of warm air I saw a familiar figure come in the town gate, pause, then stroll casually in my direction. Rather than watch his approach, I blew a smoke ring and gazed at it as it pulsed and expanded. Near me the little boy cried out in excitement, and another tiny fish plopped into the jar. The cry awakened the old man and he sat up with a jerk, looking around to see if anyone had noticed his start of surprise.

I waited until he was standing in front of me before I said, "Hello, Max. You've been following me, haven't you? I sensed you, like a bad smell."

He looked hard and fit in a blue cotton shirt and denim shorts. A navy bandana was tied pirate-fashion round his hair, but a lick of quiff had escaped and was swinging cheekily over his forehead. Remembering what Annie had said, I glanced down to see if he were wearing spurs. He wasn't. On his feet were blue sneakers with red stripes. No socks.

He grinned and I shook my head bemusedly. No matter what he did he still had the charm to coax, cajole and seduce. He possessed a quality of self-belief in his ability to beguile that blinkered criticism and kept dislike at bay. He would have made a great con man, but then again, that's probably what he was. He could certainly con me, and had been doing so for as long as I'd known him.

He nodded at the old guy at the end of the bench, then sat down between us. He placed his arms along the back of the seat and for a moment I wondered if we were meant to move into their ambit so that he could give us both a great big hug.

"Why were you following me?" I asked him. "Seems stupid to keep a dog and do your own barking."

"I wasn't following you. Would you believe me if I said I had a hunch you'd be here?"

"In a word, no."

"I thought as much."

He leaned back and stretched out his bare legs. They were tanned, muscular and hairless. He had an air of youthfulness that did smack of the Peter Pan syndrome and maybe his belief that he should be numbered among the Lost Boys was not as fanciful as it sounded.

I could sense him gazing at my face in profile. He said, "If I'd been following you, your nose wouldn't be in the shape it's in."

"It's down to you, just the same."

"How d'you make that out?"

I stubbed the cigarette out against the metal arm of the seat. Seemed a shame to be polluting the air of the park with smoke. But then I went and lit another one. I looked at the sky, so high and blue and uncluttered. A gull spread his wings against its immensity and gave a squawk of probably pure joy. The thought came to me that I could do with a drink.

I said, "You got me into a mess I hadn't bargained for. It's on your account I've been poking my nose in where angels fear to tread."

"You should've used a stick."

"A stick?"

"To do the poking."

"Is that all you've got to say? No words of sympathy? No apology ...?"

He made a gesture with his hand, tipping his forehead, his lips, his breast. "Mea culpa," he said. "For what you have

120

suffered, I'm truly sorry. I shall seek to make restitution." He sighed theatrically and crossed his feet at the ankles. "You left the Catacombs rather abruptly," he went on. "One minute you were there, the next you were gone. And I heard you redesigned the physical lineaments of a couple of bouncers ..."

"Do tell."

"So the rumour goes."

"And what else did the busy whisper circling round convey?" I turned to him, measuring him up for sincerity and coming up a few yards short. "Does it tell you that I found Chinelio in his hostelry with the spike of an umbrella impaled in his brain? Or that a trio of thugs invaded the privacy of my home a little later last night, caused me to strip down to my jocks and then castrated my nose with a sharp instrument? And that they were looking for the same thing you are, namely a roll of film negative ..."

"They told you that?"

"Not in so many words. But if it was small enough to be secreted up my arse it can't have been the treasure of the Sierra Madre."

"Who were these guys?"

"The Whacker Whelan and the doobie brothers, Humphrey and Sid."

"Doobie?"

"Do be fucking thick as elephant shit. They humiliated me. In my home, my castle, the place where I lay my head."

The old guy at the end of the seat made a clucking sound, then stared disapprovingly at us. We gazed right back and he threw us a dirty look and got up and stamped off. The woman and the boy were now at the other side of the pond, she pulling at his arm again, he resisting and obviously wishing to stay. The sun had gone in behind the only cloud in the sky as though sulking in sympathy with him.

"Now look at what you've done," Max said. "You've disturbed the equilibrium of the morning. Annoyed an old and probably holy man. Why don't you relax and let summer coming down roll over you?"

"Why don't you go and jump in the fucking lake?"

We sat in silence for a time, me scowling, he seemingly lost in contemplation. Finally I said, "You're treating all this like a comic turn. Aren't you at all worried by the fact that two men have died violently ..?"

"We live in violent times. You can get used to anything. In the prison I was in, it was a fact of life."

"Did you ever kill anyone?"

He looked at me, his blue eyes as shadowed and deep as any bottomless sea. "I may have," he said. "But you wouldn't want to know the details. I'd prefer you to think of me as a friend, the laughing boy you always knew ..."

"That's only one more myth in a long line of them. I don't think I ever really knew you."

"Why would you want to? The idea is to preserve the phenomenon. Nothing ruins a relationship more than one party being able to second-guess the moves and motives of the other. The trick is to keep and be kept off balance."

"Relationship? I didn't know we had a relationship."

"No? Maybe you'd settle for a meeting of minds? A strained affection. I'd always like you to think well of me."

"No matter what you do?"

"I'd never do you harm."

"Bullshit. Would you take a good hard look at my nose?"

"That's incidental. An unfortunate occurrence. Suffering for friendship ..."

"Well, that's it. I have suffered and I don't want any further part in it."

Max bent down and picked up a piece of shale from under the bench. He threw it up a couple of times, then scaled it into the pond. It made a dull plop and sank, causing ripples. He said, "Mossie Haly wants to see you. He sent me to get you."

"So he's appeared out of the woodwork, has he?" I dropped my cigarette end on the ground and put my foot on it. Then I thought better of it, bent over and scooped it up. When I straightened I saw Max gazing pensively at the envelope on the seat between us. I picked it up and stuck it under the flap of my waistcoat.

"He's in his office down on Usher's Island right now," he continued. "If you hurry you could be there within the hour."

122

I looked at him to gauge if he was joking, but he appeared to be serious. "You think I'm going to go rushing off to see him? You honestly believe I'd do that, jump up, salute and hightail it just to get an audience with that chicken turd? You must be out of your tiny mind."

Max shrugged, lifted a little finger and scratched around under the bandana. He said, "He merely wants a chat. He knows about yesterday and how you extricated young Archie from a fate worse than death. I think he wants to lay some thanks on you, maybe reward you for your good works ..."

"Isn't he interested in knowing if I've got the photographs?"

"Have you?"

"If I had, I might be intending holding out for a lot more money than Mossie feels they're worth."

"Like how much?"

"A nice round sum. How about half a million?"

"Why not?"

"Why not indeed."

Max grinned at me and, sore nose or no sore nose, I matched it.

"Are we talking here about some kind of understanding?" I asked him. "Entering into a partnership, maybe? The old days really revisited."

"Again all I can say is 'Why not?'"

"Why not my left gonad. I wouldn't trust you if you came wearing angel wings and singing 'The Bright Seraphim'. Don't presume on our much-abused friendship, Max; it'll buy you something, but not a lot. I know you, don't forget. We go way back ..."

"Exactly. Better the devil you know than the one you don't. I might try and cheat you of your worldly possessions, but I've no designs on your personal parts. Your nose would be safe with me."

I put my head back, tried breathing through that self-same orifice, closed my eyes tight shut, opened them and gazed into his. A dew-wet baby could not have looked more innocent.

"Tell me about the photographs again," I said. "Describe them to me. Give me all the details."

123

He shook his head. "I haven't seen them," he said. "I can only go on what I've been told. They're supposed to be of Archie and Richie plugging one another. Anything else is pure hearsay. Why?" he asked, without changing tone. "Is there something about them I don't know and should? Something you've sniffed out ..?"

"A bad choice of words there, Max," I said, ruefully fingering my hooter. It gave off a dull throbbing, reminding me it was damaged but not being overly shitty about it; that would probably come later when I had occasion to sneeze or blow it. "I know no more than yourself," I said, countering his likely lies with one of my own. "I will go and see Mossie, but not right away. I've got to get back to my office and sort out a few things. You've nothing else to tell me before I go? Like why the Whacker and his minions were sent to do me over, for instance? What is your part in this farrago anyway? And don't tell me you're just a messenger."

Max squinted into the sun. He untied the bandana and used it to wipe his face. Then he knotted it loosely round his neck. For a moment I thought he was going to tell me something of import, but he negated that by saying, "It's a gorgeous day. We should head off down the country. Into Wicklow or North Wexford. Climb a hill or a small mountain. Look at the view."

"Very nice, Max. What a simple man you are. Back to nature, eh? The sun in your hair, your arse to the wind. Straight and pure and no complications. Maybe even a youth or two to corrupt ... A thing of beauty is a boy forever ..."

"What youth are you talking about?"

I grinned at him.

"Me. I'm talking about me. You took the sweat off my innocence. You lifted stones and allowed me to look at the wriggling life forms underneath."

"It didn't do you any harm. When you know there's something there to threaten you, then you'll be ready for it. I was only trying to set you up for the bad times. With your big open face and your trust in people. Now you know what I was trying to tell you then. Everyone is suspect. Hope, faith, love, they're just words. Labels for expectations that will never be realised."

"That's a pretty drastic outlook. If there are bad times, then there must be corresponding good ones too. And people who are worth more than a telephone receiver down the throat or an umbrella spike in the eye. People who go that way need to have done some bad bad things."

"Maybe. Then again, when you go, you go, and sometimes being sent is a mercy. It doesn't much matter the form of it. Perhaps a little pain gets you a higher seat in the hereafter ...?"

"You believe in an after-life?"

"Don't you? You were born and raised a Catholic."

I was giving that some thought when Max produced a small enamelled container like a snuff box out of the pocket of his shorts. From another pocket he took a penknife, opened the blade and carefully scraped a line of white powder from the box on to it. He put this to his right nostril and sniffed. Then he repeated the procedure and sent a similar charge up the left. He licked the blade, closed it, did the same with the box and stored them both away.

"Don't I deserve a hit?" I asked him.

"With that nose? You'd need a wheelbarrow full ..."

I gazed about me. A couple, a dark-haired girl and a blond guy, were being cosy with one another on a bench down at the other end of the park. The old man, and the woman and child, had gone. But there could have been eyes watching from the undergrowth.

"Aren't you taking a bit of a chance?" I asked Max. "Slurping up the nose candy. The cops go undercover in Dublin now too, you know."

"They'd probably think I was powdering my face." He made a limp-wristed gesture and simpered. "Catch me if you can, sailor."

I made a face at him. "You know what you need, Maxie," I said. "A necessary balance. Between the black and the white. The good and the bad."

He grinned, but a little grimly this time. "It's a question of how I lean, isn't it? And of course that depends on who's pushing. I never did take to being pushed ..."

The sun had come out from behind the cloud again and was striking silent gleams off the surface of the water. I could feel its warmth on my face and it was with some regret that I said, "You're bad news, Max. The Candyman. Remember the old rhyme: Chase me, Charlie, I've got barley, up the leg of my drawers? When you and I were young ... Now the sweetness is a white powder which you push up your nose or some other orifice, and it blows your mind. Makes you feel like Jesus walking on the water. It's a funny old world."

"Isn't it just."

We sat on a while longer and contemplated that funny old world, watching the coruscation of light on water. For a few moments at least we were united as brothers, partners on the rocky road, Estragon and Vladamir, a couple of swells ... Would that we could have been two people sitting on a park bench with nothing more on our minds than the prospect of another hour in the sun, then maybe a good dinner and a dreamless sleep. Contentment surely rests in such simple pleasures.

I left Max to his thoughts and made my way back to my office through sweltering streets. Along the way I bought a newspaper. When I arrived I took off my shoes, waistcoat and sweatshirt, sat in the hot breeze from my single window and perused the paper. There was a short paragraph on an inside page about the finding of a body in the Apollo apartments. The Gardai suspected foul play but were not revealing the identity of the deceased until next of kin had been notified. Of Chinelio there was no mention.

Playing it close to their chests, I thought, seeing the hand of Superintendent George Quinlan in such an approach. I wondered when he would be around to see me. Dublin is a small town when secrets need to be kept or, more often, to be divulged, and George was an expert at keeping his ear to the ground. As soon as he got a rumble his gun dog's nose would twitch, his eyes light up and his expectation fizzle, and then he would be on my doorstep as itchy as an early morning milkman with the scent of absent husband in his nostrils.

I wound back the telephone answering machine and listened to people ringing and then hanging up without leaving any message. In the midst of the sounding silences my landlord's voice suddenly arose ghostlike, threatening to hurl me out on the street like Little Orphan Annie if I didn't hurry up and pay him his just deserts. Then Orphan Annie herself came on, like balm to my troubled spirits, to enquire how my nose was and if I had yet found her missing knickers.

I picked up the newspaper again and turned to the features section. A couple of investigative journalists were doing a series on land rezoning and the anomalies that existed in various parts of the county: green areas being left green in the up-market southside, while being built on in the more available and less influential northside. The implication was that a number of councillors were buying new suits and hats, this being an insider's way of saying they were taking bribes.

I put the paper down, then took it up again and stared at what I had been reading. It was an illustrated article, containing a picture of a half-finished housing estate in the north Dublin region, with a view of the bay and Howth Head in the background. There were some coloured maps showing existing built-up areas, proposed developments, green belts and land rezoned by county councillors.

The piece awoke something in my mind, a memory being nudged from the periphery to centre stage. I sat back, then unlocked the bottom drawer of my desk where I kept my extra bottle of Bushmills, the one only to be taken out in the direst emergency. As an aid to memory, it was the best mnemonic I knew. I half-filled a tumbler and had the glass just about to my lips when it hit me: it was in yesterday's paper, in the first article of the series, a picture of a piece of land in north County Dublin that was similar to the area in the photograph Charlie Fitz had developed for me.

I took the snaps from the envelope and laid them on the desk, then went hunting for Monday's paper. I eventually found it in the cupboard-like toilet that hid away furtively in an alcove off my anteroom. A couple of sheets had been torn off – accounted for, I presumed, by the absence of toilet paper – but the part I was seeking was still intact and relatively unsullied.

I took it back to the office and put it and the photographs side by side. Although taken from different angles, the views were undoubtedly of the same location. I read the caption under the picture in the newspaper and found I was looking at the village of Strawn in the townland of Nigalog in north County Dublin. I did a double-take at the Nigalog but, when I saw further down in the piece the names of other townlands being given as Astagob and Tobermaclugg, I realised I wasn't reading an extract from 'Gulliver's Travels' but a factual piece from a sober and serious daily newspaper.

The article explained that two hundred acres around the village had been rezoned for development – houses, a shopping mall, factory space – but as there had been so many objections from interested parties opposing the project, a stop had been put until the councillors themselves could visit the area and review the situation. A minibus load of them had gone on the jaunt and there was a picture of the bus and another blurred one of the noble men and women of the council being chased by protestors and scampering away from the camera as though urgently in need of the covering shelter of distant trees in order to relieve their feelings and anything else that needed relieving.

I turned back to the beginning and read the piece in full. It told me quite a lot about the activities of land owners, land developers, interested parties, and a professor of town planning brought in from Liverpool in the sixties named Myles Wright – afterwards memorably dubbed 'miles wrong' – who advocated the creation of satellite towns for the county in Tallaght, Lucan, Clondalkin and Blanchardstown. Most salient of all I learned that an acre of rezoned land can jump in value from £3,000 to £60,000 in the twirl of a signature.

I pushed the photographs and the newspaper to one side and leaned my elbows on the desk and my chin on my cupped hands and did some long and deep thinking. As an aid to cogitation I took the odd swig from the office bottle, in my absent-minded state dispensing with the glass.

It didn't take me long to come to the conclusion that either there were two sets of photographs or Max had been stringing me along. It might be straining the long arm of coincidence a bit to imagine a duality of incriminating pictures, but one never knew. The point was that I was in possession of one set and they appeared to be bound up with some kind of land rezoning scam.

That would make sense, for Mossie Haly was big in construction and was most likely the owner of quite an amount of prime land. At a profit margin of twenty to one per acre, we were talking here of big money, the kind that people might kill for.

But exactly where did my friend Max Morgan come in? Was he some kind of puppetmaster, pulling strings to make the rest of us dance? That was what he would have liked me, at least, to believe. He was certainly playing some game of his own, deviousness being second nature to him. What was his tie-in? To get his hands on the photographs himself and do a little discreet blackmailing? He had hinted at such when we were talking in the park. And chances were that he guessed I had found something in my poking about.

I looked at my watch and saw that it was well past one. Charlie had promised that I would have the enlarged photo, plus the negatives, by one. So, where were they? Again I remembered the sense of *déjà vu* I'd experienced when leaving his house, and this time it had the effect of making my skin crawl. I might after all have been followed to Charlie's place, and it would not take a watcher long to discover he specialised in photography and put two and two together. Stupidly I had placed Charlie in danger and had also quite likely lost evidence that might save my neck when the chips were really down.

So what was I doing sitting at my desk, gnawing my knuckles and shifting about on my chair like a bike racer with the squitters? I took one last snort from the bottle, put my shirt, shoes and waistcoat back on, and went down the stairs two at a time. In a matter of minutes I had hailed a taxi and was on my way back up the North Circular Road, my face set, determination at sticking-point, and my nose anxiously throbbing with the expectation of further damage.

I told the taxi man to drop me off at the top of Phoenix Avenue. I stuck my head around the corner and gazed down its sunlit expanse. Some children were playing hopscotch at the other end, otherwise it was empty of human life. A familiar-looking ginger tom was sitting in the bright wash of yellow light on the pathway halfway down. He was just sitting there, looking imperiously about with that gaze that cats of his ilk usually have. While I watched, his two back paws lifted and he scooted along the path on his bum. Even cats have to come down from Parnassus now and again.

From visiting Charlie in the past I knew there was a laneway running along behind the houses to allow access to garden sheds and garages. It started at the first house in the row, then made off crookedly in meandering style. I ducked into it and ran hurriedly along it. The surface was overgrown with weeds and it was also the depository for all kinds of waste matter and rubbish of a truly obnoxious kind. I got to about where I guessed the back of Charlie's house was, paused and leaned against the crumbling gravelled wall.

Sweat dripped into my eyes and ran down from under my arms, and my breath sounded harsh and laboured in the silence. The wall was hot from the sun. It was made from some kind of cinder block material and was eaten away in places so that any number of spyholes were available. I put my eye to one of them, but all I could see was an area of unkempt garden and a sagging clothes-line.

Resignedly I stood up straight, then jumped to get my hands on the top of the wall. A minor waterfall of gravel skittered down about me, but I managed to obtain a toehold and hoist myself up. I need not have bothered. As soon as the wall took my full weight it began to crumble, slowly at first and then all in a rush, depositing me in a hail of shale in the tangled wasteland of the garden.

I lay there, feeling foolish and with shards of the flinty substance biting into me. My heart was pounding, my nose was on fire, and my estimation of my worth was at rock bottom. But private detectives are nothing if not resilient, and in no time I was up again and running, ducking and weaving through the weeds and clinging nettles, staggering like a demented drunk on the trail of an olive for his martini, and probably making enough noise to alert whoever or whatever was awaiting me in the house.

I arrived at the perspex-roofed conservatory that abutted the building and looked in through the translucent side of it. Charlie was sitting in his wheelchair in full view, his head forward on his chest, immobile, with not the faintest movement out of him. A surge of panic gripped me: was this to be my hat trick of done-to-death corpses in the space of two days? Had Charlie been nutmegged like the other two, embalmed maybe in his own developing fluid?

Carefully I stepped in through the open window and approached the figure in the wheelchair. When I was close enough I put out a tentative hand and touched the meaty shoulder. It was positively glowing from the heat of the sun. I squeezed gently and Charlie's head snapped up, a "What the fuck?" spilling from his open mouth with the abruptness of a gunshot.

I jumped back, startled, but obviously not half as startled as my fat and sweating friend.

"Thundering Jesus," he expostulated, the mirror sunglasses all askew on his nose, "I nearly shat myself. What're you trying to do, give me a heart attack? And why're you back here? Two visits in one day is a little excessive, don't you think?"

"I wondered why you didn't send me the enlargements," I said meekly. "You told me one o'clock. I started worrying when the sun passed its zenith."

Charlie took off his glasses and rubbed his eyes. There were bags under them that could accommodate a week's shopping. "I must have fallen asleep," he mumbled. "It's the heat ..."

"I thought you'd gone to an even hotter place."

"Oh, why's that?"

I sat down in a cane chair and fumbled out a cigarette and lit it. The smoke wove worms of blueness in the bright light.

"Those negatives I left with you? They're rather dangerous to have in one's possession."

"Well, you can put your mind at rest on that score. I haven't got them any more. The courier came and took them. Didn't he bring them to you posthaste?"

"What time did he call?"

"A little before one."

"And the company you used?"

"You should know that. You sent him."

"Not me, mate. What'd he say exactly?"

131

"He asked for the package for Mr Blaine."

"So you gave them to him?"

"Of course. What'd you expect me to do?"

"Did you ask for any identification?"

"Identification of what? He was a courier. He had all the gear. A large motor bike. A helmet. Gloves. Little wings on his back and ankles ..."

"Very funny. How else was he dressed?"

Charlie fidgeted in his chair, the rolls of fat bouncing and glissading.

"I don't know. How d'you mean, how was he dressed?"

"Was he wearing shorts? Maybe a bandana round his head."

"He didn't take off his helmet, so I don't know about the bandana. But he was wearing shorts."

"The little fucker," I said between gritted teeth. Sweat was running down off my forehead, its salty tang irritating my wounded nose. "It was Max ..."

"Max?"

"Never mind. It wasn't your fault."

"Let me get this straight. The fellow who collected the prints is known to you, but you didn't send him for them ..."

"He's an acquaintance of mine. And the guy who hired me in the first place to get the photographs."

"So, what's the problem? Haven't they gone back to their rightful owner?"

"The trouble is that he hired me to procure a different set of prints entirely ..."

"Aha, the kinky ones."

" ... and in the process of trying to find them I stumbled across two dead bodies. That's why I rushed over here in such a dither."

"You thought I might've been the third?"

"Exactly."

"Thanks very much for putting me in such a position. With friends like you, who needs enemies ...?"

I stubbed my cigarette out in a convenient flowerpot and stood up and stretched. To add to the pain in my nose I now had a twinge in my left shoulder where I'd fallen on the wall. A soak in the sun would do me all the good in the world. I could stay here with Charlie in his makeshift suntrap, strip down, rub a little oil on, luxuriate in the heat. I could put my nose in a sling, my motive drive in neutral and my ailing ego on stand-by. That was what a man of constant sorrow like me should do.

I sighed, and Charlie, probably sussing my thoughts, said, "So what's next on the agenda?"

"I'm pretty down, Charlie. I need something to help me bounce back."

"Maybe I've got just the ticket. The print you asked me to enlarge? I did a couple of copies before I felt I had it right. They're still in the darkroom. Want to come and have a look?"

"Charlie, you're me darlin'. Lead on. Things are already beginning to look up ..."

We went into the hallway, past the array of glowering cats – I hoped they had sharpened their claws on Max's bare legs – and followed the smell of developing fluid to the darkroom. Inside Charlie switched on the safe light, fumbled about and came up with what he was looking for. He waved two large prints at me triumphantly.

I took them, noticing that one was much more in focus than the other. Peering closely at this one I could now make out the person in the back of the car being driven by Humphrey. It was Mossie Haly. He looked a little more bovine than of yore, but Mossie it undoubtedly was.

Why was I not overly surprised? It was clear to me now that what I was seeing was a pay-off of some kind, the character receiving the package probably an official of the county, certainly someone with sufficient pull to be able to affect the outcome of a rezoning decision. And there was Mossie, caught with his pants down and egg all over his face. These prints would be of much more value to a blackmailer than the ones of Archie and Michael doing the back-door rumba.

Having done so well, Charlie was now in the mood for celebrating, so he invited me to partake with him of some liquid refreshment. While he mixed a concoction of plum juice, bitters and vodka, I elected to stay with straight whiskey. He had a half-bottle of Paddy from which I poured myself a hefty slug and toasted his perspicacity in holding on to the prints.

We were now in his sitting-room, a place over-stuffed with antiques that had come from his ancestral home in Wicklow. It was an auctioneer's dream.

While Charlie stirred and slurped, I moved about, gazing at one knick-knack after another. There was an assortment of photographs, some of his family, others representative of the various stages of his life. He was there as a toddler, then in athletic vest, in mountain gear, in fancy dress, in sober formal wear; some were groupings of his time at college, while others were more recent, showing him in the company of the young people he trained and who doubled as his legs on assignments to various parts of the city and country.

I was gazing in a perfunctory fashion until one of the framed prints caught my eye. It was of a smaller group, four men and a girl clustered around a grinning Charlie, who was perched in his wheelchair with a funny hat on and clutching what looked like an award of some kind. It was the person standing left of centre, his arm around one of the other young men, who arrested my attention. Unless my eyes were deceiving me, it was Archie Haly to the manor born. His hair was longer and drawn back in a ponytail and he had the beginnings of a beard, but it was Archie: I was sure of it.

"Who's he?" I asked Charlie, picking up the photograph and holding it in front of his shades. I pointed at the Archie doppelganger and held my breath.

He uncovered a pouched eye again and squinted. "That's ... ah, Thomas Arthur Haly, known to his intimates as Archie the Brownie Basher — but we won't go into that. One of the most promising lensmen I've ever had. A spoiled brat, though. Too much money, too much of an opinion of himself, too bloody-minded ..."

"He didn't pursue the noble calling?"

"Oh, he did." Charlie sucked up half a pint of the plum juice and vodka, the sheen of sweat on his body making it appear as if the liquid was popping straight back out again. "He was very interested at first. And he was good. But his attention span was short. He wanted too much, too soon. He drifted away. I haven't seen him now for ... it must be the best part of a year."

"But he was a good photographer?"

"One of the best."

"And he had all the gear? I mean he could take long shots as well as close-ups?"

"Long, short, medium, you name it, he could do it. That boy had enough equipment to photograph an angel on the head of a pin."

"Very interesting."

"I might still have some of his work about if you're interested."

"The only examples of his work I'm interested in I've got right here in my hand."

"He took those? Why are they so important?"

"They say gelignite smells like almonds, Charlie. Have a sniff of these and tell me if it's true."

"I don't understand."

"You don't have to. And it's better that you don't. As for me, I'm off to light the fuse under a few bold bad boys and watch the marzipan hit the fan. The nose strikes back ..."

I took the envelope containing the prints out from where I'd stuffed them down the back of my trousers and added the two Charlie had just given me. Then I replaced it. I would have put them down the front only that I preferred to have my arse blown off rather than old John Thomas.

Nine

I left Charlie's place and made my way down Prussia Street. The sight of people shying away from my stitched-on nose got on my nerves to the extent that I went into a pharmacy and bought some Elastoplast and persuaded the girl assistant to tape up the offending organ. The remedy was worse than the illness, though, for the thick swathe of sticking-plaster got in my line of vision, causing me to gape, goggle and stagger about like Boris Karloff in one of his monster roles. In the end I had to tear it off, the agony being exquisite.

It was the middle of the afternoon now and the pavements reeked with regurgitated heat. The farting exhausts of the many vehicles stuck on the quays also conspired to make the air vile and the membranes of my throat were clogged from all the extra work they had to do since my smeller had become inoperative. A little liquid lubrication was in order, so I turned into a pub called The Man O'War, shuddered in appreciation of its cloistered dimness, went up to the bar and ordered a large Bushmills and a Guinness chaser from the stooped but welcoming individual behind the counter.

When my eyes became accustomed to the gloom I saw that I was in a long low room, with scattered tables and chairs, a flickering television with the sound turned down, a cigarette machine and enough seedy ambiance to keep a drunk's cup of nostalgia running over.

There was a public telephone bolted to the wall at the end of the bar and I got some change from the friendly bartender – we were the only two present, which made for a shared air of mutual amiability – and journeyed down there and rang the Sentinel newspaper. A voice answered, a nice soft female one, and I asked to speak to either or both of the guys who had penned the series on the rezoning scandals. She told me to hold on, went away and came back to inform me that neither of them was available at that moment in time.

136

"Out being measured for cement overcoats?" I enquired facetiously.

"Huh?"

I told her I was joking, gave her my name and office number and asked her to get them to call me ASAP. She breathed that she would and we rang off. Such is the way people glance off one another, I thought: for one brief shining moment our lives impinge, communication is established, then nothing. If I were to meet her in the street, or she me, we would not know one another from Adam. So it goes.

And I went back to my solitary drinking, trying to relieve my dark mood with a fiery snort of whiskey and a cooling draught of stout. My putative friend, the barman, was down at the other end of the counter bobbing and weaving like a boxer on the receiving end of a barrage of blows. What was he at? Could he possibly be masturbating? Then I saw that he was in fact moving to the rhythm of something that was coming to him through the speakers of a Walkman he had plugged into his hairy ears.

I polished off the Bushmills and drained the pint of porter. Once again I was dogged by inertia, a proselytising aura, a numbness of spirit, seeking to wean me from the proper observance of my sacrificial duties and larding my resolve with the desire to linger, to drink strong spirits, to become intoxicated, to forget. I had important things to do, more walls to pull down, an old pal to emasculate, and yet here I was courting immobility, my intentions compromised and my brain all in a frazzle. If only the human psyche could be jump started like the piston-driven, internal combustion engine.

"Hey," I called to the jiving barman, "set 'em up again. And have one yourself. And come down here till I tell you of two little boys who lived in the lovely long ago and who fell off their wooden horses and couldn't get back on again ..."

Some time later I ambled out into the declining day, this time with a happy smile on my face and an immense feeling of goodwill towards all. In short, I was as drunk as a brewery rat.

I crossed the Liffey, using a bridge but full sure, in my exalted state of glee, that I could just as well have walked on the water.

Usher's Island is an old area of the city that has been rejuvenated, burnished and fraught with new buildings that are as startlingly out of place as a three-piece Louis Copeland suit on a tramp. One of its gracious houses, now gone, featured in Joyce's short story 'The Dead' and the cobblestoned incline still rings with the immemorial chimes of the dearly departed for those who have an ear to hear them.

The new office buildings have a curiously artificial look about them, all yellow matt finish and strips of fascia-board that appear to be all that is holding them together. The frontages were so anonymous – all those windows, I thought, and no one gazing out of them.

I stopped to stare myself, leaning nonchalantly against a heavy black metal lamp standard. Shiny executive cars were lined up, noses to the curb, and a thick-set individual in a brown, gold-striped uniform and peaked cap was watching over them. He made it quite plain that he resented my presence on his patch. Was it my imagination or did he actually paw the ground?

I lit a cigarette, taking my time. As a matter of fact, I had to take my time; I was so drunk that just getting the weed into my mouth caused me great difficulty, and lighting it without setting fire to my already damaged nose took on the trappings of a minor miracle. I finally managed it and stood there, beaming and blowing smoke like a benediction, here, there and everywhere.

The guy in the uniform soon grew tired of making hostile gestures and he hitched his shoulders and came over to me. I smiled at him and waited, allowing him the first overture. He had a rough-textured, jowly face, a pair of little angry eyes and red hair pulled back tightly and tied in a pigtail. I am not a snob, but he was not a person I would have liked to be marooned on a desert island with.

"Sling yer hook," he muttered, gazing down the hill rather than at me, as if he did not wish to be seen talking to me.

"Yes, it is a lovely day," I replied. "Such sunshine. And God in his heaven. I'm only sorry I didn't join you earlier. How's the missus?"

"Hah," the pigtailed one breathed, as though confirming to himself that he was right about me from the start. He stood back

138

a pace to gain leverage.

"And the little ones?" I went on, blowing out more smoke, this time through my battered nose. "All in their father's likeness, I suppose? Might prove to be a stumbling-block as they journey through life ..."

"None o' that now," the uniform said, attempting to bluster. "Youse better get outta here fast. No place for the likes a'youse around here."

"Your wish is my command," I told him cheerfully. Saluting, I said, "If you'll just point me in the direction of the offices of one Mossie Haly, entrepreneur extraordinary – and that's not easy to say when you're as in ... in ... as pissed as I am – I'll not trouble you further."

Still glaring balefully at me he asked me to identify myself as to rank and number, and enquired of me what business I could possibly have with such as Mr Maurice Haly, king of kings, lord of lords, and boss of bosses.

In fact what he said was, "Who the fuck d'yeh think yeh are aksing for the likes a' Haly?"

"I am his private astrologer," I told him, mustering as much dignity as my damaged face and state of being tired and emotional allowed. "He puts great store in the stars and won't make a move, business or bowel, until he first ascertains which planets are in conjunction and which are not. If you get my drift."

Bullshit being his forte, a sudden gleam of wariness appeared in the angry and inflamed eyes. The thought had obviously occurred to him that he might be barking up the wrong tree by assessing me only on my state of sobriety, or lack of it. Maybe the time had come to pass me on to higher authority. He jerked his head and we marched in solemn procession to the imposing arched entrance of one of the new blocks. We entered and moved deferentially to where another likely lad was ensconced behind an ornate desk, with a bank of monitors in front of him set into an art deco fake stone cabinet.

This guy also wore a uniform, sober grey this time. He was lean and mean, his buttoned-down face proclaiming he was lord and master of his domain and that anyone who dared venture in had better have a bloody good reason for doing so. He entered into a whispered colloquy with my keeper before dismissing him with a regal wave of two nicotine-stained fingers.

We gazed in silence at one another, me teetering and most probably with a silly grin on my face, he frowning and with his hand poised over the monitor bank as though trying to imply that with one click of a switch he could atomise me and send my molecules whistling round the lobby like hail.

"You are? And wish to see who?"

"Whom."

"Huh?"

"I've an appointment with Mossie Haly," I said, deciding to get straight to the meat and potatoes. "The name is John Blaine. I'm with the IRS."

"Wha?"

"The Inland Revenue Sodality. We represent all Catholic taxmen. A bit like the Masons, only without the funny handshake and the apron. We wear a jockstrap with 'You have been warned' written across the front. Are you up to date with your balance-sheets?"

"You're pissed."

"Certainly I am. It comes with the job. The fact still remains that I am expected by the Lord High Executioner ..."

"Who?"

"Mr Maurice Haly. Esquire. The one, I presume, who hires and fires you. Is your name Cerberus?"

"I don't know no Cerberus."

"He was the keeper of the gate of Hades. A dog with three heads. He liked cake. So did Marie Antoinette ..."

"You're pullin' my chain."

"Listen you," I suddenly said, advancing on him. "I'm a busy man. I haven't got all day to be standing around here jawing. Ring through on your thingummyjig and tell Mossie I'm here. Time and tide wait on no man. Or woman or child either for that matter."

The authoritative note in my voice convinced him he should at least check with someone as to my bona fides, so he switched on his machine and began speaking unctuously into it. Whatever he heard in reply caused him to rear back as though it had bitten him. He gazed at it resentfully, his eyes unforgiving. Obviously battling with his better judgement, he jerked his head at the stairs and said, "Up to the first landing. His secretary will be waiting for you. She'll conduct you in ..."

I bowed, but resisted the urge to urinate on his shoe. He had suffered enough in having to back down. I marched over to the broad sweep of steps, feeling his eyes on me all the way. In keeping with the twenties' decor, the stairs was fake marble, the curving bannisters done in metal filigree surmounted by a wide brass handrail. Handy, in case I was in need of a quick getaway.

The first landing was as spacious as the foyer, the walls never-ending. An expensive carpet was barely held down by metal strips. Awaiting me was an equally expensive lady, groomed to the nth degree and haloed in an aura of subtle if grim efficiency. I cocked an ear for the whirr and click of machinery, but she was well-oiled and gave off no answering resonance.

"Mr Blaine?" The shellacked features cracked, the red lips drawing apart to reveal perfect white teeth. "I am Ms Haines, Mr Haly's private secretary ..."

"He's got a public one too?"

"I beg your pardon?"

Looking down, I noted her court shoe-shod foot tapping on the carpet, the heel firmly planted, the toe hopping up and down. Was she showing impatience, knocking out a message, or easing an ingrown toenail? Perhaps there was an imperfection there somewhere, some nut or bolt having come loose? Maybe she was in need of some guy to come by with a screwdriver to do a little probing? I thought of my own, underworked screwdriver and gave her a grin that was meant to be lascivious. I got a stare in return that would do justice to a deep freeze.

"Will you please follow me," the carnivorous mouth commanded, and she turned on her heel and stalked off. I watched the play of light and shade as her hips moved under the silky material of her dress, then toddled along after her. I could look even if I couldn't touch.

We went through an open-plan office that contained a number of serious people sitting at desks. Most of them were playing with

141

computers, fingers bopping keys, eyes intent, heads bent. There was an expectant hush in the room, as though at any moment someone would leap to his or her feet with a cry of 'Geronimo', brandish a wad of papers and excitedly proclaim a killing in fur-fleeced condoms. My entrance caused as much commotion as a fly peeing.

Ms Haines opened a stout, leather-padded door and beckoned for me to go in. I passed by within inches of her but found no answering warmth. All I got was an icy smile and a delicate whiff of her disapproval, all she got was the wind of a belch I had been endeavouring to suppress with ever-increasing slippage. Impatient at being chained up, it now ricochetted round the walls with unrestrained glee.

The door closed on it and her with a soft whoosh. I was in a wide and spacious office, with futuristic furniture, an odour of money and a picture-window that would allow a herd of executives to defenestrate themselves all at the same time. In front of the window was a huge silver-coloured desk and, sitting behind it doing a Benito Mussolini impression, was Mossie Haly. All I could see against the blare of light was his round head and the glint of his eyes, but it was enough. In the place of my youth, the same guy had been an ikon, he and his father and brother being almost the sole providers of work for the masses and consequent food on the table and a few pence to jingle in the pocket to let others know you were not skint like them.

Posing as beneficent benefactors, they bled the economy dry, allowed the once deep sea harbour to become silted up, and ruthlessly put down attempts by other would-be businessmen to get a finger in the door. Loyalty and life long devotion to their cause meant nothing to them, and many an employee had been sent packing after years of service without pension, position or plausibility. Max's father had been one such, a gentle, eminently honest man who had been book keeper, general factotum and confidant until the time was ripe to jettison him, call his character into question and hound him to an early grave. Old man Haly had been gaga by then, but his steely rule and indifference to the tenets of good employer-employee relationships lived on in his sons. And especially in Mossie, the older and deadlier of them.

I knew him well in his persona of patron of the county hurling team, as he attempted to buy the esteem and comradeship that his personality refused to win him. A blusterer, he was always present when plaudits were being handed out, but invisible when the slack had to be taken up and difficult decisions made. He courted me when I was in my prime, there to slap me on the back when the game had gone our way but quick to jump aside when the blood and snot of defeat were flying.

For a time I was taken in by his "good ole boy" geniality, his larger-than-life image, his expensive clothes, his big car, his seeming readiness to throw parties for the players and their wives and girlfriends at the drop of a hat. But eventually the threadbare weave of his sincerity showed through, his meanness of spirit manifesting itself more and more, and he turned out to be implacably vindictive when crossed. Forever surrounding himself with sycophants and bully boys, he liked to see himself reflected in their eyes rather than in the estimation of the few honest men around.

His vanity knew no bounds. If anyone had the temerity to stand up to him, to contradict him, or try to protect their womenfolk from his avaricious advances, he was soon brought down to size or, in some cases, ruined in business, slighted in society or physically disabled. It did not do to be known as an enemy of Mossie Haly, or even one who dared to criticise his hold on the town, his methods of business or his boorish behaviour. In short, at that time and in that place of my youth, he had things sown up and, when circumstances dictated that the climate was changing and it was incumbent on him to alter his location, he simply removed himself bag and baggage from the town and set up shop in the big city, leaving his former dependants bereft and himself still on the pig's back.

And what an apt metaphor that now is, I thought, as I moved closer to the arc of sunshine from the window and Mossie came out from behind his desk to greet me. Time had not been kind to the lineaments of either his face or figure. He was thick through the body, the well-cut suit failing to hide the meatiness of his shape. He was a tall man, maybe an inch or two shorter than my six foot two, but good living and the absence of exercise had

143

conspired to make him look lumpy and misshapen, the flesh of his hands, neck and face suety and pitted, the eyes protuberant, his nose bulbous, his mouth thick-lipped and purplish – an example of galloping obesity in full stride.

What had once been a carefully coiffured mass of shining black hair was now a greasy bird's nest, the dome of his head showing through like the shell of some monstrous egg. Possibly to demonstrate to me that the mood was good, he slid the blubber lips back off large brown teeth and gave me his version of a welcoming smile. It merely served to remind me of Chinelio's death rictus.

His desk was set on a pedestal and he came to the edge of this and stood looking at me, the sunlight framing him like a backlit spotlight. I wondered if he expected me to sink to my knees, lay my forehead on the floor and murmur, "Allah be praised". Old habits die hard and I despised myself for even harbouring the thought.

Deciding to look around instead, I did a slow three-hundred-and-sixty-degree turn. The office was luxuriantly appointed. Staying with the art deco motif, someone had been more than generous with the geegaws. There was a three-piece suite in chrome and steel in the centre of the floor, with flat cushions that looked incapable of absorbing the impact of a hastily set down backside. A number of tables with inlays and fretworked legs stood about, a varnished trunk with round metal handles seemed to have no particular use, a chest of drawers likewise, while a television set sought to hide its modernity of aspect by being housed in a softwood cabinet with the signs of the zodiac carved on its top and sides.

Abstract paintings featuring geometric patterns and set in stark silver frames hung on the walls. After turning my head this way and that to confront one of them, I came to the conclusion that it held nothing of significance for me. Ever since someone had told me that the Mona Lisa was a painting of a woman endeavouring to suppress a fart, I have been highly dubious of art criticism or appreciation.

The floor was not carpeted but was covered instead in a kind of smooth linoleum-like material, and I slid my feet along it, glided over to one of a pair of high-backed chairs that stood against one wall and sat down on it. Due perhaps to the fact that the alcohol I had consumed was losing its grip, I was feeling a mite tired, as if I'd been taken on an outward-bound trip and discovered too late that I should have been pointed in the opposite direction.

Walking the margin of the raised pedestal as though it were the deck of a ship and he the captain, Mossie came to a point near me, rocked on his beautifully crafted Italian shoes, and said, "Well now, Johnny me lad, it's good to see you, even if you have caused me a little heartache this fine day."

I contemplated my own dusty footwear, feeling slack and weary and used. My brain was hot and there was gravel in my nose. I said, "Mossie, I'm drunk. It's the only way I could come to see you. To damp down my self-loathing, I'm full to the gills. And if you start up with that stage Irish, "one of the boys" manner I'll spew the whole lot, self-loathing and gargle, over your fine handmade Italian shoes."

"Oh?" He placed his hands behind his back as I raised my heavy head to stare at him, pulled in his stomach and frowned. "I paid you to do something for me," he said sternly, the affable drollery abruptly dropped. "You haven't carried it out exactly as I would have wished."

"How the fuck do I know what your wishes are?" I asked him rudely. "This is the first time I've talked to you in years. A man's whims change. The last thing you wanted me to do was to win an All-Ireland Hurling title, and I didn't accomplish that either. Where you're concerned, my efforts always seem to end in the land of No-No."

He made a sucking sound, drawing his lips back again to show off the horse's teeth.

"Why are you talking to me like that?" he asked plaintively. "I've always had feelings of affection for you ..."

"Let's stick to the business at hand and forget the affection. I was hired to get some photographs of your beloved son doing things with another man that he should have been doing with another woman and hand them back into your safe-keeping. Who's to say I haven't done just that ...?"

"You've got them? The negatives?"

"Maybe. And then again, maybe not. It's not going to be that easy."

Looking annoyed, Mossie said, "This is not the way to do things. You seem full of resentment about something. What'd I ever do to get you all riled up? I always treated you well, didn't I? We were friends, we partied together, got along ..."

"So now you use me like an old dog to fetch for you? To clean up your son's mess, rub his stomach, put him over my shoulder and burp him?"

"Not necessarily. It was Morganthau's idea to bring you into this. I told him to handle it himself, but he said he was too involved in the gay scene to be effective. He wanted someone streetwise, with his nose to the ground."

"Do you have to mention noses?" The onset of anger had given me a headache, and there was only one sure way to ease it. "D'you have any drink around here?" I asked. "I need something to keep my head in tune."

"In that cabinet," he replied, indicating another expensive-looking piece of antique furniture, a refined item standing on carved legs, with lacquered doors and delicately inlaid patterns. This time he actually came down from the pedestal and joined me on ground level, possibly to keep an eye on me in case I took too large a wallop of his booze.

He opened the doors of the cabinet and stood back to allow me to inspect the contents.

"What'll you have?" he enquired.

A light had come on and it glinted off an array of bottles and cutglass decanters. It was like an Aladdin's cave to my thirsty gaze.

"Bushmills."

"Black?"

"Black, white, in technicolour. You pour it, I'll drink it."

While he busied himself I went over to another large article of furniture shrouded in a tasselled covering. I twitched the cloth aside to reveal a baby grand piano, its black reflecting surface throwing back a facsimile of my haggard countenance – Dorian Grey after his time had just about run out. Hurriedly I sat down on the stool and ran my fingers over the keys. The sound from the instrument was as smooth as butter melting.

"Do you play?" he enquired, coming across and handing me a glass which I was happy to see was brimful with dark amber liquid.

"No."

"Me neither. I keep it there for effect. Although sometimes I hire an old geezer to come in and give it a tinkle."

"While you're engaged on the casting couch?"

We both looked over at the sharp lines and contours of the sofa and Mossie chuckled, a nasty phlegmy sound. "You'd want to be a contortionist to fuck on that," he said.

"You should have a Bombay fornicator."

"What's that?"

"A cane chair that can be elongated to form a bed. Planters in Malaya in the good old colonial days usually kept one on their verandahs for use when they were servicing native girls."

"Is that so? Not too many people know that." Slyly Mossie winked at me, a lizard-like droop of the eyelid. Then he did an odd thing. He placed his hand on my shoulder and struck a pose. In a clotted baritone voice he broke into song, intoning the first verse of the old rebel number 'The Boys of Wexford,

"In comes the captain's daughter, the captain of the Yeos,
Saying, 'Brave United Irishmen, we'll ne'er again be foes.
A thousand pounds I'll give you, and fly from home with thee,
And dress myself in man's attire, and fight for liberty!'"

"For Christ's sake," I said, shaking myself free of both his hand and his lachrymose sentiment, "will you give over. You're making me puke."

I got up and moved away, into the full hazy stream of sunlight. Putting this gauze of brightness between us made me feel less vulnerable; I had gone down that river of the past too often for it not to have an effect. Whether I liked it or not, Mossie and Max Morganthau and other household ghosts were part of the fabric of my past, definite influences, whether for good or for bad, against which many other wraiths of memory faded into insignificance. They were factors in what had made

147

me. They had gone through the conduits of my experience as constituents of the loam of happenstance, cause and effect, motivation ... the long slow haul that had formed me and turned me into what I was. And there were pleasant memories going hand in hand with the bad ones. We had gone through good times, sad times, laughed, toasted life and the living of it, and been easy in one another's company. Even though I knew what Mossie was really like, I had still taken his conviviality and bathed in it, as had Max. We were up there, at the head of things, and when you are in that position you tend to forget to look over your shoulder. It is only later, when the penumbra spreads below the brassy glare, when the band has played for the final time and the musicians have packed away their instruments and stolen away into the night, that a true perception of thought and awareness can be achieved and people become as they really are. But by then it is often too late to hive away the feelings of guilt, of being tainted; too many bridges have been crossed, too many promises made, too many wounds opened and too hastily cured.

I knew I had it in my power to harm Mossie Haly, maybe even to deal him a mortal blow if I used the incriminating photographs in my possession to best effect. My God, the man didn't even seem aware of their existence! But in doing what I had to do, I would feel no clear and steadfast sense of triumph; rather would it be like a duty executed, a covenant broken, a connection severed. That's how it goes, I suppose, when you try to bury demons from your past.

I'll drink to that, I thought, and I lifted my glass and knocked back a tidy portion of its contents. Mossie watched me, then switched his gaze to his desk and the security it afforded him. But he did not retire to it. As though denying himself, he went over and sat in the companion chair to the one I had occupied some moments before. Was he making a statement? To show him communication was still open between us, I parked myself in the other one.

"What's it going to cost me to get those photos back?" he eventually asked me. He was sitting upright, like someone doing an evaluation of the contents of the room. He had on a grey suit with a red pinstripe, a white shirt, plain pink tie. Carefully he adjusted the knees of his trousers, first one, then the other. His jowls glistened as if he had shaved just before I entered. When I turned my head and looked closely I could see the broken veins in his cheeks.

Just as I had asked his son, I now said, "Doesn't it bother you that two men have died violently because of those very photographs? And that my person has been assaulted and my nose banjaxed ...?"

He examined my hooter critically, then he said, "I'm sorry about the nose. As to the other matter, I did hear something of Michaels being done in – about which, incidentally, I'm not too put out, as he's the one who led Archie up the garden path in the first place. I know nothing of any other fatality."

"Vincent Chinelio," I supplied. "Michaels' partner."

"Then he must have been in on the extortion too. Who killed them?"

I looked at him but he continued to stare straight ahead.

"I thought you might be able to tell me. Maybe the Whacker Whelan, for instance?"

"Who?"

I jiggled my knee, swirled what remained of the whiskey about in the glass, thought of grabbing Mossie by the nose and doing to it what he had had done to mine. The lie was as blatant as a pile of dogshit on an Axminster carpet.

"Maybe your wife killed them," I said, more to provoke a reaction than for any basis in fact. "Or had it done."

This time he looked at me, calculation etching his features. By my reading he was actually giving consideration to such a scenario.

"Louise? You're joking."

"She's a formidable woman. And she'd probably go to any lengths to keep the family out of the tabloids."

"No," he murmured, shaking his head a trifle regretfully.

"You'd maybe go to the same lengths," I went on, prodding him.

"Are you suggesting I had them murdered?"

"Perhaps. Where've you been for the last two days?"

"I was away on business."

"Are you sure you weren't lying low?"

"That doesn't even deserve an answer."

We sat and mulled things over, and it became so quiet I imagined I could hear the ice in my glass melting. To break it I said, "I can be placed at the scene of both killings. With that thought in mind I'm not giving up the photographs. They're my insurance ..."

"Fuck that," Mossie suddenly said, reverting to type. "I'm a busy man. That's why I pay others to handle problems like this for me. I'm prepared to lay out good money for those pictures and you'd better sit up and take notice. Otherwise it might be more than your nose that gets hammered."

"Are you threatening me?"

"What does it sound like?"

"It sounds like you're threatening me."

"Fuckin' right I am."

Strangely enough, now that Mossie had taken up the bully-boy stance I felt more at home with him.

"Who'll you send after me? Max Morganthau?"

Mossie stood up, balled his hands into fists and leaned down to me. I could smell his aftershave and the aroma of peppermint on his breath. Money, wealth, affluence had made him into an expensive package, but in my estimation he still trailed the mephetism of the sewer.

"Where is that little cunt?" he said. "He's the one who made a balls of this from the start. If he'd paid the money like I wanted, there'd be none of this shit. And no need to bring you into it."

I shrugged, then had recourse one last time to the Bushmills. As the raw whiskey hit my stomach I realised I had not eaten for quite a while and the thought made me feel dizzy, the sensation compounded by the glare of evening sun through the picture-window. Hurriedly I said, "How did your son get involved with these guys? Seems to me with his background he could've found a better class of citizen to sow his wild oats with."

"The ballocks," Mossie said, still staring into my face. "Sometimes I wonder if I fathered him at all. I hate the sight of the bastard. He's always done his best to get on my wick. A thorn in my side all his life."

"How did you receive the photographs?"

"Through the post. One morning a few days ago."

"Here?"

"At home. I nearly choked on my Weetabix."

"Where had the letter been posted?"

"Who the fuck cares? Why are you asking me all these questions anyway?"

"I'm looking for clues."

"Clues me arse."

"Was there a message?"

"Yeah."

"What'd it say?"

"It said the cost of the negatives was a quarter of a million. Otherwise they'd be given to the media. It also said the wages of sin is death, whatever that means. Maybe it's a clue. What d'you think?"

"Was it signed?" I asked, ignoring the sarcasm.

"Yeah. By that bumwipe Michaels. As brazen as you please."

I patted myself down for a cigarette, found one and put it in my mouth. Mossie backed away, watching me, and when I made to light it he asked me plaintively not to.

"Why not?"

"Doctor's orders. I've had to give up cigars, brandy, getting the leg over more than once a day. You name it ..."

I let my amusement show and he made a wry face. He said, "I'm overweight. High blood pressure. Maybe a dicky ticker."

"Tough titty."

"Yeah, I can see you're all broken up about it."

I kept the cigarette in my mouth, letting it bob up and down as I talked. I decided to goad him a little more. "You know, Maurice," I said, "you're full of shit. There're no snaps of a compromising nature featuring your son and heir. I think this is all about something else. I believe you're the one caught in *flagrante delicto*, not Archie."

"What're you talking about?"

Throwing me what seemed a genuine look of puzzlement, Mossie scooted over to the picture I had been scrutinising earlier. Thrusting it aside, he began fiddling with the round steel door of

151

the safe that was screwed into the wall behind it. When he had it open he stuck his hand in and extracted an envelope. He lifted the flap and took out a couple of stiff sheets of two by four paper. He left the safe standing open as he came across and handed me the prints.

I took them. They were shots of Archie and the late Richie Michaels, in full technicolour if not stereophonic sound. Parked on a bed, they were quite naked; aroused in the first one, the second showed the consequence of this arousal, a juxtaposition of arms, legs and other bits and pieces that had them in knots and me in a state of disbelief.

I raised my head, took a deep breath, then had another squint. This time I noticed the faces turned to the lens. "These weren't taken with a hidden camera," I told Mossie. "You can see from the way they're posing they're well aware of being photographed."

Mossie was building up a head of steam, his face puce, his eyes dilated. "Of course they knew they were being taken," he growled. "The pervert took them himself ..."

"Michaels?"

"No, the other one. My bastard son. He's into photography. Imagine having to look at those over your morning soft-boiled egg. He did it deliberately."

"You have a soft-boiled egg every morning?"

"For fuck's sake ..."

I got up and went and placed my empty glass down carefully on the scrolled top of the liquor cabinet.

"You know, Mossie," I said, "this conversation of ours is getting a bit like Archie and his pal poking one another."

"How d'you mean?"

"Extracting the Michael? Me pulling yours and you pulling mine. We're going round in circles. Ever-decreasing ones ..."

He was back up on his dais, looking down at me.

"I need those negatives," he said. "I need them badly. If you've got them, you better hand them over. I'm prepared to be generous ..."

"You're tempting me, Mossie. Purely in the monetary sense, of course." I pretended to think about it. "But supposing there's something more serious on the horizon? A breach in your

152

security that could do much more damage than pictures of your son browning his wick?"

I had his full attention now, which was what I was aiming at. Mossie in a stew would turn me into a vegetarian any day of the week. I added a shake of condiment: "Where did you get the money to start up again after your business in Wexford grew too hot to handle? Rumour was that you were flat broke. And why'd you get Max out of that Asian prison? One of those places where they can sniff drugs up your fundament at a hundred paces. You can make a lot of friends with the help of drugs ..."

"Piss on that for a lark," Mossie replied enigmatically.

"Then or now?"

"I'm a respectable and respected businessman. What's past is past."

"Oh, no. The past has a nasty habit of resurfacing, like a well-greased turd. Once a crook, always a crook, Mossie. You get a kind of fascination for standing with your legs apart while the chasm widens. Is it the scent of danger?"

"No, it's the satisfaction of grinding know-alls like you down into the dirt. You think you're so smart? You couldn't even protect your own nose ..."

He stepped down from his ledge and marched over to the liquor cabinet. Pulling out a cutglass tumbler that sparkled in the sunlight, he poured in a libation of Hennessy brandy and knocked it back. He coughed, leaned on the press for support and gave a good impression of someone who had just been kicked in the kidneys. While he was in extremis, I pocketed the photographs he'd shown me.

"I thought you were supposed to keep off that stuff?" I reminded him.

"Balls to you, Jack."

I shrugged, found a match and lit my cigarette. Might as well let him have the benefit of some passive smoking to go with the brandy.

"So what d'you think of my putting two and two together and getting a bingo call?" I asked him. "If Max went to prison while on drugs business for you, you'd be in honour bound to get him out again."

"Honour-bound?"

"Nah, you're not into honour. Well, let's try this instead. Max was always one to cover his rear, if you can say that about someone with his sexual orientation. He probably had enough on you to send you down the river for an indefinite stay. You had to spring him. But the consequence is that now you can't trust him. That's why you've had Whelan and his two thugs on his trail. And by being on his trail, they're also on mine. Hence the threats and the nose job."

Mossie was still leaning against the cabinet, his mouth opening and closing as if he had to search for and trap each breath he took. He could only have been in his early fifties, yet he was beginning to look like the one-hundred-year old man. His eyes were muddy, his colour awful, his normal heartiness muted. The big office, the expensive accoutrements, the well-cut suit, they were merely ostentations to draw attention away from their owner's destabilisation. For whatever reason – and it was probably a combination of them – Mossie was on his way down, and if I wanted to get in my shove, I would have to be snappy about it.

Now once more he did something to surprise me. Pushing himself upright, he came over, took the cigarette from between my fingers, put it in his mouth and dragged smoke deep into his lungs. He held it, then let it out with a pleasurable sigh. After a second inhalation he handed the weed back to me.

Still standing eyeball to eyeball, he said almost caressingly, "You'd be better off dealing with me. Once upon a time I had control over the people who worked for me. Some of them remember. There was a certain ..."

"Fear?"

" ... respect. Nowadays they're all young lions, eager to rend and tear. You put your hand out to shake on a bargain and you're lucky to get it back all in one piece. Everyone's trying to prove something ..."

"My heart bleeds for you. Not to mention my nose."

"Take that Maxie Morganthau for example. He's playing a deep game. You know him better than me. What's he on about ..?"

"Maybe he's trying to get a bit of his own back?"

"How's that again?"

"Jesus, Mossie, d'you ever see any further than the end of your prick? You ruined his father. A good old man who never did any harm to anyone. And you were the cause of his being thrown into a Malayan jail to wank in lonely splendour. Do you expect him to be grateful to you? Light candles in church on your behalf? Storm heaven with prayers that you'll have a long life and a happy death?"

Mossie frowned and pulled at his lip. He said, "Maybe you've got something there. Maybe I should review his situation."

"You'd better be quick about it, if so. He's out to do you. And he's not the only one."

"There's someone else?"

"Yeah, your son."

"That little cocksucker."

"Plus me, of course."

"You're out to screw me as well?"

"In a manner of speaking."

"Why?"

"If you don't know, then I can't tell you. Take a good look in the mirror tomorrow morning and ask yourself truthfully what you see."

Again he came down from his pedestal and went and stood with his elbow on the grand piano, looking like Leonard Bernstein after a night on the tiles. He said, "You know, I'm sick and tired of people making demands on me. My wife, my family, assorted go-by-the-walls and gombeen men ... shit-loads of other bums and losers. I pulled out before and started up again. My mistake was in not divesting myself of all the freeloaders. I'm a man of vision. I get things done. People like me are necessary. We're the movers and doers. I shouldn't have to account to anyone. I'm above the common herd ..."

I eyed him, my hand already on the door to take off. It occurred to me that I'd misjudged him: he was not just any old lunkhead with too much money and no proper sense of morality. In fact, he obviously entertained some sort of God-image, seeing himself as a manipulator of other people's lives. To him human beings were pawns and if they fell off the board or were pushed aside he would not unduly worry about them. His point of reference was how he himself felt about things; that was the lit match, the spark that motivated him. Arguing with him or endeavouring to get him to see your point of view would be like kneading empty air. All he would ever understand was the blow that shatters, the snip of the wire to bring him to ground. And doing it to him, trying to execute a finality where he was concerned, would be like chasing a blob of mercury about on a shiny surface: when you thought you had him, he'd already have squirted away in a different direction.

He laughed now, not very pleasantly, still standing by the piano. He was shiny, padded, obese, all tucked into his expensive suit. He said, "I'll give you twenty-five thousand quid for the negatives. No names, no pack-drill, and no questions asked. That's instead of sending someone round to stick them up your arse and have you shit them out in shreds. It's your choice, and I wouldn't even be giving you one if it weren't for old times ..."

A number of things went through my mind as I stood there holding the door. Most of them were the colour of anger. But in the end I said nothing and did nothing. I merely left, feeling a bit like a cur with his tail between his legs. I didn't even bang the door in my wake.

Ten

I went back to my office to see if there were any messages on my answering machine. There weren't. My feet felt as if they were suffocating, so I removed my shoes and socks and propped my bare tootsies on the windowsill. Evening was coming down over the city and the air had a tired, shoulder-flexing unease to it that suited my mood perfectly.

I decided I was feeling morose. I was also hung-over, grubby and hungry, and my nose ached. To have something to do, I poured myself a small measure of Bushmills, but I merely rolled the glass around between the palms of my hands, admiring the amber swirl of the liquid and the way it appeared to be winking knowingly back at me.

The photographs were on the desk in front of me, still in the envelope. Two different lots, but which lot the more valuable? I had the distinct impression that one set was being used as camouflage, to keep Mossie looking in one direction while someone crept up on him from the other to stab him in the back.

As for myself, I was as usual caught in the proverbial cleft stick, not knowing whether to protect my client's or my own rear. It was a matter of some puzzlement to me that the minions of the law hadn't been around to pay me a call. Of course there was the possibility that young Archie had kept quiet about my involvement, that I had left no fingerprints behind at either of the two murder scenes, that no one had recognised me going or coming. The fact that I was scuttered most of the time had probably worked to my advantage: who pays any attention to a drunk?

And what of Max Morgan? Had he now everything he wanted, the negatives to both sets of photographs, the knowledge to use them, the driving power of vengeance to urge him on? It didn't require inspired guesswork on my part to come to the conclusion that he intended holding them over Mossie's head, his own personal sword of Damocles, ready to descend whenever he felt like it.

I tried a sip from the glass and the whiskey sizzled in my trachea, causing me to gasp for air. When I surfaced I stared at the telephone through watery eyes, It was a modern, pink affair with buttons that one pressed. I bought it from a salesman with prominent teeth and an overbite that continually placed his chin in danger, on the supposition it would brighten up the otherwise rather taciturn nature of my office furnishings.

Maybe I should ring someone? Annie, perhaps? Come to think of it, there weren't too many people I could turn to in search of succour, a cheerful chat, a bit of bucking up. My father down in Wexford, a few public house acquaintances, my former lodgers who had bunked with me when I still owned the big house up on the Cabra Road, a couple of fellows I'd worked with in the insurance company – they would be glad enough to hear from me, but if I started getting into anything heavier than basic jollity they would soon roll their eyes and scarper. If you want someone to listen to your troubles nowadays, you have to hire a therapist by the hour and give him or her the shirt off your back for the pleasure.

As though I had willed it to, the phone suddenly whirred. I was so thrilled I had it lifted before it could buzz a second time.

"Max?"

There was a pause, then a voice said, "No Max here, mate. What would you say to a Fred?"

"I'd say, 'Hiya, Fred, how are they hanging?' Are you a Fred of my acquaintance or just any old Fred?"

"Fred Wimbush. I got a message you wanted to see me. Or my partner, Tim. Hacks with the Sentinel. You gave the impression you might have something of interest for us on the land rezoning scams. Or am I making that up ...?"

The penny dropped and I said, "No, that would be a reasonable supposition to make. When can I see you, and where?"

It turned out both of them were available, so I made an arrangement to meet them in Destry's in a half-hour. I was so excited about not feeling morose anymore that I was halfway down the stairs before I remembered the photos on the desk. I trudged back up to retrieve them and stuck them down the rear of my trousers, held tight against my spine by the restraining belt.

A blast of air that could have come from the mouth of an oven did nothing to instigate an evening coolness. Pedestrians looked rattled, as though pressurised by the heat, and had that squinty-eyed, sore appearance that gave the impression they would take offence at the first hint of provocation. I stepped it out carefully, with frequent glances to left, right and centre, but no one seemed to be treading in my footsteps, with fixed stare and orders to terminate with extreme prejudice.

Cedric was at his post as usual, sour as gone-off milk. A few early evening drinkers sat up at the bar, but the tables were mostly empty. I got myself a pint of lager, shrugged off a guy I knew slightly and who wanted to tell me about the state of his internal plumbing, and went and sat at a table near the back of the room.

The level in the glass had slipped down to about halfway when two characters came in who were new to me. They stepped up to the bar and engaged Cedric in conversation. I wondered why they looked familiar, then it struck me they resembled forties' comedians Abbott and Costello, one short and roly-poly, the other cadaverous, of serious mien and wearing a straw hat.

Cedric pointed them in my direction, then went back to rubbing the counter, as intent as Lady Macbeth trying to out her damned spot. The duo approached, the short one employing a fat man's waddle, the other tipping it out disdainfully as though afraid he might step in something nasty.

"Blaine?" the Costello clone enquired when he was near enough to be heard. "I'm Wimbush. And this is Kosegan. You wanted to talk to us?"

"Sit down. Have a drink." I waved at chairs, grinned to offset my injured nose, did my welcoming host bit.

Wimbush smiled, rubbed his hands and sat down carefully in a chair that protested slightly at having to bear his bulk. The other one, Kosegan, took out a handkerchief and fastidiously dusted the seat of his before deigning to lower himself into it. He took off his hat and laid it beside him on the table. He had a bony skull fuzzed by about a centimetre of hair. He did not look particularly happy, in contrast to his companion who fairly oozed high good-humour and bonhomie.

"A pint of Guinness and a packet of crisps for me," Wimbush said. He rubbed his chubby hands together again and winked at me. "Stout man," he complimented me, the beam on his face ready to take off and fly around the room.

I glanced at Kosegan, who gave me a pained response. "A glass of still water will, I think, be sufficient."

"Ice and lemon?"

He thought about that, grinding his teeth. His lips were so thin it appeared as if someone had drawn his mouth with a designer's pencil. He was the kind of man to whom haemorrhoids would have been endemic.

I called Cedric over and gave him the order, and Wimbush and myself chatted about this and that until he came back with the drinks. Kosegan centred his carefully on the cardboard coaster, his fingers long and thin, the nails beautifully squared and manicured.

Wimbush, on the other hand, dived straight into his. He came up for air with a moustache of froth decorating his upper lip and asked me, "So, what've you got for us?" His little baby hands tore greedily at the cellophane bag of crisps, his tongue in the corner of his mouth in anticipation.

"First I'd like to know a little more about this rezoning lark," I told him. "Is it a true scam?"

"It can be. When it's abused. There's a lot of money to be made when land is redesigned from agricultural use. More money than people realise."

"Enough to kill for?"

They both stopped what they were doing, Wimbush stuffing his face with crinkly crisps, Kosegan glaring wrathfully at the bubbles in the mineral water that Cedric had probably deliberately given him by mistake, and stared at me.

"A figure of speech," I explained, waving a hand apologetically.

"Many a true word is uttered in jest," Wimbush breathed. He held up a curl of crisped potato and examined it studiously. "The kind of money involved would cause even a millionaire to bend his knee in reverence."

"Really?"

"Really."

"I know roughly how it works," I said. "It depends on how many councillors you can grease, would that be right?"

This time they glanced at one another, but I caught no hint of what the look contained. Up at the bar someone laughed loudly and I also heard Cedric's answering whinny.

"We've been working on this for quite a while," Kosegan spoke for the first time. "As you can appreciate, we have to tread carefully. It's difficult to get people to talk. Landowners, land developers, members of the various county councils ..."

"There's a conspiracy of silence."

Kosegan put out a hand, palm downwards, and examined his fingers. He burnished a nail on the lapel of his light summer jacket. "Which are you?" he said, looking at me frostily.

"Which what?"

"What's your interest?" Wimbush put in. "We looked you up. You're a private investigator, God help us. Have you a client who's been ripped off? A councillor who didn't get what he felt he deserved? We have to be careful. The last investigative journalist was shot in the thigh. We'd like to know where you stand before opening our hearts to you."

I drank some beer to give them the impression I was considering coming clean, opening my own heart. Then I said, "I may have something for you. Photographs. If you can convince me I should give them to you, I will. And with no strings attached."

"What kind of photographs?"

"Ones showing a pay-off?"

They did the quick glancing at one another routine again, then looked hastily away. Wimbush emptied the last of the crisps into his mouth, then burped loudly. His partner threw him a censorious look, then returned his gaze to where his hands lay flat on the table beside his untouched drink.

"Tim doesn't approve of my manners," Wimbush explained. He giggled. "Or of my eating habits. He's into organic food himself. And food combining. Scrambled tofu on aubergine toasties, that's his style."

"Sounds about as appetising as a barium meal."

Kosegan looked at me keenly but said nothing.

"I'd still like to know a bit more about how it works," I told them earnestly. "There's been talk about money being passed around in brown paper bags."

"He wants to know how it works," Wimbush said musingly. He stroked his chin. His skin was smooth and unblemished, his hair thick and curly and well nourished. "Are you one of the good guys or the bad guys? In for what you can get out of it or a conscientious citizen eager to do your duty?"

I drank some more of my beer, then reached around and liberated the envelope from the grip of my trousers. Carefully I selected the print of Whelan handing over the parcel to the prim-looking number in the long overcoat and hat. I passed it across the table to Wimbush. He took it expectantly, perused it, then whistled softly through pursed lips. Without making any comment he handed it to his partner.

"I presume you're not going to tell us where you got that?" he said to me, little points of light dancing in his eyes.

"You recognise the people in the photograph?"

"Of course."

"Then give."

"One of them is the Whacker Whelan, a well-known hoodlum and enforcer of the old school ..."

"And the other?"

Wimbush took the print back from Kosegan and studied it. He laid it down on the table and said, "You asked me to tell you something of how this scam works. Well, most of the councillors are on the up and up, even those who consistently vote for rezoning. They argue they are providing employment and are furthering economic development. There's a kind of knock-on effect: members are guided by local advisers in a particular area as each district comes up for rezoning. Opponents of the plan are accused of being influenced by a hostile press" – Wimbush smiled deprecatingly and placed a hand on his ample chest – "and that they only see 'green' issues instead of the more pragmatic ones. It's pretty complicated and there's a lot of smoke and flak flying around."

"But you've established that some councillors can be ... ah ... swayed?"

"Not conclusively. But with the help of that photograph and,

162

better still, the negative, we might just have the missing piece we've been seeking."

"Why?"

Wimbush took the print up again and indicated the guy taking the brown paper parcel from Whelan.

"You see him?" He pointed with a stubby finger. "He's one of the most powerful people on the council. We've had our suspicions of him for a long time. If he's dirty it'll explain quite a few of the more dubious rezoning decisions. He wields a lot of influence."

I took the photograph back and gazed at the man in the coat and hat. He did not look like a very powerful figure to me, and I said as much to Wimbush.

"Don't be fooled by appearances. He's very clever at hiding his light under a bushel. He's a bachelor, lives frugally, keeps his head down. But he's a true fixer, well-connected and smoothly efficient. And he's got friends in high places ..."

"Would he be gay by any chance?"

They both stared at me, tension suddenly palpable.

"It's a possibility," Wimbush hedged.

"Is he or isn't he?"

"It ties in with something else you know?"

"What's with this answering a question with another one? There, you have me at it now ..."

I lit a cigarette and blew out smoke, and Kosegan nearly dislocated his neck muscles jerking away from it. He looked as discomfited as if I had grabbed him by the crotch.

Wimbush gave a phlegmy chuckle. He said, "Kosegan abhors smoking. He also drinks vegetable marrow juice and wears organic underwear. He's an all-the-year-round swimmer and he's into alternative medicine. He believes I've got worms."

We both stared at him, Wimbush grinning slyly, me with my famous gimlet squint. Kosegan, for his part, looked as if he had swallowed a wasp. He glared, twitched, rumbled, but then rapidly lost momentum when he saw that neither of us was impressed. Eventually he lowered his gaze and began rearranging his already perfectly-positioned glass. He still had not taken as much as a sip from it.

"Look," I said to Wimbush, "I haven't pulled all the threads of this together yet. I've a little more sleuthing to do. When and if it pans out, I'll give you first shot at it, but I want it to be airtight and shock-proof where I'm concerned when I deliver it to you. And there's someone else as well as the queen of the council that I want to bring down ..."

"That's very interesting. What kind of time span are you putting on it?"

"Huh?"

"When can we expect to hear from you?" Kosegan asked nastily. "And how much is it going to cost us?"

"I've already told you you can have it free gratis."

"Tell that to the marines. The paper won't pay ..."

"Oh, no?" I gave him back nasty on the double. "Then what about you personally? How high are you prepared to go? A ton of wheatgerm stuffing? A giant crock of ratatouille? A couple of million almond balls? I've been on the track of the recipe for tabbouleh for months. Any chance you could provide it? I'd look more than kindly on that."

Wimbush sniggered, while his partner flushed angrily. His long horse's jaw tightened, the skin of his face open-pored like the rind of an orange. I would have been prepared to bet that he shaved at least twice a day, probably with a cut-throat razor.

"What the fuck is tabbouleh?" Wimbush enquired.

"Ask the good food man."

"It's a cracked wheat dish," Kosegan said reluctantly, although he seemed slightly thawed by the fact that I knew about it.

"Sounds to me like a musical instrument. One that you might thump with your gizmo" – it was obvious Wimbush got an amount of relish out of needling his partner.

Kosegan snatched up his hat and jammed it on his head. "I'm getting out of here," he said. "I don't have to sit and listen to this kind of bullshit. Just because I lead a clean and healthy lifestyle ..."

"You don't have to stuff it up other people's wholesomes," I finished for him. "Live and let live, that should be your motto."

"Hear, hear," Wimbush agreed. He nodded at me. "You're lucky you don't have to work with him. He gets on my wick like

164

a lighted match." Watching as Kosegan walked away, his imitation leather shoes clack-clacking on the wooden floor, he went on: "Much as I'd like to stay and shoot the breeze, I'm afraid I have to scamper. Maybe I'll hear from you sooner rather than later? That stuff you've got is good, maybe even potential dynamite. You'd better watch your back. Some pretty evil people are implicated in this business. They always surface when big money is at stake."

"Thanks for the warning. I'll be careful." I saw him looking meaningfully at my nose, so I said, "Once bitten, twice shy. The noses have it, or maybe I should say have had it. The next time I'll go in bazooka first ..."

"Or at least wear a face-mask? Like those martial arts people wear? Bring the sword as well."

We both stood up. His eyes were on a level with my breastbone. As broad as he was long, he was build for stamina rather than speed.

"Not a pretty sight, eh?" he said, looking down at himself. "I haven't seen my mickey in years. Have to rely on touch to know that it's still there."

"Touch-and-go? Sounds like the guy who suffered from premature ejaculation."

Wimbush laughed. "That's a good one," he said. "I like it. Give us a call when you're ready to trade and we'll tie one on together. I've a feeling you're a drinking man ..."

Nodding in the direction of the departed Kosegan, I said, "What's with the name? Is he Russian?"

"Something like that. His people were Russian Jews. Came to Ireland and started up in the pawnbroking business. That's why Kosegan still thinks he's got three balls. He's a rare sourpuss, but a brilliant investigative journalist. He's so sour himself he doesn't mind stepping on other folks' toes. I come along afterwards and rub on the soothing syrup. Works pretty good."

We shook hands and he waddled away. I watched him go, then knocked back the remnants of my beer. It had gone stale and flat. I debated having another, but decided one more might lead to a legion. Anyway, it was time I had a little tête à tête with Archie Haly and maybe shake some sense out of him. I badly needed to talk about the art of photography, its uses and its misuses. And whether a two-dimensional image on stiff paper could be a true representation of real life or merely the murky echo of a lie.

Before heading out to the boondocks, I went back to my office one last time in the hope Max had seen the error of his ways and contacted me. I went through the outer room and opened the door of my sanctum and there was Mary Haly sitting in the visitor's chair in the spill of light from my standing electric lamp. She looked cool, poised and composed. She was wearing a wrap-around white dress with red piping, silver sandals with tongs to the knee and a discreet sheath of perfume that made me want to climb into her lap and salivate messily.

"You don't exactly keep office hours," she said. "I've been ringing on and off all day and I do like your nose."

"Why didn't you leave a message? That's what answering machines are for."

I pushed in past her and sat in the swivel chair behind my desk. It seemed like a good idea to put it between us. I took out my cigarettes and offered her one.

"I don't smoke."

"Mind if I do?"

"Would it matter?"

"Yes, it would. I'm of that old-fashioned type of persuasion that values chivalry as a dying art."

"Well, bully for you."

I stuck the Dunhill in my mouth, but I didn't light it. Bending down, I unlocked the bottom drawer and took out the bottle of Bushmills. "How about a drink?" I asked her. "A little whiskey to institute a spirit of companionship."

"I can drink you under the table."

"Can you now?"

I gazed at her and she smiled back at me, her tongue in the corner of that bee-stung mouth. I thought of letting out a 'Yippee' and doing a cartwheel over the desk, but decided the strain it would put on my trousers might leave me defenceless. Instead I fished out two tumblers and poured a couple of ounces of spirit into each. I pushed one of them across to her.

She shifted in the chair, a mere susurration, and crossed her legs. I fought the urge to look and lost. This caused her right eyebrow to lift and a gleam to switch on in the green eyes.

She took a sip from the glass. She didn't grimace as the raw whiskey bit, the clean line of her throat merely pulsed a little as it went down. Maybe she was telling me the truth when she said she could drink me under the table. To impress her I took a hearty swallow. A mistake. It left me gaping like a fish who had taken in too much air. Round one to her.

When I had got my breath back I took up the cigarette, lit it and blew smoke. I said, "When I was much younger I had a hurling coach that I looked up to. He was a charming man of infinite patience. And he was great company. To my young eyes he was one of the most glamorous of men. He stood out among his peers. Even my own father faded in comparison. He was my role model, the man I wanted most to be like when I reached my maturity."

Mary Haly jiggled her foot in its silver sandal. She held the whiskey glass under her pert chin and arched her neck. Somehow I got the impression she was not very interested in what I was saying.

"Why are you telling me this?" she asked. "Has it some relevance to why I'm here?"

"Why you're here?" I scratched my nose, remembering the old adage that an itchy nose meant the imminence of a fight. "I don't know why you're here. What I do know now is that my old coach was a wifebeater and that he had an incestuous relationship with both of his daughters. A street angel and a house devil. Goes to show how much one can be blinded by affection, and even more so by love."

"Am I supposed to get something out of that?"

"Well, it seems to me that sometimes you set someone up as a figure of admiration, only to be let down badly when he or she turns out to have feet of clay."

She took a minute to digest that one, eying me the while. Her hair was thick and oiled, but a lock of it had still come loose and hung over her forehead. I barely resisted the urge to lean across and tuck it back into place.

Maybe divining my irresolution, she smiled sweetly. She said, "You know, in some societies it's the custom when a girl comes of age to have her virginity taken by her father. Don't you think that's ... interesting?"

"Interesting? I find it bloody obscene."

"Why? Who better to initiate a girl into the wonders of her body than the man she has probably most looked up to?"

"I hope you're not trying to tell me something."

"What d'you think?"

"I think you're trying to bug me. Getting in fast with a winning stroke. Don't you know I've been shock-proof since puberty?"

She tossed her head and the lock of hair danced. She looked young and fresh and fair, too much so to be engaging in the kind of insinuations she was purveying. I wanted our repartee to be light and innocent, but the turn it had taken left me feeling moth-eaten and ragged at the edges. I said, "I've been wandering the streets of Dublin for the last two days like the shade of Leopold Bloom. I've unearthed not one but two dead bodies. Count them: one, two. Both done to death in horrible ways. I've been lied to, cheated, had my nose rubbished, and all for what? I'll tell you. To keep a quite unscrupulous and probably corrupt man in the manner to which he's become accustomed. And to babysit his equally degenerate son ..."

"You're talking about my father and brother, aren't you?"

"If the cap fits ..."

She held the glass of whiskey out at arm's length, and I thought she meant to throw it at me. But then she abruptly knocked it back. It caused her to cough and shake her head. This had the effect of lowering her defences and for a moment I felt a touch of remorse. What I had just said to her was not very nice, but the fact of the matter was that I was pissed off, not merely with her but with all of her family. And with Max Morgan too for getting me involved. They were an unwholesome lot and I was truly sorry I had got mixed up with them in the first place.

To get things back on a more even keel I said, "I came on to you a little hard there. It's not your fault you were born into such a set-up ..."

Suddenly all pretence at coquetry vanished. A dark flush suffused her features and the green eyes blazed. "Such a set-up?" she said in a choked but tightly-controlled voice. "What're you talking about? How dare you presume to sit in judgement on people you know fuck all about. My prick of a brother gets into messes, that I admit, but it's weakness that causes them, not wickedness. As for my father, he's powerful and wealthy and charismatic, and such men will always have snide enemies who will try to drag them down. And you, you're not even fit to be a doormat for him to wipe his shoes on ..."

I sat there and took it, admiring the play of light on her face, how her expression took on delineation with the force of her anger, the way the flap of her dress in her agitation fell away from her bosom. Who knows what delights might have been showered on me if I had played the game, assured her her father was a paragon of virtue and that I was the white knight riding to his rescue? Possessing principles can be a terrible downer at times.

"I have reason to believe he's bribing county councillors to rezone illegally land that he owns," I told her feebly.

"What's so reprehensible about that? A minute ago you were hinting he was responsible for two murders. Everyone goes in for a little bribery now and then."

"Is that what you came here for?"

"I beg your pardon?"

"Your mother and father tried to buy me off with money. What're you offering?"

"You bastard ..."

She surged to her feet and I had to admit she looked magnificent. Her eyes were on fire, her skin a rosy hue, her bosoms swelling in twin globes from the front of her dress. Glaring around, obviously with the intent of making a definitive gesture, she spotted the cabinet choked with sets of false teeth that the former occupant of the premises, the dental mechanic, had left behind. She advanced on it, hooked both hands in behind it, and brought it crashing down on to the middle of the floor, the teeth clacking and chattering in protest as they were unceremoniously strewn in all directions.

The unholy din shocked both of us into dumbness. When it subsided, the silence thrummed with its echo. We stared at one another and, for a second, I thought the enormity of what she had done might nudge her into some form of contrition. I was way off the mark. Working her mouth, she stuck out those beautifully beestung lips and let fly a silvery spit in my direction. It fell short and hit the colour photo of Annie that held pride of place on my desk top straight in the kisser. I gulped and waited for the sound of sizzling.

Possibly feeling she had made her point, Ms Haly then turned on her heel and stalked out, the sound of her rapid steps on the stairs like the rat-a-tat-tat of gunshots.

She left me poised in my chair, my forearms pushing hard against the arms, my backside lifted a couple of inches from the seat, the very model of a man in extremis. Drumming up a sigh, I allowed myself to sink back. When the bough does finally break, I thought, I'm bound to be sitting astride it.

I sat, taking time out to assess my situation. The last rays of the sun were inching in under the halfway-pulled-down blind and fighting a losing battle with the spill of light from the standing lamp. I gazed at the mess on the floor, then got up and resettled the cabinet in its place. The glass doors were cracked, a pleasing mosaic like frost on a window pane. I thought I would leave the sets of teeth scattered about as a kind of surreal addition to the meagre furnishings. Give the place a bit of colour, an individuality of counterpoint to remind casual visitors to return and have another look, just to be sure they were correct the first time.

The inclination was strong in me to stay where I was and let the world and its tribulations fend for themselves. After all, I still had about one third of the Bushmills to finish. And the remains of a pack of cigarettes. I placed the packet in front of me and shook the contents out on to the desk. Nine cancer sticks. Enough to get me through the next hour at least.

I picked one up and stuck it in my mouth, then I took the rest and crushed them between the palms of my hands. Little worms of tobacco squeezed out and curled back on to themselves as if they possessed a life of their own. I opened my hands and smelled their aroma, the nicotine pungent enough even to penetrate the bruised membranes of my nose.

I dusted the tobacco on to the floor, then I stood up and walked around a little, my feet mashing a set of false teeth into the threadbare carpet *en route*. Patience may be a virtue, but it was one I was in short supply of at that moment. My skin crawled and my brain felt hot, as if the sun had been cooking it all afternoon and it was now contracting and complaining about it. I could sense the alcohol in my blood, thinning it and shrinking the veins. As for my stomach, it was as slack as an empty sack, gassy and full of wind. In short, I was not in good shape, and the thought, allied with the feeling, made me want to do damage of some sort: what a restorative it would be to get my hands around someone's neck and apply considerable pressure, enough to cause a seizure, engorgement of the facial muscles, protrusion of the tongue and a pleasing bulging of the eyeballs.

An image of what such an action might effect on Archie Haly's prissy mug reminded me that I had intended journeying out to the family residence to see him. There were a few matters that boy could clear up for me before I finally took some definitive action.

I was on my way through the outer office when I heard the sound of footsteps on the stairs, loud and heavy and authoritative and decidedly not the feet of a troupe of ballet dancers. Hurriedly I stood in behind the door, clenching and unclenching my hands and wishing I had had the foresight to grab a couple of sets of teeth to bite the intruders with. A ground-under-repair sign would also have been useful to hang on my nose.

I need not have worried, certainly about the prospect of further physical damage. The first person to shoulder in through the door was Superintendent George Quinlan of the Dublin Special Branch, and he was followed by another bulky specimen I guessed was one of his tried and trusted acolytes. They made purposefully towards my inner sanctum, affording me the opportunity, if I so desired, to dodge out without them seeing me and scarper.

I did consider it, but then decided I would have to face them at some stage and now was as good a time as any, especially seeing as it was good old George in person who had done me the honour of visiting.

I followed on after them, readying a quip or two to break the ice and put them at their ease. I was knocked out of my stride, however, when I saw the face and form of George's companion. It was the guy from the gay underground nightspot, the good bouncer with the nicely-waved chestnut hair and the little pubic moustache that I had poked in the cakehole with my trusty elbow.

He was showing the effects of my love lump: a nose size somewhat similar to my own and a purplish knot on his left temple that made him look as if he had been dehorned by a blunt pliers. He recognised me at the same moment I recognised him but, after an initial double-take, he gazed right through me as if I had taken on a cloak of invisibility. I received the distinct impression that he did not want George to know anything about our previous little contretemps, probably because the bouncer job was a moonlighting affair that would be hotly frowned upon by such a stickler for the book as the good superintendent.

"How's it going, men?" I greeted them, as they both stared at me. "I was just on my way out, but I'm sure I can spare you a few minutes from my busy schedule. Is this a social call or that old devil, business?"

George looked glum, a perennial expression with him. The only time I ever saw him happy was when he was sighting down the barrel of one or other of his sporting guns. He shared with Cedric, the barman in Destry's, an inordinate hatred for all forms of wild life, and was only truly content when he was blasting some game bird out of the sky or preparing to blow some unsuspecting rabbit's arse through the front of its head.

He was tall and cadaverous, with a bony outcrop of forehead shadowing deep-set, steady grey eyes. This evening he was attired in a crumpled check sports shirt, sagging knitted cardigan, baggy cotton trousers and sandals with no socks. Not a man to pay much heed to his wardrobe, he probably put on whatever came to hand in the morning. The consequence was a nondescript appearance that ideally suited the impression he liked to cultivate of himself: a bit of an old plodder who could easily be taken in.

Nothing could be further from the truth. George was one of the most astute policemen one could ever hope to come across. Blessed with infinite patience when in pursuit of some miscreant or other, he allied an intuitive mind with attention to detail and in the process solved many an intricate case while others were still circling around it. As a result, he was admired and envied by his peers, and made much of by his superiors. George, though, went on his singular way, paying little or no attention to either laudatory comments or denigratory ones; as he saw it he was merely doing his job: prosecuting and persecuting the criminal classes, and putting a spoke in the revolving momentum of wrongdoing in all its shapes and forms.

I met him through being in the same gun club, and we had done a little hunting and fishing together. We got on, much in the manner of two people who were willing to step aside to give one another space to breathe in, but there was nothing intimate about our friendship. We never visited each other's homes, did not socialise together, had no common interest other than our mutual preoccupation with firearms and a desire to clap as many crooks as possible in the cooler. At the same time I sometimes suspected now and then that George felt a grudging stir of affection for me, a kind of looking back over his shoulder to see if I had fallen into a hole or been run over by a truck. Whether he would hurry back to pull me out or pick me up, of course, was another matter entirely.

Now I went around behind my desk and sat down, indicating that the other two should also seat themselves. George stepped cautiously over the fallen sets of teeth, but he made no comment. He eased himself into one of the two clients' chairs, crossed his long thin legs and gave a sigh as if he were deep down, bone-weary tired. Knowing him, I took this as merely another part of the act, an interview technique that told many an anxious wrong-doer if he did not hurry up and confess, George would keel over and fall asleep out of sheer boredom.

My friend from the nightclub did not sit down but instead stood against the wall with his arms folded. He was wearing a cool-looking linen suit, a cream silk shirt, tasselled loafers.

Sartorially he put George in the shade, a matter I'm sure that grieved the superintendent deeply. I caught the guy looking at me and I winked, and he quickly transferred his gaze to the middle distance like a sentry told to attend to his business.

"This is Detective Garda Smythe," George said. He twisted his head to gaze at his subordinate, then he looked back at me. "Smythe with a 'y' and an 'e'." He allowed a pause for me to make a smart remark, but I said nothing, so he went on: "He and I are following up a matter that you might possibly be able to throw some light on."

"Indeed?" I shifted my foot nervously and kicked a set of false teeth halfway across the floor. "You know you have only to ask ..."

George stared at me, his jaw muscles bunched, his eyes as empty of guile as an infant's. It was disconcerting having to meet that kind of look and still contrive to appear innocent of all matters pertaining ... to what? I had no idea how much or how little George knew of my involvement in the murders of Michaels and Chinelio. For that matter, he might have called on another errand entirely: possibly the dental mechanic had got wind of the despoliation of his precious, hand carved false teeth and had lodged a complaint, or maybe my longsuffering landlord had sent them in ahead of the bailiff to read me my rights.

"If I can be of any help at all, Superintendent," I offered, barely refraining from placing a hand on my heart to demonstrate the depth of my sincerity.

"There's been a couple of murders in the city over the last two days ..."

"Only a couple?"

The jaw muscles tightened a bit more and the brows came down like shutters.

"Two gay people. Friends. One named Michaels, the other Chinelio. Ring any bells?"

I tilted my head and assumed a listening attitude. Smythe gave in and glanced in my direction, while George sighed and danced his sandal-clad foot up and down. The light was fading fast outside, but summer warmth still lingered. I could feel myself perspiring and smell its musky odour. The thought of a shower and a change of clothes bled into my mind like a cooling

174

mountain breeze. I felt as grimy as a coalman at close of day.

"Not a chime, I'm afraid, George," I said, in answer to his question. "Is there some specific reason why I should have heard of these two deceased gentlemen? Are they on my Christmas card list? Dressed by the same tailor, perhaps?" I gave him what I hoped was a quizzical stare. "I don't normally move in gay circles."

I sensed rather than saw Smythe shift when he heard that one, but furtiveness won out over duty and he held his tongue.

"You'd be pretty obvious with that nose," George responded, mildly enough. "What happened to it anyway?"

"A pig fell on it."

"A pig?"

"Don't you remember the story of Graham Greene's where a porker was being fattened on a balcony in some Italian city? Was it Venice? No, Naples, I think ..."

George frowned and recrossed his legs, a sure sign that I had him slightly off balance.

"I don't recollect."

"Well, anyway, this Englishman was passing underneath, the balcony gave way, the pig fell on him, and in no time at all they were both rasher material. Quite a messy affair. Ever afterwards the guy's son was loth to tell people how his old man had kicked the bucket."

"Why was that?"

"They'd laugh at him, wouldn't they? In spite of themselves."

"Not surprising." George pinched the bridge of his nose between thumb and index finger. He rubbed gently, his head moving in rhythm. When he grew tired of that he circled his lips with the same two fingers, pursing them and staring into space. "So, what's the point?" he eventually asked, by now cradling his chin in his hand.

"The point is that pigs can fly. Never underestimate them, George. They may look dumb, but they've sometimes got hidden resources."

"Hidden resources, eh?" He glanced at Smythe, who was regarding me with such a look of malevolence I felt as if I were being fried under a grill. "What d'you make of that, Detective

Smythe?" he asked him. "This man is trying to convince us that a pig fell on his nose. Could it be the same one that landed on yours, I wonder?"

"Sir?"

George sighted along his index finger, his head back, his Adam's apple prominent. He said, "This is a friendly call really. A chat between old pals. I could have had you pulled in. Sent an official escort party for you. But instead I chose to do it this way because I wouldn't like to embarrass you in front of your ... putative clients?"

"Putative. Now that's a nice one, George. Maybe I should write that one down ..?"

"I'm pleased you're pleased. Now, if you have anything to tell me, off the record or on, about these murders, or matters relating ..." – he let the rest hang, like a piece of knitting unravelling.

Taking up the slack, I said, "I appreciate it, George. I really do. It's not often my humble office is graced by the presence of a Superintendent of the Garda Siochana. But what can I tell you?" I spread my hands and shook them to show I was concealing nothing. "I don't know these two unfortunate men, certainly not by name. Perhaps if you were to show me photographs? Or take me down to the morgue to view them? Although I'm inclined to feel decidedly queasy where violent death is concerned. How did they die anyway? Shot, garrotted, or hit with a spade?"

Ignoring the question, George said, "Are you working for someone at the moment? The whisper is you were seen in the company of a known pervert and ex-jailbird named Max Morgan, that you visited a certain house out in an affluent part of the city, and that you also dropped in on the house's owner at his place of business ..."

I did my best to appear shocked.

"Where'd you get that kind of information? You're not having me followed, are you?"

This time he tapped the side of his nose, tilted his head forward, gazed sternly at me under those beetle brows – he was a great man for body language. "We have our sources," he said. "Ways and means. Dublin is a small place and people like to talk. You can't hope to get away with something and not expect to be rumbled."

"Come on, George." I fumbled for a cigarette, then remembered how I had mashed them and thrown them on the floor. I stuck a finger in my ear and rotated it, the finger not the ear, as a small addendum to George's sign language. "You know the trust that exists between a private eye and his client is sacred. I do admit I'm engaged in an operation, but it has nothing to do with the deaths of these men."

"Why don't you tell me about it and then I can be the judge?"

He waited, gazing at me. When he shaved he left a little tuft of black wiry hair high on each cheekbone. This imparted a saturnine appearance, like a clergyman whose special province is the Old Testament. George would be good in a pulpit, preaching fire and brimstone.

"It's to do with ..." – inspiration was lacking, so I decided to leak a little of the truth – " ... land rezoning. I'm looking into an allegation of vote rigging. The Green Party is concerned ..."

This had the effect of setting George's teeth on edge: he equated the Greens with animal rights and the like.

"You're working for them?"

"Don't spit, George. They didn't set themselves up specially to annoy you. Anyway, I'm not getting anywhere."

"Really?"

"Yes, really. Really is as really is. I don't think you're being fair to me. If you've got some concrete information that links me to these murders, then maybe you should trot it out?"

"Why? I'm under no compunction to tell you anything. You're the one who should be doing the telling. I've good cause to be sitting here questioning you. That's all you need to know, and all you're going to know."

I essayed a hurt look, squinting to show how painfully direct I found his tone. "What're you getting shirty about?" I asked him. "I'm willing to cooperate. It's just that I know fuck all about two queers being murdered. Maybe it was a mutual suicide pact? Or a duel? Dildoes rampant at dawn. Gives a whole new meaning to the expression 'Get stuffed'. What d'you think, George? Am I warm?"

"Sir?"

We both turned to gaze at grim-faced Detective Garda Smythe,

George ruminatively, me measuring him up for possible seepage of information that would be deleterious to my present state of health and wellbeing.

"If you were to step into the other room, sit down, put your feet up, smoke a cigar, and I had a chance to speak to Mr Blaine alone? There might be things he'd tell me that he'd be too shy to say in front of you. And if there were any untoward noises, why that'd merely be the two of us doing a bit of shadow-boxing and shaping up."

I transferred my gaze back to George, and he returned the look. "Untoward?" I said. "What kind of word is that? Why can't you call a spade a spade, Smythe, as the ditch digger said to his shovel? Are you threatening me with the third degree? In front of a superior officer? Shame on you!"

Smythe coloured, at the same time throwing me a look that would have driven rivets into a wall. The knot on his forehead was blazing like a Belisha beacon. He bit his lip, then said, "Sorry, chief. I got carried away. It's not my usual inclination to offer violence to a ..."

"To a what?" I looked from one to the other of them. "Am I a suspect in something? Have you grounds for arresting me? Because if you haven't, I'm going to walk on out of here. I'm tired, hungry and badly in need of some quality time. And I intend having it." I banged my fist on the desk and a set of false teeth that had landed there jumped in the air. "Are you hearing me sweet and clear?"

George blinked, then stared at me solemnly. He wasn't fooled for a minute by my show of pretended anger, and it was not his way to respond in kind. Better to shut up shop, toddle away, do a little more poking and prying and return when the atmosphere was a little more conducive to give and take. George emulated the wisdom of the tortoise, slow and seemingly ponderous but in no doubt that he would get where he was going eventually.

I watched him as he made up his mind, got out of the chair and stood leaning slightly forward in front of me.

"I know, I know," I said. "You'll be back. Maybe I'll have more to tell you. Then again, maybe not. We live on different sides of the fence, George ..."

"Yes." His heavy-lidded eyes looked almost asleep. "But my hand is extended in friendship."

"It's the other one I'm worried about," I told him, not without a wry grin. "The one you've got behind your back. You could be flexing your fingers preparatory to tearing my nuts off ..."

"Not me." George turned and looked fondly at Smythe. "I leave that to others. I'm the one with the cotton wool and the salve and the soothing words. I'm like the confessor into whose ear you pour your sins, small, big, or indifferent."

"I'm aware of that," I said, nodding my head. "And when I need absolution I'll come looking for you. Until then, though, I'd like to be alone. My yoga hour is nigh and I wouldn't like to have an audience when I'm arranging myself into the lotus position."

Eleven

I stayed as I was, thinking how it was becoming a fixture in my life listening to the sound of departing footsteps. Soon I would be left on a promontory with no one to keep me company, or up a pole like those hermits of old who then had trouble getting rid of their waste matter.

My life had not turned out to be the success story I had once willed it to be: myself and Annie awash in the social whirl, a town house, a *pied-à-terre* in the country, a top-of-the-range Volvo, buying wine by the crate, regulars in Lillie's Bordello, featuring in Kathryn Rogers' social column, and calling the members of U2 by their first names ... come to think of it, what are their first names?

I hunted about and found a cigarette butt in the wastepaper basket. Lighting it, I singed my already damaged nose. The tumbler was empty, so I took a swig out of the bottle, the whiskey sliding down like liquid fire. I turned the chair around, reached out and caught hold of the cord of the blind. A couple of gentle tugs elicited no result, so I gave it an almighty yank. The blind snapped up, rattled on its roller, then fell off the wall and skittered away out of sight. I didn't bother going after it. Instead I gazed out over rooftops glazed by twilight's last flurry, a hotch-potch of dips and corners, chimney pots and television antennae, a church steeple sticking up in the midst like an admonishing finger. A furnace glow of light low down in the western sky drilled colour in radiating spokes, crimson shading into lighter, more pastel pinks, then losing out altogether as it pushed higher into the heavens. There was a brooding silence, the sound of traffic distanced and far away, as though held out there on a rim by some supportive coordinator.

Sometimes I imagined the city to be a wild beast, its component parts atavistic, crouched with fiery breath and menacing teeth, ready to leap out and rend the lone traveller courageous or foolhardy enough to perambulate its mean streets.

And sometimes too I saw myself as that singular figure, the last honest man, the Lord of La Mancha transposed to O'Connell Street and preparing to tilt at a few strobic windmills. A fixation of intent all too obviously false, of course, but still a sustaining bolt in my ever more rusty and corroding armour-plate of protection against a naughty world.

Looking out at the sky submitting to night coming softly down, I thought about Annie, and of how our relationship had soured so drastically, and I wondered if it is ever possible for two people to be selfless in one another. It implied a negativity, this obligation to sublimate individual desires and rinse them of their immediacy. And maybe having to move in the direction of becoming a paper person, with consequent curling and blackening when the flame takes hold?

The awful transience of love was what always got to me; you think you have a style of ownership on it and it slips away between your fingers like blood dripping inexorably down. The more of it you have, the more you need, and that need eventually tips over into a set of diminishing returns, with a demand once subtle assuming the proportions of a stern and unrelenting expectancy.

Perhaps only in the charged thrust of mutual orgasm do real knowledge and vindication lie, and the thought led me to a vision of Annie with drowned eyes and the strained rigidity of her thrown-back head. With no other woman had I achieved such repletion, such a sense of the rightness of things, yet a true permanence eluded us.

The cigarette stub suddenly burned my fingers and I flung it from me so that it burst against the window in a shower of sparks. They fell, winking into nothingness on the way, and the analogy of their brittle brevity of life and the ephemerality of the thoughts I'd been kicking around was not lost on me.

Suddenly night was upon the city, lights, movement, car horns honking and the explosive roar of a motor-bike exhaust. The cacophony reminded me that if I didn't get off my butt and go and do something about the mess I was in, I would be trading ideas of love, life and destiny with the prisoner in the Château D'If.

I went out and found an Italian café and had a meal of green lasagne, garlic bread and a side salad liberally embellished with radishes and onions. If I were to come face to face with any villain, I'd poleaxe him with my breath.

I bought some cigarettes, then made for the taxi rank in the centre of O'Connell Street. The driver of the cab at the top of the line was a woman with shoulders like a docker. She wore a baseball cap turned back to front, and a cheroot drooped wetly in the corner of her mouth. She turned her head and stared at me under her lashes, her face flat and broad and expressionless. Cab drivers have a facility for quickly summing up their passengers: it is a defence mechanism to guard them against future shock and a necessity for survival in a trade that is becoming ever more hazardous.

I gave her my honest look and instructed her to take me to The Beeches, Old Pond Road, out in Rathfarnham. She put the car into gear and we glided away and I felt as safe with her as I once had with my Granny Blaine, who also looked like Marie Dressler in a huff.

I must have dozed off, for it seemed like no time at all before my lady driver was shaking me to tell me we had arrived. I sat up and saw that we were indeed parked outside the gate of The Beeches, the road lonely and ill-lit, the shadows under the trees full of menace.

I got out and paid the fare and, feeling generous, added a sizable tip. It might be the last generous act I'd ever have the chance to make. In the glow from the dash I could see her name and picture set into a small frame.

"Thanks, Gertie," I said. "You drive like a dream."

She took the cheroot out of her mouth – could it possibly be the same one? – and bent her head to get a better look at me. She said, "Don't shake my chain, Jack. I'm stuck in this moving shithouse until six in the morning. When I get out it takes me half an hour to unwind. My arse is as flat as a pancake and I've been constipated since last St Patrick's Day. Twice in the last month I've been done over, and I'm in court next week for wrapping a tyre iron round a third perp's head. It looked a bit like your nose when I'd finished ..."

"The tyre iron or the head?"

"Grab a line, soldier. What d'you think?"

"I think it's a tough old station but that you can't afford to give in. Keep the faith, Gertie."

I stood back and she crashed on out of there. I was sorry to see her go, each new leave-taking like a little death. I was beginning to feel like Job, alone and solitary and fit only to lick my sores.

The walk up the driveway helped to staunch my sense of grievance. The moon had appeared, round and fat and smarmy, and it was sitting in the sky like half a pumpkin head, grinning an inane grin. Under my feet the grass verge was soft and pliable, and the scent of night blooming flowers was balmy on the air. The statues had a silvery sheen in the moonlight and their placid immobility imparted a comfortable emanation. No fear of any of them creeping up behind me and whacking me on the head.

I followed the sweep of pathway and came around a final bend and into sight of the house. It was lit by sodium bulbs, set at ground level, a harsh white brilliance that hardened surfaces and gave a patina of sharpness to what in daylight had seemed soft and snug and homely. Mossie was clearly cognisant of the need for security: I could see remote control cameras and the luminescent shape of an alarm centre peeping out of the climbing ivy.

Avoiding the main door, I journeyed around the side of the house, my feet scraping on the concrete surround. The ivy had spread and was growing with a determined abandon that would soon pose quite a challenge to any reproving shears. It smelled stale and mildewed, and it rustled protestingly when I brushed against it.

A lighted window drew me to it. Curtains were half-pulled but I could see a strip of mustard carpet and a polished table with a bowl of fruit centred on it. It was no trouble to me to lever up the sash and scramble into the room. It was a nice room but I gave it merely a cursory glance as I swanned across to the door, opened it a fraction and applied my eye to the gap.

I was gazing into the same hallway I'd traversed the day before. It still registered an air of haughty disdain, the refined aura of a place that had grown accustomed to the gentle swirl of ballgowns and the creak of evening wear. Mossie might be a

183

conniving git, but I had to give him credit for purveying his villainy with style.

I pushed the door further open and padded into the hall. I heard the low murmur of conversation from what I knew was the drawing-room, but I passed on that and ascended the stairs instead. Something seemed to be drawing me up there, some sixth sense telling me of the correctness of taking that route. Was I about to complete the hat-trick of dead bodies? I wondered, the mausoleum-like silence of these upper regions adding to my sense of foreboding. If so, I might be in line for some sort of prize from the union of undertakers.

I pressed my ear to a number of closed, ivory-painted doors on the first landing and behind the last one on the right I heard a little scuffling sound, like a mouse joyfully skating on a shiny surface. Turning the handle, I went on in.

Archie's flat-top hairdo was bent over the glass surface of a dressing-table, his right nostril fluttering to the tune of a line of white powder as it carefully ingested it. He was using a thin glass tube, like an eye dropper with the end cut off, to suckle the cocaine, and the snuffling sound he made reminded me of a piglet with his snout stuck in the feeding trough.

He finished, then raised a couple of enlarged and watery eyes and gazed in my direction. I flipped a hand in greeting, but I could have done a triple back somersault and landed on my little finger and old Archie would have given me the same uninterested stare. He was spaced out, off the wall, as high as Mount Everest; if he needed his tonsils seen to or his appendix whipped out, now was assuredly the time to do it.

Giving him a moment to compose himself, I looked around. The room had a soft feminine feel to it. The bed was valanced in cream satin, the furnishings white on black, with metal drop handles on the drawers of the dressing-table. I counted five lamps, all of them with pink shades that gave a rose-tinted glow to the light. A built-in wardrobe had a sliding mirror as its door; this was pushed back to reveal rows and rows of brightly coloured leisure wear. Peeping out from under this array were the toes of innumerable pairs of shoes. Archie did himself proud where raiment to adorn his body was concerned.

While I had been making an inventory of his belongings, he had been sitting on his haunches, opening and closing his mouth in an effort to break into speech. He finally managed to squeeze out a "Fucking hell ...", then frowned as if that was not what he had intended to say at all.

"Do not faze thyself, noble sir," I told him. "I do not intend staying long. And neither have I designs on your virtue. I merely wish to converse on divers topics close to both our hearts."

He stared at me, then gave a croak like a thirsty man in a pub with no beer. This also served to surprise him and he fell back on his arse between the double bed and the dressing-table. As he struggled to right himself, he knocked jars and other containers off the glass surface. All this time the tube was stuck in his nostril, like a solidified snot.

He finally made it onto the bed, where he stretched out and closed his eyes. He was wearing a mauve silk dressing-gown and a pair of thick white woollen socks. As I watched he carefully arranged the folds of the wrapper about his thin shanks, extracted the glass dropper, shut his eyes and gave a sigh like someone settling down into sleep at the end of a long and fruitful day.

There was no way I was having that. Perching myself on the end of the bed, I took one of his stockinged feet in my hands and twisted it gently but firmly. He rose up like the late Vincent Price from the crypt, an expression of exquisite agony replacing the vacant look on his face.

"What?" I asked him. "You don't want to play one little piggy went to market?"

He looked at me with venom.

"Let go of my fuckin' foot."

"I'll twist it off and stick it up your back passage," I told him sternly. "How dare you invite me into your boudoir and then lie down and go fast asleep."

"I never invited you."

"Didn't you? Then it must have been someone else. No matter. Now that I'm here we can use the time well. *Carpe diem*, as they say."

"What?"

"Seize the day. Just as I've seized your foot" – I gave it another

185

twist and he emitted a yelp like a puppy dog when someone stands on his tail – "If you want it back still attached to you, you'll have to answer a few questions."

He gritted his teeth and made to sit up, but I applied more pressure and he desisted. Turning sideways, he took a mouthful of the satin quilt and began chewing on it.

"I want to know about the photographs," I told him. "Both sets. Those of Richie Michaels and yourself, and the other lot of the Whacker Whelan and your Da handing bribe money over to a prominent member of Dublin County Council."

He stopped gnawing on the counterpane and I relaxed the pressure on his foot, enabling him to turn and face me. A look of craftiness now vied with incipient bravado as he struggled into a sitting position. He was as easy to read as a pop-up book and nowhere as three dimensional.

"I don't know anything about photographs," he said. "And if you don't get out of here and leave me alone I'll ..."

"You'll what?"

"I've got influential friends. They're the kind who'd feed you into a meat grinder and have you come out as a string of sausages."

"Yah boo to that," I said. Breathing onion and garlic at him, I began playing with his toes. He tried to pull away but I held on. "You may as well tell me what I need to know," I continued. "It'll save you some pain and me an amount of heartache."

"Fuck off."

"Don't you know any other swear words?"

"Get out of here, you red-nosed cunt."

"Aha, a change of direction. I know what you're at, you're trying to get me angry. Then, when my attention is diverted, you'll chew through your ankle bone and limp off, leaving me holding the foot. Ingenious, but it won't work. I've a collection of foots – sorry, feet, owned by guys who tried that same manoeuvre on me."

"Really?" he said, looking interested.

"I have them mounted. In a glass case. They make for an unending topic of conversation."

"You're pulling my leg."

"Jesus Christ!" I said, flinging his foot away from me. "You're one for the birds. When God was giving out brains he short-

186

changed you to the point of going into the minus quadrant. Don't you realise that two people have been killed because of those photographs? And that you're involved up to your eyebrows? You could be next for the chopper. Even if you go to the law and prostrate yourself, you'll still probably do hard time. And you can imagine how hardened cons will view your good looks and tight little behind. You'll be bent over so often you'll look like an S hook."

He blanched, a sign I hoped that I was finally getting through to him. I pushed home my advantage: "Now, if you were to tell me all you know, get it off your chest as it were, the possibility exists that I might be able to help you."

"Oh yeah?" he said, trying and failing to maintain a cheeky-boy attitude. "What will you do for me then?"

"I'll try my best to keep you out of it."

"Why?"

"Why what?"

"Why would you want to do that for me?"

Putting on my genuine and caring expression, I said, "You're a young man, just starting out in life. If I can give you a helping hand to keep to the straight and narrow, stop you from wading up to your neck in shit creek, why I'm only too glad to be able to do it ..."

Archie had been looking at me suspiciously; he now made a face, putting out his tongue and pretending to gag. "Stop it," he said, "you're making me sick. I've never heard such a load of cobblers.." The sick-making look turned to one of craftiness again. "I know why you've got a hard-on to help me. Why you'd like to put me and the family under a compliment ..."

"Why?"

"Because you'd like to poke my sister. I saw you putting the eye on her. You want to get into her knickers."

I stood up from the bed and went and leaned against the wall. I was afraid of what I would do if I stayed within reach of the little fucker. Sticking his head up his own gable end was only one of the myriad of possibilities that occurred to me.

"I'll give you one last chance," I told him. "Tell me about the photographs, right from the beginning, and I guarantee I'll protect you. You're in need of a friend, matey. Especially now that Michaels and Chinelio have passed over."

He sat up, once again arranging his nice silk dressing-gown about his bare thighs. The effort to think was causing his eyes to become crossed.

A silence descended on the room, with him cogitating and me fuming. I spent the time thinking up ways of doing him serious injury if he didn't come across. Bust his head, break his arms, block his apertures with quick-drying cement – and if I couldn't find any quick drying-cement I'd use whatever was to hand: toothpaste, hair gel, a wire hanger. I'd tear him into strips and make of him the first human stir-fry. I'd baste him, lambaste him, screw him to the wall and throw paper darts at him. The notions floating into my mind were so satisfying that I felt an acute stab of disappointment when he nodded his head, signalling, apparently, that he was at last willing to make me into his father confessor.

"All right," he said, "I'll tell you what I know. But you've got to promise me you'll keep me out of it. Otherwise, it's no go ..."

"That must have been an effort for you."

"What?"

"Putting three coherent sentences together. Getting that soft-boiled egg that you call a brain to stay still long enough for you to crack it open." I was handling this badly, but I didn't give a damn: he'd frustrated me to the point where it was immaterial whether he talked or not. He was a toerag, and being in his company made me feel sick to my stomach. "I'm making you no more promises and telling you no lies. If you want to unburden yourself, fine. If not, you can go piss up a gum tree. The choice is yours."

He dithered, probably wondering whether to sulk, whinge or stamp his foot. His eyes were dilated, most likely because his hourly feed of nose candy was coming round again. He shifted, shuddered, drew the gown about him. Finally he spoke: "The photos of Richie and me began as a joke, a way of sticking it to Da. We didn't intend extorting money from him. But then Maxie Morgan got in on the act and it was he who put the idea of blackmail in our heads. He said why shouldn't we make Mossie pay up, give with the shekels, the cash, the bread ..."

"And did he?"

"Not at first."

"What'd he do?"

"He laughed. Said we could strip bollock-naked and do it on top of Liberty Hall as far as he was concerned. Told us he'd stand and laugh and clap with the rest of the punters."

"But he changed his mind?"

Archie shrugged. He was beginning to sweat, a dewy film just under his hairline and across the bridge of his nose. He said, "I guess so. Eventually."

"In the meantime why didn't you try your mother?"

"How d'you mean?"

"Did you attempt to get money from her?"

"Why should we do that?"

"Isn't her money as good as anyone else's?"

Archie looked shocked.

"But she loves me. I love her."

I rolled my eyes, then decided to hurry things along a bit. I said, "Okay, Mossie didn't bite at first. What happened then?"

"Well, he changed his tune, didn't he?"

"How come?"

"I think maybe Morgan convinced him his place in society might be threatened if photographs of his son getting his weenie roasted were displayed on public notice-boards."

"He agreed to pay up?"

"I believe so."

"Well, did he or didn't he?"

"I'm not sure." Archie used a fold of the dressing-gown to wipe the sweat from his face and I saw he was not wearing anything under it. It was not a sight to set my pulse racing. He went on, "Morgan said he did, and he's not someone to argue with."

"You're afraid of him?"

The old blustering Archie returned for a moment and he said, "No way, José. He's only a piss artist." The protestation didn't serve to convince either of us.

"Tell me about the second set of photographs. The ones you took out in north County Dublin."

189

"Again it was Morgan who wanted those. I didn't know what the fuck it was all about, but he insisted and we went ahead and did it."

"But Michaels and Chinelio had a good idea about what was going on?"

"Maybe."

I changed tack again and asked him if he knew the Whacker Whelan and his pals Humphrey and Sid.

"I know Whelan," he admitted. "I've seen the other two with him but I didn't know their names."

"They work for Mossie?"

"In some capacity. I told Morgan he'd probably set them on us if we didn't give up on the blackmail idea."

"But you still went ahead and took the second lot of pictures?"

"What choice did I have? I was between a rock and a hard place. That Morgan is a dangerous fucker ..."

"You've seen him in action, haven't you?"

"What d'you mean?"

"Don't come with the innocent stuff again. It was he who killed Michaels, wasn't it?"

Archie swung his feet off the bed and planted them on the floor. He had to make a physical effort to prevent them running away across the carpet.

"I told you the truth about that one," he mumbled. "I was so out of it I noticed nothing. It could have been Morgan. It probably was ..."

"Why would he have done it, though?"

"How would I know?"

This time part of the shiftiness seemed to come from the answer he had just furnished me. I said, "You, Michaels and Chinelio were trying to cut him out, weren't you? The boys were greedier than you. They saw the chance of a really big score and their palms started to sweat. I can imagine Max not taking too kindly to that arrangement. And you were caught in-between. You must've felt like the boy on the burning deck ..."

"Which boy is that?"

"The one with his feet full of blisters." I lit a cigarette and blew smoke about. Now that I knew how deeply Max was

190

involved I felt more than ever like walking away. The suspicion had been festering in my mind that he was responsible for the two deaths, but I had refused to face up to it. Now it seemed inescapable, and the knowledge formed a sour knot in my heart. I always knew he was capable of extremes, any person whose sense of survival was so strong had to be. But if I thought about it at all, I imagined his cockeyed view of morality would lead him in the direction of harnessing his ruthlessness for good rather than for evil. Shows what an over-the-top optimist I am, in spite of all.

I said, "Chinelio is dead. He was shafted with the iron spike of an umbrella ..."

The flat statement shook Archie, but he still had gumption enough to ask, "What happened to the negatives of the second set of photographs? They were supposed to be in his safe-keeping."

"That doesn't concern you, now. Have the Guards been to see you yet?"

"About Richie, you mean?"

"No, about the dog you buggered last Michaelmas Day."

So help me, a guilty expression fleetingly adorned his immature mug — could he have been into dogs? I shook the thought out of my mind, giving a little mental shudder to help it along.

"No one has been to see me about anything," he said, avoiding my eye. I noticed he was stealing quick, hopeful glances at the dressing-table. Guessing he was in need of another jump-start, I mashed out my cigarette on the glass surface of the bureau and began opening drawers and rummaging in them. Over my shoulder I said, "They mustn't have come to your name yet, but it's only a matter of time before they call. The guy in charge of the investigation works like the mills of God, slow but exceeding fine."

However, Archie had more on his mind than the machinations of the law. He was concerned with what I was doing, pawing through his silk monogrammed underwear and unearthing an assortment of uppers, downers and middle-of-the-road mind blasters. There was a hoard of amphetamines, glazed and shiny and multicoloured like naughty Smarties, innocent white tabs labelled MDMA – but which I knew under the more popular designation of Ecstasy – something called Methaqualone, a jar of blood-red capsules of codeine, bottles of Paxipam, Ativan, Librium, Valium – a chemist would be scratching his head to recognise them all. I also found some sachets of what I presumed was cocaine, and a cellophane packet of perforated squares of lint, each with its sweet little heart of acid, like individual drops of yellow pus.

I placed the lot in a heap on the top of the dressing-table, then sat back on my heels and looked at it. There was enough there to send Nelly the Elephant into orbit.

Behind me, Archie gave a nervous cough, cleared his throat and enquired what I intended doing with his medication. He said, "They're mine and you've no right to them. I'm of a delicate disposition." When I turned to gaze at him he amended that to, "Take half and leave me half. You'll still make a fortune selling them on the street."

To be honest, I didn't know myself what to do with his junk. Flushing it down the toilet seemed the obvious move and give the rats in the sewers a treat. I emptied a designer boxer shorts out of its plastic cover and swept the various odds and ends into the see-through sack. It made a sizable package. I knotted the top, then stood up with it swinging from my left fist. Immediately Archie made a grab for it, but I held it out of his reach and the momentum of his move deposited him on the floor. He sat on the carpet looking distressed, his legs stuck out in front of him, his feet ridiculous in their woolly white socks.

He looked so down I almost relented, but not quite. It would do him good to detox, even if only for a couple of hours. Suffering, they say, is good for the soul, and I should know.

I left him crying into the lush pile of the carpet, went out the door and was halfway down the stairs before I spied Humphrey and Sid standing four-square in the hall, like two garden gnomes someone had taken in out of the night air. They stared impassively up at me, showing no emotion whatever, but what they stirred up in me engendered an agitation too deep for words.

We formed a neat little gathering in the picture-book setting of the Haly sitting-room. We might have been actors on a set:

myself the centre of the scene, sitting in a wing chair flanked by Humph and Sid, the Whacker Whelan facing me on an exquisitely carved straight chair, Mossie Haly standing in front of the fireplace, his wife and daughter side by side on the sofa, and Archie chewing his nails and aptly enthroned on a well-padded pouffe. All that was needed was the director's call for "Action", but Humphrey and Sid would probably provide that in due course.

Whelan was not one to wait on instructions, however. He had already called me a number of names – bumfuck, arsewipe and nose-browner being the mildest of them – and been rebuked by Mossie, who told him to watch his language in front of the ladies. The ladies looked suitably pained, but the Whacker showed no signs of remorse whatever.

Now he got up and stood a little way from me. I hoped he would come closer so that I could sink my teeth into his bulging crotch, but he was alive to such an eventuality and kept his distance. He was wearing brown boots, light beige summer trousers, a waisted cotton shirt and a yellow cravat pulled through a gold bangle. A thick, linked chain was solid around his tanned neck, an identity bracelet drooped from the wrist of his raised right arm, and a thin Cartier watch and a signet ring gleamed on his left arm and hand. As usual he was done up like a dog's dinner, but for me he still resembled its transformation after it comes out of the canine's rear end.

Suddenly he came in sideways, offering me only the bone of his hip as a target, caught a wad of my hair and forced my head back. At the same time Humphrey and Sid came alive, grasped one of my arms each and held on for dear life. As the ham in the sandwich I prepared for the champ of hungry teeth.

Again Mossie came to my aid. Still attired in the navy blue pin-striped suit and white shirt, he had made only one concession to the heat of the summer night by loosening the pink tie and allowing the top button of the shirt to come undone. Admonishing Whelan to tread carefully, he said, "I don't want any rough stuff, certainly not here in my home ..."

"In my home," Whelan mimicked him, still holding on to my forelock. "So will we take him outside and kick the shit out of him?"

Mossie jerked his head, like a gannet endeavouring to swallow an extra large fish. He looked angry, his fleshy face flushed, his open pores gaping. Always one to keep violence at a respectable distance, it plainly irked him now to be part of the Whacker, Humph and Sid show.

He moved over to where I was sitting and leaned in so that I could get a good view of his perspiring countenance, and asked me if I realised the position I was in.

"Not one from the Kama Sutra anyway," I responded, feeling the tendons in my neck strain under the effort.

"So what d'you intend doing about it?"

"Hang loose like a goose and honk for Jesus?"

The Whacker wrenched my head back further, taking my breath away. On either side of me Humphrey and Sid were as immovable as ballast.

"Let's try that again," Mossie said. "And if you give me another smart answer, I'll do you an injury myself."

He made a gesture and Whelan loosened his hold slightly, enabling me to tense my jaws and listen to them creak. Sweat was salty in my eyes and my wounded nose had begun throbbing again. If purgatory really existed, I was rapidly cutting off chunks of my time there.

I essayed a few preliminary croaks, then tried out my voice with: "Let's be fair about this, Mossie. You haven't asked me anything as yet. Lay your cards on the table and I'll tell you if you've a hand of trumps or a bum deal. Can't say better than that, can I?"

There was a silence in the room, a pregnant silence if I were any judge. Then Mossie said, "I've only got two questions for you. Answer them to my satisfaction and you're away out of here and free ..."

"And they are?"

"Where is Maxie Morgan, has he got the negatives of a certain set of photographs, and if so, what does he want for them?"

I widened my eyes at him in as close an approximation as I could come to a look of reproach.

"Come on, Mossie, that's not fair."

"What isn't?"

"You asked me three questions when you said you were only

going to ask me two. I could've handled a couple, but a threesome is going a bit far."

Mossie breathed deeply but said nothing, so I went on, "Any chance you'd instruct your pet gorilla to release me, so that I can test out my neck muscles for flexibility? I think I heard a vertebra snap."

He made a sign and Whelan reluctantly let me go. The other two, on the other hand, dug their heels in like anchor men on opposing tug-of-war teams.

"That's better," I said. "But now my nose is itchy. Maybe you'd scratch it for me?"

"I'll tear it off your fuckin' face," Mossie said. "You horse's arse ..."

"Now, now," I counselled him, "remember the ladies." I looked at them, where they were perched on the sofa. Madame Louise was avoiding my eyes, gazing around the room as if attempting to come up with a new colour scheme, while the daughter glared at me, licking her lips and giving the impression she would like to see my thumbs being screwed into the light sockets and my willie light up like the element in an electric fire. I shifted my gaze back to Mossie and said, "You know, I've got a very low pain threshold. So, the fact is that if I could answer your questions, I would. The truth is that I don't know where Maxie is holing up, nor do I know if he's got the snaps of Archie and his pal or the negatives. That's it in a nutshell. Take it or leave it."

The eyes staring at me narrowed, the mouth compressed itself into a thin line, and a look of calculation appeared on the fleshy features. Mossie was either puzzled, thinking, or had experienced a sudden dart of abdominal wind. After a suitable pause for reflection he said, "Fuck those photographs. We're into a new ballgame now. I've just been informed by my associates that certain other prints exist which could prove to be much more damaging to my business interests. They're what I'm after. And I mean to have them."

"Can't argue with that."

"So you'll help me?"

"To do what?"

"To find Morgan. He's the key to this. Always has been. He talked me into bringing you into it when I still thought it was a simple case of knocking the pansies about a bit to make them forget about trying to blackmail me. You took my money. So in theory you're still working for me ..."

"Don't you think you lost any claim on my services when you sent these gay old boys here around to rough me up?"

"Gay?" Whelan said murderously. "Who's he calling gay?"

"Forget it," Mossie snapped. "That's an old ploy, trying to make us angry. He's not going to tell us anything unless a little persuasion is used. But you can't do it here. Take him out to the site. You know where. There'll be no one there at this time of night, not even a watchman. Do what you have to do."

"That's it, then, is it?" I asked. "I'm expendable. And after all those nice things you said about me this afternoon. Reminiscing about the good old days in Wexford." I turned my head and gazed at the women again. "What about you?" I enquired. "You know this is a question of guilt by association. That's why Mossie's got you here. Think about it. These guys are going to kill me. I know too much. They could do me serious injury, but if they let me live there's always the chance I might talk. The dead don't tell tales. You're going to be party to a murder. And for what? To maintain your shitty lifestyle? Your place in society? They won't be worth a damn to you when your consciences start at you. Or am I presuming too much by entertaining the idea that you have consciences ...?"

There was a collective withholding of breath, as if each and every one of them was awaiting some judgement to be made in answer to my plea. Then Archie decided to take a hand. Not on my behalf, though, but rather his own. Using the moment of hiatus to his advantage, he bounced from where he was sitting on the leather pouffe, grabbed his plastic bag of goodies from the lacquered table where it had been deposited, and hared up the stairs. As he went, his dressing-gown swirled out in his wake and the twin globes of his buttocks twinkled in derisory salute.

My God, I thought, can this be the end of Blaine, his last memory a vision of a poofter's bare arse? If anyone ever needed the clarion bugle of the rescuing cavalry, I needed it at that moment, but strain as I did my ears, not a pip-pip did I hear.

Twelve

I was in my accustomed position in the back seat of the Datsun, with Sid to keep me company and the silhouettes of the heads of the other two in the front to give definition to my forward view of things. Some months before I had made a similar trip, but I'd survived to tell the tale. This journey might have a different outcome.

"Have you a feeling of *déjè vu?*" I asked Sid, by way of passing the time.

"Wha?"

"The notion this has happened before. An intimation of your past life recurring. Or maybe the possibility of parallel worlds, with one impinging on the other. Old Arthur C Clarke, the science fiction writer, was a great one for writing about them."

Sid thought for a minute, then he said, "I knew an Arthur once. A great man with plastic. When he did a blow job, it stayed blowed."

"A blow job?"

"Could take the plug outta a lock like the cork from a bottle. Never left a mess. And yeh could be in the next room and yeh'd never hear a t'ing."

I glanced at Sid's profile, was reminded of a pit bull terrier and wondered why he wasn't wearing a muzzle.

"What happened to him?" I asked.

"Who?"

"Arthur the dynamite man."

"Blew himself up, didn't he? Everyone told him he was past it, but he just hadda do that one last job. Charge hit him straight in the mush and knocked his friggin' head off. A guy was with him said he danced around like a headless chicken. Blood everywhere. And bits of Arthur. Gave him a proper turn, I can tell you."

"Not half as much as it gave Arthur."

Sid nodded, but his mind was still grinding away. "Then there's that character on the tele. He's an Arthur too. Arthur Daly.

197

Always on the con. Keeps a minder named Terry ..."

I detected approval in his tone, so I said, "Fancy old Terry, do you? See yourself in his image and likeness? A hard man. Putting the boot in and the screws on. Watching the fright come up in the punter's eyes and how he pisses in his pants ..."

"Worse sometimes," Sid agreed, wrinkling his nose.

"Is that how you get your kicks? By kicking someone else? I'll bet you loved pulling the wings off flies when you were a boy. Have you ever given a sucker an even break, Sid? Faced up to someone your own size and engaged in equal combat?"

"Shut your cakehole," the Whacker suddenly said from the front seat. He twisted around and gave us a view of his beautifully capped teeth as the lights of a passing car flashed off them. "If you don't give over with the bullshit, I'll have Sid sit on your face. And that's not an experience Listerene would cure in a hurry."

We lapsed into silence and I turned and stared out the window. We had crossed the Liffey and were heading in a northerly direction. The moon was still up, but paling against the steely blue of the sky. Traffic was light – I wondered what time it was but was afraid to move my wrist to look at my watch in case Sid mistook the gesture as a threat.

We bypassed Santry and hit the airport road, and soon in the middle distance I could make out the glow from the vast conurbation of buildings. It held the promise of hustle and bustle, the pull and drag of human activity. Fervently I wished I were part of the colour and the noise, maybe meeting someone or, better still, waiting to board a plane to take me to Acapulco or far Bombay.

The last holiday I had taken had been with Annie: two weeks in Playa del Ingles in the Canaries, walking out each morning to the beach at Mas Palomas to sunbathe in the nude and let the warm wind and hot sun lull us into lethargy.

At the end of the fortnight we had been so fit, from a combination of walking, swimming and lovemaking, that our view of life had become of the rarest. We floated, inured in each other's happiness and in a present habitual that was as smooth and ungapped as the long sunlit days. Our bodies tanned and languorous, our minds keen and aware, we drifted through billows of goodwill, so allied as to be indivisible. We communicated through look and gesture, and words were as superfluous as colour thrown into a kaleidoscope.

But all good things come to an end, and on our last day a wind sprang up, hot and dry and rattling in the fronds of the palm trees outside our window. When we made love, I surprised the wet snail-track of tears on Annie's face and I knew that our golden time had finished and that we were being dumped back into the bumpy path of the commonplace.

And so was the Datsun. I started from my reverie when the car turned off the main road and began rocking along a more rutted one. I fancied I could smell the sea, but then again it might merely have been Sid's bodily fluids, stirred up by the vehicle's rough passage. The moon had given up and gone home and I now had to rely on starshine. Ahead all I could see in the glare of the headlights was a pitted road surface, a grass verge, and crouching trees like evil old men beckoning.

Soon the gravel surface gave way to hard-packed clay and I was able to discern the low humped shapes of sand dunes. And then indeed I was certain I could smell the sea, its briny tang and the iodine smell of seaweed. We were close to the coast, somewhere to the north of Malahide, maybe near Rush or Donabate. By the absence of welcoming lights I presumed it was a lonely stretch, not much given to being traversed, even in daylight, except by cheese-and-wine imbibing, disclaiming poets and bird-watchers with powerful binoculars and designer wellington boots. Would that I were of their kin at that moment!

We continued on, Sid breathing like Puff the Magic Dragon beside me. The idea occurred to me to twist the door handle and hurl myself out of the reasonably slow moving car but, Sid and I by now sharing the same telepathic bond, he immediately sussed out my wavering intention, stretched out an arm like an iron bar and clamped me securely against the upholstery.

The road began to climb and in the glimmer of starshine I could now see the glint of the ocean laid out below us, flat and placid and giving off romantic emanations. I cocked my ear for the sound of Rudy Vallee crooning 'Ramona', but all that was borne on the night-time zephyrs was the low purr of the car's engine and the swish-swish of its tyres on the track.

We turned and came to a fenced-in area, and a white painted board with black lettering warning trespassers to beware. A gate barred our way. Humphrey stopped the Datsun, let the engine idle and folded his arms on the wheel. No one made any attempt to get out and open the gate.

"Shall I get out and do the necessary?" I enquired, after a length of time had passed.

"Stay where yeh are," Sid counselled me, laying a fatherly hand on my arm.

"But we could be arrested for loitering."

"Shaddup."

Some more time went by, then Humphrey sighed, opened his door, got out and jerked the rickety gate aside. He pushed back in behind the wheel and drove through the gap. He was continuing on when Whelan suddenly ordered him to halt.

"What's up now?"

"You've left the gate open."

"So?"

"Supposing some suspicious fart sees it and comes in to investigate?"

"That gate wouldn't keep out a drunk with the head staggers. What's the point in closing it?"

"It looks better closed. This is private property and we don't want to be disturbed."

"So why don't you get out and do it? Have you become paralysed or what?"

Beside me Sid chortled and administered a companionable poke with his elbow to convey his merriment.

"Fuck that for a lark," a plainly piqued Whelan muttered. He raised his arm and for a moment I was hopeful he was going to give Humphrey a belt in the ear, but he was only using the attached hand to smooth down his already well-manicured hair. "I'm not getting out there," he went on. "That's your job. I might step in something. Have you any idea how much these suede boots cost me?"

Humphrey grunted as if he'd been hit a low blow in the

kidneys and again my hopes of a diversion arose, but then he lifted his shoulders resignedly, got out and went back to carry out his chore.

While we waited, I asked Sid if there was any chance I might light a cigarette.

"About as much chance as me asking you to foxtrot," the Whacker answered for him. He twisted around to face me. "You're taking this pretty cool, I must say. You must have been at the son's dope shit. I hope you're feeling numb, otherwise you're in for some pain."

I sneered at him, then decided a little goading might be in order. I said, "No use having a fit of the vapours until there's a need for it. I reckon we're all guys together and can sit down and talk this problem through. Why get excited about it? It only leads to spots and hot flushes."

"Is that so?"

"Didn't you learn that at your mother's knee?"

"Leave my mother out of it."

"And your father?"

"What about him?"

Pushing the needle in a little further, I said, "Tell me, Whacker, were you ever let in on the secret of who he was? Story goes that he was a prize boar who broke loose and galloped up behind your old lady when she was bending over. Went to his execution with a smug smile on his porky chops ..."

Whelan stared at me in disbelief, his jaws working and his eyes popping out of his head. To make it worse, Sid began heehawing like a jackass. I was preparing myself to repel boarders when the oblivious Humphrey came back, got in, started up the car, and drove on.

Play suspended, to be resumed after tea.

We rattled along over rough ground until finally coming to a halt on what appeared to be a forty-five degree angle of slope. There was a structure of some kind: from the outside it seemed like a shed, probably a storehouse for the tools of the building trade. Behind it in orderly rows were the roofless shapes of dwellings in the process of being completed. I guessed we had arrived at a parcel of the controversially rezoned land that Mossie Haly owned. From our elevated position there was a splendid view of the starlit sea, while on the horizon the darker bulk of an island or maybe the inward curve of the northern aspect of Dublin Bay brooded hump-backed.

It must have been well after midnight and the early morning air had a chilly cut to it. I shivered in my thin slacks and waistcoat as Sid prodded me ahead of him and out of the car. The Whacker went first and unlocked a padlock, the stout wooden door of the shed rasping along the ground as he pushed it open. We went inside and someone clicked a switch to give light to the hanging electric bulb.

The place was as I had surmised: a shed for assorted shovels, picks and other such implements. In the centre of the cement floor stood a badly constructed table, its unplaned surface the repository for innumerable tea-stained mugs, empty milk cartons, overflowing ashtrays, and a loaf of bread that sprouted a rather becoming beard of blue mould. Not a place in which one would choose to linger, never mind die in.

An old wardrobe with a spotted mirror leaned drunkenly in one corner, and Whelan stood in front of this and began arranging his hair with a bright yellow comb, the same colour as his cravat. With his back to the rest of us he said, "It stinks in here. It's like a Russian's armpit." He turned, blew on the comb and put it away in a soft leather case. Next he took out a small vial of amber-coloured liquid, uncorked it and stuck it up each nostril in turn. He sniffed appreciatively, while Humphrey and Sid gazed at him and looked vaguely embarrassed.

"Take a seat, apeshit," he told me, indicating a paint-streaked chair that was drawn up to the table. Overhead the bulb swung on its frayed cord, casting large and uneven shadows. These had the effect of making the interior of the shed sinister and threatening, and I was reminded of descriptions I had heard of the lock-ups where the Shankill Butchers had plied their trade. I had the urge to spit but couldn't summon up enough saliva even to moisten the inside of my mouth.

I sat down, the seat of the chair rough against my backside. It set me to thinking of George Orwell's account of the condemned native in Malaya who stepped barefooted over early morning pools of rainwater on his way to be hanged. Even the fear of imminent death, it seems, cannot make one deviate from mundane and trivial acts – or does one treasure them all the more in such a situation?

While the Whacker continued to posture, Humphrey and Sid took up their usual 'pretending to be stone pillars' disguise. I thought about a cigarette, thought about a drink, thought about Annie and the new and sainted lifestyle I was going to lead if and when I managed to get out of my present difficulty. I even threw a pious ejaculation in the direction of the ceiling in the hope that St Jude, patron saint of lost causes, might be in a listening mode.

Seeing my lips move, the Whacker leaned down, his ear cocked. However, when he saw the condition of my nose at close quarters, he hastily took his own back out of biting distance. Casting a quick glance at the other two, he said, "Now, what's it going to be? The hard way or the easy way? Either is okay with me, but you might like to have a say in the matter."

I shifted on the chair, careful not to get splinters in my bum. The Whacker was looking at me, waiting for an answer, so I said, "Could you spell it out in simple terms? What exactly d'you mean by 'hard' and 'easy'? Are you telling me you'll let me go if I give you the information you want? Or am I presuming a bit there?"

"You're presuming, yeah. Either way you're going to end up talking to the fishes, but there's a clean or messy manner of operating. That's what's on offer, the chance to go quick and sure."

I placed my hands on my chest and took a deep breath. Talk about teetering on the rim of the lion's den! I said, "You guys are not killers. Hard men who like to cause pain, yes, but not ones for the ultimate sanction. You're bluffing ..."

I raised my head and watched him as he took another couple of sniffs from his magic bottle, screwing up each eye in turn as the charge hit home. Whatever he was snorting, it gave a healthy blush to his features, a lively thrust to his gaze. He saw me looking and once more presented me with the razzle-dazzle of the cosmetic teeth. He said, "This time it's personal. You've stuck your nose once too often into my affairs. I'm going to top you and enjoy doing it. And we'll weigh you down so that when they fish you out of Dublin Bay it'll be the year two thousand and there'll only be enough of you left to fit in a matchbox."

"We? Humph and Sid are going to help you out?" I turned to look at them. "What d'you think of that then, boys?" I asked, hoping they might shake their heads and violently demur. No change there, though; they stared back at me with all the emotion of a brown paper parcel – two brown paper parcels, to be exact.

"Let's stop this larkin' about," Whelan suddenly said. "We want that merchandise and we're going to get it. Plus Morgan. Or the next best thing ..."

"The next best thing?"

"His whereabouts. His address. Who he hangs out with. His usual haunts. Where he can be reached out for and squeezed."

"His jockstrap size?"

"I'll leave that to you and the other fairies. You clusterfuck. You backdoor bandit. You ..."

"Whoa," I said, holding up my hand. "I'll give you whatever I can. Starting with this" – so saying, I reached down the back of my trousers and got hold of the envelope containing the photographs; by this stage it had slipped so far I was sitting on it. I held it out to him.

He eyed it suspiciously, especially after seeing where it had come from. Turning to Humph and Sid, he said, "Which one of you two gumballs was supposed to have searched him?" he asked. "Can I not trust you to do anything for yourselves?" He indicated the envelope and gestured for one of them to take it. "It's impossible to get good help nowadays," he grumbled, shaking his head in mock sorrow.

Sid did the necessary and slid the glossies out on to the table. Whelan scrutinised them, poking fastidiously with a beautifully manicured forefinger. I saw his lips move and wondered if he was going, "Eeny, meeny, miny, mo." Seemingly satisfied, he got up and began rummaging about in the corner. He unearthed a battered steel bucket, came back with it and dumped it on the floor. Then, with due ceremony, he took out a thin gold cigarette lighter and set fire to each of the photographs in turn, holding them over the container and letting the curls of ash drift down into it like dirty flakes of snow.

When he was finished he dusted off his hands, put the lighter away, unzipped his fly and urinated into the bucket. His flow was energetic, but he was inclined to splash, and I was happy enough to observe some of the pee ricochet as greyish drops and stain the lower legs of his expensive slacks. Eventually he shook himself off and packed his weapon away. I had to admit, though reluctantly, that it was an impressive piece of apparatus.

Pleased with himself, he said, "That's fine as it goes, but they're no use without the negatives."

"Afraid I can't help you there, chief," I said. "The negatives took flight. I did have them, but then they disappeared into the vortex."

"The vortex?"

"Matter rotating round an axis to form a big black hole, said axis in this case being one Maxie Morgan. As you surmised. Find him and Bob's your uncle. You've got the negatives, the cookies, the cookie jar and, who knows, the pot of gold at the end of the rainbow?"

"Morgan, eh? I knew it. I told Haly from the start he shouldn't have trusted the little cock-browner. When I get my hands on him ..."

"Beware of him. He's as sharp as a ferret. If he manages to grab hold of your essentials, nothing'll persuade him to let go. He'll rot hanging out of you, but he'll never let go."

"Fuck him. He's in the future." Whelan grinned a grin at me that was pure wolf. "But you're here. And the time has come to give you a keepsake, something to prepare you for what lies ahead ..."

"I thought you'd given me one already," I said, touching my nose.

"Naw, that was only a little love tap. What we need now is something that'll really have you going ouch, ouch, ouch." He had recourse to his magic bottle again, emitting a couple of wet snorts. "Now, what can we think up? Maybe you might even like to help us out with a few suggestions? No? Oh, well, we'll just have to do it all ourselves then."

He went over to the pile of tools in the corner. Picking up a shovel, he gave it a few experimental waggles. He put it down and came up with a pickaxe. "It has to be something special," he went on, looking from the implement to me and back again. "Something we can all remember when we're old and grey and full of beer ..."

I was beginning to experience a decidedly squelchy feeling in the region of my bowels and my heart was going pocketa-pocketa like a jackhammer. There was no doubt in my mind that the time had come to make a stand, cause some damage before I was rendered incapable of movement. I rose up from the chair with the intention of throwing the table at Whelan, but before I could do more than bend and grasp the edges of it Humph and Sid were on me. For such seemingly slowwitted turkeys, they could move like blue streaks when they had to, and they were also as strong and hard as whipcord. They sat me back down in the chair and held me as if I were bolted into it.

The Whacker advanced on me, a hammer held aloft in one hand and a six-inch mortar nail in the other.

"I'm going to tell you what I'm about to do before I do it," he said. "That way you'll be able to look forward to it as much as me." He paused and raised the nail so that the light reflected off it. Then he made hitting motions at it with the hammer. "I'm going to nail you to that table," he said, a dreamy expression on his face. "I'll start with your hand, but there're plenty of nails and many bits of you. I might even dump you in some public place for all to see. It'd be like a punishment penance, in the manner of those guys of old who went about throwing dust in the air and whipping themselves. What d'you say to that, pisspot head?"

My immediate reaction was to open my mouth and yell bloody murder, at the top of my voice and at some length. The only effect this had was that it induced Sid and Humphrey to tighten their grip, while, if Whelan did jump a little, it was not high enough to hit his head on the ceiling and knock himself out.

The shouting was merely sound and fury signifying fuck all. In the god-forsaken spot we were in, it was probably only denizens of the wild who pricked up their ears at my entreaties. When I stopped to draw breath, Whelan leaned in closer and commanded me to put out my hand. much in the manner of a teacher about to administer the cane. A drop of sweat glinted at his hairline, then slid across his forehead and wobbled to the end of his nose. I watched it intently, trying to focus on it to the exclusion of everything else. But, like a lot of things that have served to let me down, it hung only for a moment and then gave up the ghost and fell away out of sight.

"Get his right arm out," Whelan was telling Sid, as I lunged and jerked like a gaffed fish. He did as he was bid, forcing my arm out slowly but inexorably across the splintered surface of the table. I kept my fist closed, leaning back against Humphrey and trying to use his body as leverage. Even in my panic I could still smell his body odour, and the sour stink from the battered milk cartons.

Whelan came in closer, hammer and nail poised. He was breathing in short gasps, but it was the excitement of what he was about to do rather than his present exertion that was causing his elation. He was a typical bully-boy, getting off by exacting pain on others.

"Open your fingers," he whispered, his body blocking out the light. "Otherwise I'll smash them, one by one." To emphasise his threat he tapped me lightly on my clenched knuckles. "You'll never play the piano again," he intoned. "Bing, bang, bong ..."

Reluctantly, with Sid's grip like a vice around my wrist, I relaxed my fingers, watching them curl open on the table top. I had never given much heed before to those self-same appendages, but now I experienced a sudden rush of love for them, a crooning, drooling doting, a flame of adoration for their vulnerability and usefulness. What would I do if my itty-bitty fingers became incapacitated? Never again to be able to use them to count on, light my cigarette, caress an erect nipple, wipe my arse ... What a work of art are fingers, I thought, what truly complex tools.

Then I gave up thinking as Whelan applied the first tentative tap to the nail head, followed by the second, more authoritative wallop as a crashing encore. A searing, white-hot lick of agony shot up my arm, along my shoulder and leaped by way of the big muscle in my neck straight into the most tactile region of my brain. From there it may well have gone out my ears, through the roof and into orbit, but by then I had blacked out, my sense perception unable to cope any longer with the unexpected anguish of being presented with the first instalment of the stigmata.

Slowly I came back to the land of the living, although fighting vigorously against it. I also had no wish to associate myself in any way with my right hand, but still felt drawn to it, as one is pulled fearfully towards the edge of an abyss.

Trying to control a surge of nausea, I felt the acidic sting of bile rise and cause my insides to heave. The urge to scream was also strong in me, but I had been down that path and I was damned if I was going to give my companions the added pleasure of hearing me again.

Slowly, out of the corner of a semi-shrouded and unwilling eye, I gazed at where my hand was now attached to the wooden table top. Whelan had driven the six-inch nail to the hilt into the centre of my palm. There was very little blood, but the flesh around the puncture was purple and puffy-looking. I slowly tried to close my fingers, but the pain was excruciating and caused me immediately to desist.

Along with the agony I experienced a feeling of shame: my body should not have been subjected to such an abject humiliation, such a degrading intrusion on its normal functions. And if it had to be so traduced, it should have happened out of the glare of prying and spiteful eyes; in the sterilised confines of an operating theatre, perhaps, under anaesthetic and the quiet expertise of caring and curative hands.

Gritting my teeth, I concentrated on banishing the red mist that rose and fell in front of my eyes. At all costs I must retain some semblance of the reasoning faculty. I would not descend to the level of an animal. Trying to still my breathing and bring my heart back to a normal beat, I began counting, one, two, three ... until slowly my sense of panic abated and I was able to think in a normal manner once again.

Whelan was still standing over me, the hammer now laid on the table. He was regarding me closely, as someone might scrutinise a scientific experiment he was conducting. I tried to work up a ball of spit to lob at him, but my mouth was as dry as attic dust.

The goons had let go of me, obviously seeing no further need to expend their energies now that I was so firmly fixed to the table. They stood, their hands hanging, no expression whatever on their unholy mugs. My pain was making as much impression on them as a mouse attempting rape on an elephant.

"So, how's that feel?" Whelan asked me. "Not bad for a first shot, eh? I'll probably get better at it as I go along. Although I have to admit, I never was much good at DIY. The nail always seemed to bend. Or the wood would split. I'll keep trying, though ..."

I attempted to come up with an answer, but my store of smart remarks was as bare as a nudist's backside. Instead I turned my head and gazed at the single window that the shed boasted. Grainy grey light was beginning to seep in, squeezing itself up against the grimy panes as the last rubbings of night dissolved. Soon a new day would break, but would I be alive to see it? For some reason the words of an old song my father sometimes sang drifted into my mind:

"Yesterday, the skies were grey,
Look, this morning they're blue,
The rising sun tells everyone,
Come and start life anew ..."

There was no doubt the pain from my hand was making me light-headed, but was it solely the cause of my spying an upside-down goldfish bowl with eyes outlined in the rectangle of dawn light in the window? I blinked and looked again and the apparition had disappeared.

A giggle escaped me, bringing a grimace of disappointment to Whelan's features.

"Putting it up to me, are you?" he said. He motioned to Humphrey and Sid. "Grab hold of him again. We'll drive one through his other hand. Then maybe we'll hoist him up and nail his pecker to the table. That'll really give him something to be happy about."

209

Once more they laid hands on me and, in spite of knowing better, I tried to shoulder them off. Pain the like of which I couldn't even dream about placed a burning band around my perception and began drawing itself tighter and tighter.

Mercifully I was on the point of again blacking out when the door of the shed suddenly flew open and crashed back against the wall. Through dimming eyes I beheld RoboCop framed in the entrance, with what seemed like a miniature cannon aimed phallic-like at the room at large. What an imagination you've got, I told myself, but then I became aware that the other occupants of the room had seen him also, for they were turned away from me wearing expressions of extreme surprise.

As my senses partially returned, I realised that what I was seeing was someone clad in motor-bike leathers and wearing a helmet with its tinted glass visor closed. It did not require much more inspired supposition on my part then to come to the conclusion that Mad Max Morgan had arrived, hopefully with the intention of freeing me, roping the bad guys and leading them off for the sheriff and his posse to collect.

Slowly, and with all our fascinated eyes following its progress, his free hand rose and dislodged the visor. Sure enough, Max's face with ironic grin intact was revealed. He lost the grin, though, when he saw my bleeding hand where it was fixed to the table top.

"Let him go and stand back," he instructed Humphrey and Sid. "Against the back wall." He motioned with what I now perceived was an Ithaca M & P handgrip shotgun, probably the one with the eight-shot feed. A lethal weapon and, in the confines of the shed, absolutely devastating. "You" – he motioned with the gun at Whelan – "get away from the table. And if you make a move towards the hammer you'll be picking it up with a stump. You've done enough business with it."

They did as they were told, Humph and Sid as expressionless as ever, the Whacker's face working and his hands clenching and unclenching by his sides.

Max edged around until he could get a better view of my face. "How you doing, kid?" he asked. "Sorry I was so long in getting here. I had to scout around and make sure there was no lookout before I barged in."

"Oh, I'm okay," I said. "Just hanging around really." There were tears in my eyes, either from pain or relief, which I had to blink away. "I'm in agony, Max. I don't know if I can stand much more of it."

"Hang on in there. I'll be with you in a minute. First I've got to shorten the odds." He levelled the gun at Humphrey and Sid. "It's goodbye from me, fellas, and it's goodbye from you ..."

I knew what was about to happen, but I still couldn't prevent myself from rearing back when he let fly. In the close quarters of the inside of the shed the blast was all fire, noise and shocking velocity, as the charge hit Humphrey in the bridge of the nose and tore the top of his head off. Blood and pinkish matter and bits of bone fountained everywhere, the initial spray followed by a fine mist that hovered in the light like rosewater thrown as a bouquet. His feet did a little shuffle, his hands hanging limp like an Irish traditional dancer's, then his body fell over sideways against the wall. It was still on its way down when the shotgun blared again, and this time it was Sid's turn to do a buck-and-wing, the concentrated blast taking him amidships, blowing a hole in his mohair jacket and an even bigger one around the region of his belly button. Again there was a crimson explosion, a small geyser that became red sails in the sunset for Sid as he was driven back against the same section of wall that the partly decapitated Humphrey was half-sitting, half-lying against.

The detonations drummed and reverberated in the room, and cordite smoke swirled and coiled back on itself. My ears were deafened, but, as the waves of sound lessened, I began to hear the beat of Whelan's voice as he kind of keened, over and over again, "Ah, Jesus, no. Ah, Jesus, no. Ah, Jesus, no ..."

I looked at him, seeing him as though at some distanced reality, registering the fact that he had sunk to his knees and was extremely distressed, but not able to comprehend his reasons for so doing and being. I was still too taken up with trying to assimilate the enormity of Humph's and Sid's carnage-strewn passing.

Max stepped across to the stricken Whacker, stood in front of him and then just looked at him. Like a penitent, the kneeling man continued to stare straight ahead through unseeing eyes, the same monotonous phrase, like some kind of mantra, spewing from his lips.

Eventually Max raised the gun and brought the barrel down with force across Whelan's skull. That put an abrupt end to his pious ejaculations. He wheeled over sideways and curled up quietly on the floor in the foetal position, his limbs clenched, his mouth drooling into the sawdust.

Max leaned the shotgun against the leg of the table and reached up and took off his helmet. His face was flushed, the hair plastered flat on his bony skull with sweat. Otherwise he appeared not in the slightest fazed by the bloody destruction he had effected; no trace of regret etched his face, there was no wringing of hands, no dip of the knee in sorrow.

"Max?" I said, the single word emerging as a croak through blood-flecked lips – in my extremities of pain I must have bitten a little too keenly into them.

"Yes?"

"Will you poke around in Whelan's shirt pocket and see if you can locate a small brown bottle? When you've got it, bring it over to me. I think it contains magic drops."

He did as I asked and came up with the brown vial. Carrying it over, he laid it down beside my skewered hand, Using my good one I picked it up and, with my thumb as lever, popped the cork. I put the bottle to my still enlarged nose and took a hefty snuffle. Whatever pick-me-up was in it shot up my nasal passage like a charge from Max's shotgun and blasted its way into my tactile regions. I felt my eyes bulge, my neck tendons stretch, and then I was floating on a soft scented mattress of air that pulsed and undulated in the manner of a water bed when two consenting adults are consenting on it. The genie of the bottle had done his work without my even having to make a wish.

While I was busy pumping up my morale Max bent down and looked under the table. I took notice of him when he sat back on his heels and gazed at me.

"The nail has gone right through. I'll have to tap it back up before I can extract it from your hand. It's not going to be pleasant ..."

I frowned, seeing three of him. When I closed an eye the three

212

faces became one; when I opened it they began to drift apart again. Hurriedly I instructed him to fire away: "It can't hurt anymore than it did going in. Anyway, as long as I've got my magic bottle you can do whatever the fuck you want. Nothing can spook me. I'm inviol ... inviol ... as numb as a stepped-on spider. Wow-ee ..."

I took another hit, drawing the fumes up my nose and then deep into my brain, feeling their good vibrations induce an almost pre-orgasmic sensation. After I was fully restored to health I would have to look into this drugs business; it appeared as if I had been missing something all my life. With that thought in mind I held on to my nose wanking bottle and motioned Max to do whatever he had to in order to free me.

At first he tapped gently, but that only drew out the agony. I took a couple more shots of regenerating fluid and told him to get it over with, then watched as he made a more definitive swing. The head of the nail shot up in front of my watering eyes, too small to cause so much pain.

I thought I might be able to work it out myself, but it was too firmly embedded. Max had to fit the claw end of the hammer around it and heave. This time even the bottle failed me and I passed out. When I came to the glistening spike was lying on the table, while Max was busy wrapping my hand in the Whacker's yellow silk cravat.

"Does it hurt much?" he asked me solicitously.

"What d'you think? The fucking thing's on fire. First my nose, now my hand. If I keep on at this rate I'll have the spare body parts shop emptied. Do you know, he was going to nail my John Thomas to the table ..."

"Lucky I arrived when I did."

"Lucky? If you hadn't come back into my life in the first place none of this would have happened. I can do without that kind of luck ..."

I pulled my hand away and cradled it against my chest. Shakily I got to my feet. Putting one foot carefully in front of the other and averting my eyes from the ever-widening pool of blood seeping from the tattered bodies against the back wall, I shuffled towards the door. The time had come to say toodle-oo, cheerio, good bye-ee.

213

"Hey, where are you off to?" Max called from behind me.

I ignored him and continued on my way. It needed all my concentration just to stagger along. Once, not too long ago, I had been a reasonably fit and healthy human being. There had even been a bit of a spring in my step. Now I was old, Father William, older than tears, remorse or jurassic dust. When the fabled Oisín came back from Tír Na Óg, the land of youth, and the girth of his saddle broke, throwing him down on to the clay of his native place, he had aged in an instant, turning into skin and bone before the horrified gaze of the onlookers. I had no audience, but I could still feel the heaviness of the years pressing down on me in like manner. Never again would I experience the salmon-leap of youth exultant in my veins, never realise the rapture as spring broke the brittle stick of winter and flooded my supple body with all its impending joys ...

"For fuck's sake," I muttered out loud as I forced my battered body along, trying to dam up the tide of self-pity that was threatening to engulf me.

I made it to the door and stood leaning against it. In time I might be able to summon up the energy to walk on through. Sensing Max moving about, I turned to look at him. He had hoisted up the inert Whelan and was half-dragging, half-carrying him towards the table. My curiosity level had dropped quite a bit, but I still felt impelled to ask him what he was about. Then again, maybe I didn't have to ask, and it was my blank stare and leaning attitude that gave the impression I wanted to know.

"I'd tie him up if I had some rope," he explained, dumping the semiconscious thug in the chair I had lately vacated. "Can you see any rope around?"

"Rope?" I said, my head juddering, then again, "Rope?"

"That's what I thought," Max answered, nodding in confirmation of the utter absence of any such commodity. "The problem then arises, how are we to keep him subdued until we've some further use for him? Have you any ideas on that score?"

I waved away a haze of mist from in front of my eyes and fumbled the bottle to my nose. Just as I was about to take a snort, the bloody thing fell and tinkled away out of my sight. To hell with it!

"My hand hurts," I said, gazing at it balefully in its yellow silk bandage.

"Exactly," Max said. "I see what you mean. It's only fair that shit-in-the-river here should experience some of the pain and sorrow you're going through. I get your message loud and clear. Pass me the hammer."

"Araghhhh," I coughed, again trying to find the moisture to spit. "You're on your own with that, pal. I'm out of the crucifixion business."

I continued on my way out the door, my impetus and the slope taking me along at a steady trot. Under my feet the ground was muddy and squelchy and the fear of getting bogged down brought me to a halt. Although the night was just about done, it still lingered in shadowed pockets like an unloved guest. The air was thin and cold, and it didn't take it long to edge inside the makeshift bandage and caress the wound in my hand like an inquisitive nettle.

Behind me from the shed I heard an ominous banging, then a high-pitched scream like a cat being poked stirred me once more into motion. I crab-walked sideways, not lifting my feet but shuffling them along so that I would not suddenly fall over something. The ground was rough and full of shale now, and it grated unpleasantly under my shoes. In my throat the breath see-sawed, rasping in counterpoint with the gravel.

The Datsun was still parked on the brow of the hill, standing dark and motionless but somehow safe-looking and sturdy. I came to it and leaned against its reassuring solidity. The metal was cold and smooth and I bent down and laid my cheek against the bonnet. Its chilly touch against my nose and the side of my face was so soothing.

I was in the same position when Max came out, stretched and stood gazing down at me. The greyness had climbed higher into the sky and objects were becoming clearly defined. A predawn wind had got up, full with the smell of the sea. I could feel it slide along the metal under my ear, making a slight shushing sound.

In his creaking leathers Max walked down the incline until he was standing next to me. I followed his progress with my one available eye, trying not to blink.

215

As he had with Whelan he hoisted me up and, for one horrible moment, I thought he was going to take me back inside and nail me to the table beside the stricken gangster. He didn't. Rather did he half-support, half-carry me until we came to what I saw was an old double car seat, set advantageously back a little on the hill to catch the morning sun and possibly a panoramic view of the sea. It was most likely where the foreman on the site and his best boy took their elevenses.

Max sat me down, then plopped himself into the seat beside me. We leaned on one another, as companionable as two old friends with nothing on their minds except the intention of greeting the dawn together.

Strangely enough, I felt at peace with myself. In spite or maybe because of all the pain and sorrow, the horrors I had experienced, I was happy enough to be there on that promontory, in that deserted place, waiting for night finally to fold its wing and daylight to use its forbearance to bring the landscape and the sea into focus.

I felt no need, no want. There was no craving in me for stimulants, no longing for a drink, a smoke, or further snorts from the Whacker's magic bottle. This must be the peace that passeth all understanding, I thought, an interlude where necessity becomes an irrelevance and present time coming down the only requisite. Artifice, I told myself, all artifice, but like some large, unwieldy box kite the sectioned thought flew away and left me merely pulling on the string. Then suddenly I was running through knee-high grass, with the sun on my skin and the wind in my face and the terrors of the world spiralling away behind me as twists of smoke. No longer did I feel old and used – what winy tang had invaded my mind to lend me such an exhilaration, what grace under pressure to give me pause to sit and wait? Relief from stress, most probably, the delicious release of giving in, not having to continue the fight, being able to own up to one's inadequacies and failings. In short, I was out for the count, pole-axed, the towel fluttering into the ring as a flag of surrender. Stripped bare, I could only arise, phoenix-like, a happier and a wiser man.

Out over the flatness of the sea fingers of pale colour were beginning to nudge at the horizon, and a crescent-shaped

216

opalescence was pushing up seeking attention. I turned my head and gazed at Max in the pallid morning light.

"You were pretty hard on those guys in there," I said. "You could have taken them out of commission without making it permanent. And the same goes for Richie Michaels and Vincent Chinelio. They were lollipops. You could've sucked them dry using only your spit. They'd have given up the photographs without your using extreme prejudice. Why'd you do them in, Max? And in such ghastly ways ..."

He stretched out his legs, sighed, turned and gently patted my cheek. In the morning light the skin of his face was tight and bloodless, his eyes no longer merry, his whole aspect hunched and clenched. It was as though, Doctor Jekyll-like, he had drunk the awful elixir and was on the point of changing into Mr Hyde. This was a new Max, one who only bore a passing resemblance to the one I had known in happier times. My mood darkened again and I felt a terrible foreboding, a sense of something even worse than what had gone before about to shoulder its way above the horizon along with the rising sun.

He tried out a grin, but in the monochrome light his features resembled a charcoal sketch, a caricature. He was truly hurting, and I felt a pang of sorrow for his genuine pain. Or was it for my own genuine pain? And did it matter? In the aftermath of the highly charged situation we had been in, emotional reassurance was about as difficult to assess as the fluctuations in one's bowel movements, and just as messy.

Holding my injured hand against my chest in a Napoleonic gesture, I rocked back and forth, waiting for Max to speak, hoping he would shape and redefine things for me, lend coherence to a fall of events that blooded my mind with anger and unforgiveness. Rescuing me from the clutches of Whelan and his thugs had gone a long way down the road, but other perspectives would have to be attempted before reconciliation became final.

I could see he recognised my perception of the state of play and was about to attempt some form of holding action. He said, "I've always had this need to best everybody. Maybe it came about originally from the fact that I was born into a minority station. I was a Protestant among Catholics, a homosexual among heterosexuals, short in stature ... Out on the edge always attempting to break in, always seeking footholds, is a precarious position to be in. It leads to a desperation of intent and plays fuck with your moral outlook. The consequence is that I've a pretty warped conception of what good and evil entail. It's like being in a race where getting to the finishing line is the be-all and end-all, and all bets are on the winner. You can push and shove, kick, bite and gouge, knock down and walk on the other competitors, until you're out there in the lead and running free."

He paused and we sat and gazed at the scene in front of us. Small, ridged clouds were now backboning a mother-of-pearl sky. The sun was still just below the horizon, but it was sending out feelers of peach light, a blush of colour whose texture was of the most delicate and fragile. Reflected on the sea, its mirror image teased itself in the sky.

Staring out into all that peal of radiance. I said, "I'm listening, Max, because we go a long way back and we were like brothers once, but don't expect me to endorse your actions with forgiveness and some form of absolution. To my knowledge you've slaughtered four men, none whose deaths were particularly necessary. Maybe the first two were for gain, the second lot for revenge? Who elected you their judge and jury? And executioner ..?"

I could feel him looking at me but I didn't return his gaze as he said, "Maybe I believe in an Old Testament scheme of things. An eye for an eye, a tooth for a tooth. Michaels and Chinelio and their ilk did for me before I did for them. And as for the two in the shed, they're cannon-fodder. It was only a question of time before they died violently. You know that as well as I do."

"Do I?" I rubbed my face with my left hand, feeling the rasp of stubble along the jawline. When I moved my tongue around in my mouth it was as if I were using it to investigate the contents of a dirty ashtray. "What I don't understand is why you got me involved. You were well able to take care of things yourself."

I felt the car seat creak as he moved his body. He said, "It's to do with old ghosts. A harking back to an ideal, where the past is the best place of all. Mossie Haly got away with too much for too

218

long. He ruined my father and for that alone he deserves retribution. But there are wider issues too. I felt myself cast in the role of an avenger, an angel of death with a flaming sword ... To right the wrongs done to those I loved."

"Loved?"

"Love, hate, sometimes it's a very narrow margin between the two. I loved our friendship, the closeness of the bond, but I hated the adulation you got while I had to dwell in the shadows. That's why I wanted you with me at the end, to be my witness."

"The end? The end of what?"

Suddenly Max was on his feet and standing in front of me. He began to divest himself of his leather gear. He unzipped his tunic and let it fall to the ground. Then he stepped out of the padded trousers. He took off his sweatshirt and bared his torso to the streaming morning light. There was a grim intensity about his movements and I feared whatever revelation was coming, but when he was stripped down to his white jockey shorts and boots he was the Max of old, thin and wiry but with ropes of muscle laddering his chest and arms.

"Look at me," he said. "Tell me what you see."

"A well-preserved specimen of physical manhood?"

He shook his head. Stretching his arms out in the cruciform position, he said, "That's outward show. Inside I'm tainted with the scourge of God. Soon there'll be night sweats, dystrophy of the muscles, a breakdown in my immunity system, open wounds that won't heal, slackness of the mind, vacancy, and a slow and agonising slide into oblivion."

"You're telling me you've got AIDS?"

"Game ball, Johnny boy. The ultimate horror. Michaels and Chinelio had already killed me before I killed them. They share in a collective guilt. Mossie too. He was the cause of my being imprisoned in the charnel house."

He grinned at me, but this time it was a rictus that encompassed more than I could ever understand. Then he began to make stylised mime movements, the kind that Oriental people practise in the morning before they go out to face the routine of another day. The red ball of the sun had glided into view, turning the eastern sky into a heart-stopping chimera of roseate hues, coral and damask at the edges leading into flushed pinks and a central rubied tone. Against this backdrop of stippled brilliance his movements took on a highly formal air, a fixed monumental aspect as though he were calling down a curse or enacting the death song of some tradition-gripped tribe.

"Stop it, for Christ's sake," I cried, caught up myself in the awful fear of the intangible, but he continued to gyrate, turning and twisting against the blood-red sky, until his form and figure took on the guise of something elemental, a nature spirit at one with the sun, the sea, and the dawn breaking gloriously all about.

Thirteen

It needed something as bizarre as Max's death dance to break the spell and that was what we got. With an almighty roar, the Whacker Whelan came shooting out the open door of the shed. The transformation from fashionable man-about-town to whirling dervish was complete and he was something to behold.

The effort needed to tear his hand from the table had to have been phenomenal, and it showed in his pain-racked visage and wild man appearance. His hair was standing on end, his eyes darting from his head. He held his injured limb aloft as though demonstrating his anguish to the gods, while in his other hand he brandished the demon hammer.

I doubted he actually saw us as he came steaming forward, although in his agony-crazed brain there must have been the desire and the will to exact revenge. I flinched, cradling my own wounded hand, but he shot past me where I was sitting on the car seat and ran straight into Max.

For one splendid moment they were silhouetted against the back blaze of sky, entwined like some straining Rodin couple in the throes of passion, then they went over backwards, hit the ground and began rolling down the slope.

The wild excitement of the scuffle took hold of me, and I jumped up and went charging after them. They came to rest in a small hollow, slick with the wetness of morning dew. Max had hold of the hand with the hammer, endeavouring to wrest it free, while Whelan beat at him ineffectually with his other, bloodied one.

It was an uneven contest from the start, for Max stayed cool and calculating, while his opponent had lost the run of himself. Still holding on to the Whacker's arm, Max started butting him in the face with the top of his head. Bright red blood rained in a pointillistic frieze through the clear air, and I had to dodge about to avoid it.

Eventually the battered Whelan had to let go of the weapon

and, as he did, the now enraged Max hit him on the temple with it. As he raised it for a second blow I caught hold of its blood-slicked head and held on. Max looked at me, the fire went out of his eyes and he released the hammer into my keeping.

The sun was now fully above the horizon and was touching the air with fingers of brilliance. A gull shrieked out over the sea, the sound harsh and abrupt in the sudden silence. Further down the slope there was a stand of lupins, the yellow flowers like tears, and I could make out the light-reflecting glint of Max's motor-cycle where he had partly hidden it in the bushes. Further on again the land fell away in a sheer drop and from where I was I could observe the heavy swell of water over submerged rocks at its base.

"That's enough," I said. "It's over." With infinite care I laid the bloody hammer down in the grass. "All that violence ... It's not worth it. Let there be an end to it."

Max disentangled himself from the unconscious Whelan, sat up and cradled his knees under his chin. He gazed about him, taking in gulps of air, then he said, "You know, it's going to be a beautiful day. Reminds me of those long summer days when we were young. Remember? They seemed to go on forever. And all the people who lived in them. The Boiler Brown, Blacklead, Jimmy Harris, the guy we knew as Rashers and Bacon, and Ned Fenlon with his horse and cart and his cry of 'Rags, bones and bottles'. Is there ever a time so good as when you're young? The blood singing in your veins, your outlook unblemished by shadow or substance, all possibilities laid out before you. It's like a drop of water trembling on the point of falling, a quivering moment you just fail to reach." He looked at me and his old familiar grin was back in place, lopsided but so engaging. "Then it falls, plop, and you've gone past it, but all the time looking back over your shoulder, regretting what could have been while obliged to continue on into the future. I slaughtered those guys because I blamed them for infecting me with something that's always been there, its seeds planted way back. A disease of the soul ..." Rocking backwards and forwards, he raised his face to the light, the tentative rays of the sun outlining his profile in a blink of brilliance. "Why aren't we given another chance?" he said softly. "Just one more shot at the side of ham at the end of the greasy pole ..."

"You think we'd do any different? It seems to me that things always turn out the same. My life is a mess too. I'm not proud of how I've let myself slip. But you go on, doing the best you can, trying not to dislodge a flowerpot on to your neighbour's head. You look for a little light at the end of the tunnel, while trying to ignore the sound of the approaching train's siren. It's a question of doing what you can with what you've got ..."

I looked to Max for a response, but in my heart I knew we were not talking to one another now but to ourselves. We were old friends who had run out of ways of saying, "I'm sorry."

At the same time I could not just let him walk away. I would have to make some effort, no matter how irresolute, to bring him back with me. There was a reckoning owed.

But he took that decision out of my hands too. Still clad only in jockey shorts and boots, he got up and went down the hill. He walked with a jaunty swing as if he hadn't a care in the world. I thought about going after him as he pushed into the clump of bushes, but the sudden coughing to life of the motor-bike engine stalled any move I might have made. In a moment he came riding out from cover, urging the machine up the hill towards me. He had unearthed a white stetson and was wearing it, pushed to the back of his head. He was grinning and going 'vroom, vroom' in tune with the sound of the engine.

I scrambled to my feet as he drew up beside me in a shower of pebbles. I could see the glint of sweat on his forehead and a certain tightness in his bearing, but otherwise he was Cowboy Max, out for fun and frolic, merry-making and whatever else might come his way.

"I can't let you go," I said, feeling foolish but yet determined.

"No?"

"I have to make the effort."

"There's no effort required. I'm not going anywhere. There's nowhere really to go. I might do a few circles and figures of eight, but I'll be back. You know I always come back."

I looked him in the eye and said, "It's over, Max. You know that, don't you? Whatever you have against Mossie, it doesn't matter anymore. Now it's your turn to pay the ferryman."

The muscles standing out on his arms, he hoisted the bike up on its stand. He dismounted. The light was a silent blare now, the sun majestic, the sea reflecting its glory. The air felt newly minted, tremulous with the approach of heat. On such a morning one should be full of expectation of new beginnings.

"Myself and the Whacker are going to take a little spin," Max explained. "He's in need of a bit of jollying up."

Without any help from me he put the unconscious Whelan sitting on the saddle of the motor-bike, then climbed on behind him. Running his hands out underneath the other man's arms, he rested them on the handlebars, revved the engine, tipped his stetson and took off. With wheels spurting grit, and doing elaborate slides and turns, he went in and out among the various obstacles of the building site. The harsh roar of the engine bit into the quiet of morning, throwing up echoes that reverberated off the cliffs and along the distant sea like skipping stones.

I walked down the slope towards its edge, not looking at Max or what he was up to; perhaps he was merely marking out the aimless contours of his life by the directionless pursuit of his progress. A thin pathway was worn along the rim of the cliff and I stood on it and leaned forward to gaze over the edge. There was a drop of some hundred feet to a small, pebbled beach. The tide appeared to be coming in and silvery ripples were coursing through the stones and hitting playfully against the base of the escarpment. The lone gull had been joined by a friend and the two of them swooped and glided, graceful parentheses against the enormity of sea and sky.

I heard the thud, thud of Max's bike grow louder and he drew up beside me and let the engine idle. The sun was still shooting colour into the pale vault of the heavens, redness being the predominant hue, but there was a myriad of other pigments also, tints of off-white, bronze and warm golds, mustard and vermilion, a Joseph's coat spread out against the sky. Nature was really putting on a show.

Max sat and watched with me, hat on the back of his head, a sheen of sweat on his bare chest. There were bright patches of blood also, like war paint, but this was probably from Whelan, who was covered in it.

I patted my pockets out of habit, in search of cigarettes and a lighter. All I came up with was a spent wooden match which I put between my lips and chewed. Somewhere to our right, in towards the city, there was a sudden flash of light as the sun glanced off a reflecting surface.

"There's Indians in them thar hills," I said.

Max grinned. "Isn't there always?" he said. He reached up and settled the hat forward over his eyes. "Remember how I told you the time would come when I'd be ready to make that one great and definitive jump? I think that time's arrived."

"You figure?"

"Yeah, why not? If I make it, I'll never have to look back over my shoulder again. I'll be out in the clear, on a straight and level plain, heading towards distant hills, with loads of guys in my wake but none of them with the slightest chance of catching me."

"If that's what you think," I said, shrugging. I chewed my match and gazed again at the panorama of sea and sky. "If you want to give it your best shot, I won't try to stop you."

He was grinning broadly now, a real happy look as if a great weight had been lifted from him.

"Just watch my dust, old friend," he said. "When I get there, I'll send you a postcard."

"From hell?"

But he wasn't listening any more. He turned the bike in a wide semicircle that took him halfway up the slope. There he paused, revving the engine until its thunder was all about. It even woke Whelan out of his daze and he began rocking from side to side. Max rose up on the pedals behind him, then let the throttle out.

The bike surged forward, rising up so that the front wheel was off the ground and, for a second, it appeared that the riders might be deposited back into the fantail of dust and gravel it was kicking up. But then it settled and was moving with vicious intent. It shot past me and sailed out over the edge of the cliff, and for one beautiful and balletic moment it seemed as if Max had taken off and was indeed flying. He had cut the engine and there was no sound except the rush of air and the distant swish

225

of the sea. Out and out machine and riders went, in a truly astonishing leap, an arrow hurled from a magic bow, Shem the Penman's famed, 'shot from a shovel'.

But then reality set in, gravity took hold, and the bike and its burden reached the apex of its flight and began its descent. I felt a sickening click in my throat, and a whirl of dizziness as if I too were in free-fall and could see the ocean and the rocks coming up to meet me.

I closed my eyes, refusing to register the actual moment of impact, but I could still hear the watery thump, hard and abrupt, and indeed definitive. When I did look, all I could see was a foaming geyser of water, then a rainbow of iridescence as the wing of water was caught in the slanting rays of the sun.

I remained watching, hoping to see heads bob up, but the sea was keeping its own on this occasion. Except for a widening ripple nothing showed but the slow motion swirl and curl of the tide. Max had gone to join the flawed immortals, those sadly misappropriated men who took a wrong turning in their early years and could never ever again find a way back.

Rather than go inside the shed to look for the keys of the Datsun in the dead Humphrey's pocket, I hotwired it and drove in along coast roads until I came to the outskirts of Malahide. I abandoned it in a lay-by, wiping down the steering wheel and any other surfaces I felt I might have touched with a chamois I found in the glove compartment. I took the rag with me when I left.

It was still early when I got to the village. My watch had stopped, the face starred and pitted. However, an ornate clock over a jeweller's shop told me it was exactly twenty minutes past six. I walked down to the seawall and sat in the sunshine, watching sailboats at anchor rise and fall in the swell, their fog bells tolling in solemn chant. The sea sucked and eddied against the cement pilings, carrying a detritus of oil slick and accumulated debris, but I was afraid to look down in case I saw Max's submerged face staring back at me.

It was pleasant sitting there in the sun. I had supped full with horrors and it would be a long time before the events of the night faded from my memory. My skin felt sticky, and I imagined the pink spray that had erupted from Sid and Humphrey's shattered bodies still clinging to it. But time is a great healer, and already my mind was settling into old and tried routines, my body chiming in with protesting aches at the injuries done to it.

There was a scent of ozone and salt, a "down to the sea in ships" smell that reminded me of Wexford when I was growing up, its silted-up harbour, the ballast bank, and the warm feel of the wooden boardwalk that bordered the inlet. Once a large splinter had transfixed the ball of my bare foot, and Max had carried me all the way home and extracted it with the care and solicitude of the grieving friend he was. Now I also owed him my life.

I must have dozed, sitting there in the sunlight, for I suddenly started to the abrupt thump-thump-thump of an outboard motor as it was coaxed into life. Below me a grizzled old sailor in fisherman's jersey, overalls and wellington boots was uncoupling the rope of his single-masted ketch from where it was tied to an iron ring set into the harbour wall. He winked up at me, then steered the boat out carefully between the other vessels, pipe clamped between his teeth, face jutting forward and his eyes squinting into the morning light as though hopeful of catching sight of flying fish on the starboard bow.

I got up and walked back into the village, and the clock over the jeweller's now informed me that it was seven-thirty. A number of sleepwalking commuters were queueing for a bus and, feeling in the mood for company, I joined them. When wishing for anonymity, always seek out a crowd. The bus arrived and I got in, took a seat downstairs and slept all the way into town. I disembarked on the quays, then got a taxi to the North Strand and rousted Leo Quinn once again from his virginal bed.

He didn't seem particularly surprised at my bringing him new business. Unwrapping the silk cravat, he cluck-clucked over the wound in my hand and asked if the nail had been new, or old and rusty. I told him new, which appeared to please him. He cleaned the wound with surgical spirit. splashing it on to the injury and causing me to rise up on tiptoe and beg for mercy. He offered to cauterise it with a hot needle, but I passed on that. Finally he dusted it with antiseptic powder, covered it with lint and put on a bandage. He rigged up a makeshift sling and instructed me to come back and see him on the morrow.

"D'you think it'll become infected?"

"If it turns yellow and black and swells up ..."

"Yes?"

"Then you'll know it's poisoned."

"What'll I do if that happens?"

"Put your head between your legs and kiss your arse goodbye."

"Very funny."

"No, come back and I'll lance it for you."

"Christ!"

"It might get gangrenous."

"What?"

"Then I'll have to take it off altogether."

I leaned against Leo's padded table and felt myself grow dizzy. Seeing my distress, he said hastily, "Just my little joke. You should be right as rain in a few days." He took up the flask of alcohol, swirled the clear liquid about, then regretfully put it back into a glass-fronted cabinet.

"You've got a heart transplant operation later on?" I asked him, but he ignored my attempt at sarcasm and showed me to the door.

I decided to stroll back to the warehouse in Sheriff Street, but about halfway there I got a fit of the shakes that forced me to stop and lean against a shopfront. Eventually I got going again, only to find when I arrived that my landlord, Lester, was unloading goods and boxes from a transit van. Hurriedly I packed a bag, trotted across the road and checked into the North Star Hotel. The room was at the back, bright, clean and containing the usual furnishings. I thought about a shower, but waves of tiredness were breaking over me and the bed looked like a couch fit for a king.

I took two sleeping pills, drew the curtains and stretched out, grimy clothes, shoes, sling, the lot. I went out like a light and dreamed of playing hurling on a field on the side of a cliff. Max was there, a member of my team, while Sid and Humphrey were in the ranks of the opposition. When I ran with the ball on my stick, they converged on me, but Max got there as well, swung, and decapitated them like someone skulling turnips. The disembodied heads soared into the air, then began bobbing up and down, at the same time giving a running commentary as the match progressed.

I awoke at some stage and the room was dark. I staggered to the toilet, peed for an interminable time, took two more sleeping pills and passed out once more. This time I sank into a velvet-lined casket that Dracula must have left lying about, and my dreams were so shifting and shadowed that I pushed them aside and drifted into a pit so deep and dark that even the wise virgins with their lamps would not have been able to find me.

The next time I started into wakefulness, bright light was knifing in where the curtains had not properly come together. I got out of the bed and promptly experienced a bout of the staggers that deposited me back in it. I tried groaning, listened to it critically, felt it could be improved upon and spent some time doing just that. When I thought I had it about right, I made another try at getting off the bed.

I walked around the room, shuffling like an old man. Trails of vapour curled at the edges of my vision, but, when I turned to confront them, they were not there any more. I resumed my walkabout, from the bed to the wardrobe, across to the door, then back to a bedside locker whose top contained a leather-bound bible, a brochure advertising the delights of Dublin in full living colour, a book of hotel matches and a glass ashtray.

These last two objects awoke a longing and I fumbled the phone off its stand. I dialled different combinations of numbers until I got room service, then told the squeaky voice at the other end of the line that I needed a pot of tea, a plate of scrambled eggs, a ton of toast, and twenty Dunhill cigarettes. The inside of my mouth felt as if it had been painted with distemper, with my tongue as the brush, so I also put in a request for a jug of Buck's Fizz, iced to the gills.

I was sitting on the bed thumbing through the bible and seeking an appropriate passage to assuage my vexation and worry when a discreet knock on the door heralded the arrival of the

229

goodies. A venerable old party in grey waistcoat, black trousers and patent leather shoes creaked in behind the breakfast trolley. By the look of him, it was as well he wasn't trying to carry a tray.

Avoiding my eye, he laid out the various bits and pieces, all the while clucking away to himself like a broody hen. When he was finished he stood back to survey the scene. He nodded and rubbed his hands together, making a dry rustling sound like whispers from another room.

All I had left in my wallet were two ten-pound notes and I was damned if I was going to bestow one of them on him. So I stared him out until he blinked, muttered some kind of curse on me and mine, and shuffled off. I listened for his departing footsteps, but all that greeted my ear was the tempting buzz of the Buck's Fizz in its iced container.

I had a glass of it, gasping as its coolness bit. Then I had another, which I sipped more slowly. It made me feel light-headed, so I started in on the eggs and toast. Then I drank some tea. Then I had more Buck's Fizz. Then I lit a cigarette, drew in the smoke, gagged, and just made it to the bathroom where I chucked up the whole caboodle, food, drink and hopefully the bile and badness of the past few days, into the toilet.

I went back and lay on the bed and, at last, shed a few tears. I'm not ashamed to admit it. Real men may not eat quiche, but they sure can cry up a storm when the moment is opportune. I lay there for a time bawling my heart out, and when I was finished I felt so much the better for it that I was able to get up, have a shower and a shave, and dress all by myself.

I returned to the bedroom and drank some of the lukewarm tea and ate the remainder of the toast. This time it stayed down. I had brought clean underwear and socks from the warehouse, but I had to climb back into the grubby shirt, waistcoat and trousers of the day before. I discarded the sling and let my hand hang at my side, where it felt as if it was nailed to my hip-bone.

Thus fed and clothed, I went downstairs and paid my bill by Access card. I had to sign with my left hand and the receptionist looked long and hard at the signature before she accepted it. Bright sunlight was again the order of the day and I walked up

Talbot Street with a jaunty air. Stopping at a kiosk, I bought a newspaper and was staggered when I saw the date on the masthead and realised I was standing in the middle of Thursday morning. I had either mislaid Wednesday or slept right through it.

Banner headlines on the lead page told of gang warfare on a building site in north County Dublin. The story outlined the finding of two bodies in a hut and also the dredging from the sea of a third corpse. Names were given: the two in the shed were identified as Sidney Jeavons and Humphrey Butt, while the one from Davy Jones' locker was tagged as Edward Mary Whelan, popularly known as the Whacker. The report stated that they all had records and went on to list some of the more outstanding achievements of their careers. The Gardai were quoted as being of the opinion that the slaughter was the result of inter-gang rivalry. Of Max Morganthau there was nary a mention. Did this mean, I wondered, that at some stage in the future he would make another of his miraculous appearances?

I was about to continue on my way when I spied some familiar countenances staring at me from the cover of the latest Hello! magazine on the stand. It was a grouping of the Haly family, the two ladies sitting, while Mossie and his idiot son stood leering in the background. The setting I recognised as being their chintzy sitting-room and the blurb accompanying the portrait stated that there was a feature inside on the members of the family and full colour pictures of their beautiful home and gardens.

I bought a copy of the magazine and stuck it under my arm along with the paper. It gave me food for thought as I walked towards my office. Once again it seemed that Mossie, like a dog shaking off fleas, was going to rid himself of possible disasters. Without the incriminating photographs I could not hang the rezoning scam on him, and the man who had them was presumably swimming with the fishes in polluted Dublin Bay.

I arrived at my business premises, scooted past the open door of the video shop downstairs, ascended, unlocked the outer and inner doors, opened the window in my sanctum, sat down and put my feet up on the desk. This is where I came in, I thought, and I peeped through the vee to see if Max was standing there. He wasn't. But someone else was...

It was the postman, a thin sardonic character in navy blue uniform with green piping, a fine head of Brylcreemed hair and an expression that said lip curling was back in fashion.

"You'll have to sign for this, chief," he told me, showing but keeping a firm hold on a large brown Jiffy bag. "It's registered."

Laying his form flat on the desk and taking the proffered biro, I signed once more with my left hand. He gazed curiously at my nose, then at the bandage on my hand, but he didn't ask about either and I didn't tell him. Tucking the form and the pen away in his tunic pocket, he flicked a finger at his visored cap and departed.

I let the parcel lie for a time on the desk top. I got up and collected the scattered sets of false teeth and put them back in the cabinet. The crack still ran down the glass like a jagged scar and I made a mental note to get it repaired. The blind was lying in the corner, so I picked it up and placed it gently back in its socket. I thought about rewinding the answering machine and listening to whatever it had to tell me, but decided to postpone that pleasure to another day.

Finally I fingered the postman's gift, turning it this way and that. It was addressed to me, John Blaine, with the location of my office printed below in anonymous block capitals. I was not expecting a registered parcel, nor was I in the habit of receiving any such. Could it be a bomb? I wondered, and I held it gingerly to my ear to see if it ticked. It didn't.

I got up again and walked around the desk. I sat down and lit a cigarette and took an experimental drag. The smoke went down into my lungs like a scouring cloth and began busily rubbing away. After I had ceased coughing I took another look at the parcel. I twisted it about, hefted it, and finally began unwinding the tape that sealed it, hoping that it wouldn't blow off the one good hand left to me.

When I had it unwrapped I carefully sorted out the contents and laid them on the desk. Contained in sheets of tissue paper were two sets of photographs: the ones of Archie and Michaels doing their last tango in Ballsbridge, and the set of Whelan

232

handing bribe money to the county councillor, with Mossie in the back of the car, his face visible at the window and, more importantly, when blown up, easily identifiable.

The negatives were also present, and a metal object that rolled on the desk top with a merry little tinkle. I looked at it and saw that it was a bicycle bell.

There was a single sheet of notepaper, which I picked up and read. When I was finished I shook my head and read it again.

It went:

Dear Johnny,

   Thought you might find a use for the enclosed. Make sure they get a good home. Should be worth a heap of money if you go according to your head rather than your heart.

   The bell is from the bicycle I stole from you all those years ago. I kept it, hoping to attach it to a new and shining model, which I would then lower down your chimney one snowy Christmas night. Alas, it never came to pass.

   As you know, I never was much good at saying goodbye, always going on the premise that like the bad penny I'd turn up again some day. This time though it may well be "adios".

   Don't think too badly of me,
   Your friend,
   Max.

I gazed at Max's last will and testament for a long time, then I lit a match, put it to the corner of the notepaper and watched it shrivel up and be consumed. It turned into ash and shivered in whorls along the desk top. I blew at it and it rose in a cloud, and disappeared in little darts of light as the rays of the sun played with it.

I tried to think of a suitable epitaph to match the act, but my mind was frozen on the memory of Max's last noble leap into oblivion. "Geronimo," I whispered into the silence of the room and from somewhere, away above and beyond the confines of this mundane world, I fancied I heard an answering echo, accompanied by a rakish grin and a retreating, waving hand.

"So, what did you do with the photographs and the negatives?" Annie asked me. "Will you tell me before I die of curiosity."

We were sitting in Clery's basement cafe, me eating a rock bun and drinking tea, she with an untouched white coffee in front of her. She was wearing a plain cotton summer dress and white sandals. Her pale skin was dusted with freckles, her hair was glossy where it dipped over her forehead, and her expectation was all aquiver with eagerness to hear the conclusion of my story.

I had given her an account of almost everything else, glad to be able to get it off my chest. She listened, once or twice looking as if she might be about to interrupt, but then going back again to stirring her coffee. She was an amazing lady, for she took it all in, the description of Mossie Haly's perfidy, my removal to the building site, the nailing of my hand to the table, the shooting of Sid and Humphrey, and Max's final grand leap into eternity, and still contrived to seem as if she were merely listening to the plot of some film or play.

Curiosity had now got the better of her, however, in her desire to know what I had done with the treasure trove Max had bequeathed me. It also probably had something to do with her continuing assessment of me and of how I stood in her regard. It was important to her that I retain some shred of integrity – important to me too; after all, it was about all I had left to help me preserve a semblance of self-esteem.

I said, "I packed up the photographs and sent them to the journalists Wimbush and Kosegan. Then I forwarded the negatives to George Quinlan. That way Mossie should get it in the neck from two fronts, the newspapers and the fraud squad."

"Will they know where the material came from?"

"With the reporters, it won't matter. They think of themselves as holding the same portfolio as the priest in confession. George may have a good idea of the source, but he won't make a fuss about it. Why should he? Pulling Haly down will be a feather in his cap. Even if it wasn't, George'd still be pleased as punch. He likes sticking a pin into stuffed-up shitheads like Mossie Haly."

At last Annie picked up her cup and drank from it. When she put it down she left a line of froth along her upper lip. I reached across and removed it with my finger. I was getting quite adept at using my left hand. It's an ill wind that doesn't blow some good: I might end up ambidextrous.

"You could have made a lot of money out of blackmailing Haly," she said, almost wistfully.

"Is that what you'd have wanted me to do?"

"No, of course not. It's only ... well, money is always useful. Especially now ..."

"Now?"

"I've got something to tell you." For a moment her eyes left mine and she frowned down at the table. When she looked up again, though, she was grinning. She said, "I'm pregnant."

"Pardon?"

"I'm in the family way. With child. I've got a bun in the oven."

"Seriously?"

"You can't get more serious than that."

I said nothing and she gazed at me with a raised eyebrow and a waiting expression on her face.

"Aren't you happy for me?"

"I'm over the moon. Delirious."

"No, you're not. You're sitting there wondering whose it is. Am I right?"

Now it was my turn to stare at the table.

"Well, you can't blame me for that, can you?" I said. "Considering the peculiar circumstances of your relationship with Harold and myself."

"It's yours."

"How d'you know?"

"I just know, that's all. This is one you'll have to trust me on, big boy. Isn't that good enough for you?"

I thought about it and surprised myself by quickly coming to the conclusion that it was good enough. If I ever had faith in her, now was the time to show it.

I reached across the table with my one good hand and clasped hers.

"Annie ..." I said.

"Johnny ..." she said.

And we both burst out laughing.

When the spluttering ceased I said to her, "We'll go down to the Gresham Hotel and crack open a bottle of champagne. Then we'll get a room and crack open some more."

"But I've got to get back to work," she protested.

"Not today, you haven't."

I led her out and up the stairs and into the sunshine of O'Connell Street. Then a thought struck me.

"There's somewhere I want you to come with me. It'll only take a minute."

We turned right, down to Marlborough Street and along by the railings of the Pro-Cathedral and in the main door. The sudden shift from light to shade took both of us by surprise.

"Have you got religion all of a sudden?" Annie whispered, but she went willingly enough when I guided her over to the shrine where one lit blessed candles.

Standing in front of the banked rows with their tiny diamond flames I said, "I want to light a couple for remembrance."

As I reached into the container, Annie said, "Just light the one. As a sign of continuance. A death followed by a birth ..."

I set fire to the wick of the candle, then screwed it into its holder. It caught immediately and burned with a strong vibrant glow.

"If it's a boy, will we call him Max?" I asked her.

Annie looked at me with an impudent grin and said, "Maybe we'll name him Harold ...?"

"Over my dead body."